The sound came ba................................n,
deafening, grating l................................n
clamped his hands ....t
at the road. Darke.................................w
was advancing on t......

'No . . . Jesus . . .'

Don saw it close, enveloping the wheels.

'God Jesus . . .'

He flailed his arms around his face, beating back the surreal horde that was starting to engulf him. Screeching, half-insane from the noise and the fear, he switched on the engine and threw it into gear, thrusting the vehicle forward. He steered with one hand, shielding his face with the other as the obscene swarm enshrouded his head.

Something mad happened to the road. It became three roads – one going left, one right, one straight ahead. There was no way he could tell which was real. The tyres squealed . . .

By the same author

The Outsider

HUGH MILLER

The Dark Side of the Sun

Based upon the BBC TV series by Michael J. Bird

GRANADA
London Toronto Sydney New York

Published by Granada Publishing Limited in 1983

ISBN 0 586 06016 2

A Granada Paperback Original
Copyright © Michael J. Bird and Hugh Miller 1983

Granada Publishing Limited
Frogmore, St Albans, Herts AL2 2NF
and
36 Golden Square, London W1R 4AH
515 Madison Avenue, New York, NY 10022, USA
117 York Street, Sydney, NSW 2000, Australia
60 International Blvd, Rexdale, Ontario, R9W 6J2, Canada
61 Beach Road, Auckland, New Zealand

Printed and bound in Great Britain by
Cox & Wyman Ltd, Reading
Set in Times

Granada ®
Granada Publishing ®

Night. A high moon bathed Rhodes in chill, pearl light and laid a shimmer across the wide bay. Mingling sea sounds added their measure to the shrilling of the cicadas, making rhythms to augment the fragrant breeze.

On its high stone peak the Crusader fortress stood out in sombre relief, immutable against the luminous water. Jutting gargoyles along the walls hung in mute subservience to Asmodeus, the Hebrew devil carved by the main gate, surrounded by the effigies of lesser demons.

There was movement inside the fortress. A man – a Greek, slim and shabbily dressed – was running up the steps towards the wall, the urgent thudding of his feet echoing off the stonework.

When he reached the wall he stopped, breathless fumbling for the rope he had attached to the battlements. Locating it, he hitched his canvas satchel higher on his shoulder then swung himself up over the edge, holding tightly to the rope.

The wall was steep. The man eased himself down slowly, moving his feet cautiously on the craggy stone, his breathing sharp and anxious, eyes tensely watching the pavement below.

A few feet from the bottom he released his grip on the rope and dropped to the flagged path. He misjudged his angle; his right foot struck the ground an instant before the left, unbalancing him and sending him sprawling sideways on the ground. The satchel flew off his shoulder and its contents – four hand-chased goblets, gleaming dull gold in the feeble light – clanked out on the paving.

On his knees, panting, the man began gathering up the vessels, his fingers trembling nervously on the cool, precious metal. Above him the countenance of Asmodeus, abiding, malevolent, scowled steadily into the gloom.

The man stuffed two of the goblets into the satchel. He was holding the third when he stopped suddenly, startled, his fingers tightening on the goblet's stem. The cicadas had gone silent. The sound had simply cut out as if a switch had been thrown, leaving a silence that seemed to press on the man's ears.

He jerked his head from side to side, scanning the shadows. There was still the rumbling of the sea, he realized, but without the accompanying insect noises it seemed distant and chilling. He moistened his lips nervously, looking around him once more, then he dropped the third goblet into the satchel.

Fumbling for the remaining goblet he froze again. There was a new sound, faint and disturbing, an urgent rustling that seemed to grow louder with each accelerating beat of his heart. It was like nothing the man had ever heard before. As it grew it changed, the urgency of it swelled and became tremulous, the angry chattering of something unimaginable, an invisible, dangerous horde.

The man turned his head. He was convinced the sound came from the direction of the main gate. And it was getting nearer.

Frightened, he snatched up the fourth goblet and shoved it into the satchel. Before he could rise he was held again, paralysed. The undergrowth at the foot of the fortress was moving wildly, churning. A deep shadow began spreading along the pavement, a carpet of amorphous, agitated movement without identity or proper substance. As the thing moved faster towards the man the sound grew, hammering the air around his head.

With a whimper he looked up and saw that the walls were infested with the same dark, pernicious thronging, pouring over the battlements in a cascade.

The sound grew to a roar. Panic seized the man, throwing

him to his feet, the satchel dangling from his hand. He began running – running for his life, he was sure, crazily pumping his legs along the pavement.

His breathing was out of tempo, too shallow and irregular for running. A sudden pain in his side made him stop, gasping as he threw himself against the wall. He looked back, wild-eyed, seeing the murderous shadow closing on him, the sound travelling before it in a shrouding deafening roar. The man hurled the satchel into the heart of the tumult and began running again, terrified, howling his panic into the dark air.

The gibbering noise seemed to enter his skull, making him dizzy. He ran no more than a hundred yards before he tripped, stumbled a few paces and fell. In an instant the shadow closed over him.

The man screamed and pulled himself to his feet, flailing his arms as if he were beating off an attacking swarm. He took two blind steps, teetered, then plunged backwards over the cliff edge. His scream trailed after him down the swift, five-hundred-foot fall to the rocks.

The malignant babble halted on the instant. There was no longer an engulfing shadow, no sound beyond the sighing of the waves. After a few seconds the cicadas began again, suffusing the night with their music.

A man was standing by the battlements of the fortress. He was grey-haired and handsome, with an ageless, dispassionate face. He stood motionless, gazing out to where the thief's body lay on the rocks, the dead eyes wide and frozen in terror.

Chapter One

The Tierney's house stood on one of the quiet roads leading off Hampstead's Rosslyn Hill. It was a spacious home, comfortable, furnished carefully in an expensive blend of old and new that deliberately avoided trendiness.

The sitting room, in particular, evoked the couple's individuality. Tables, chairs and cabinets had been selected for their attractiveness and functional quality; nothing was included to impress outsiders. The paintings on the walls, mostly landscapes, were there because either Don, or Anne, or both found them particularly appealing. They had never believed that a famous signature on a canvas could be an automatic criterion of value.

No vanity motivated the presence of the three framed magazine covers, either. They were from *Paris Match*, *Life* and *The Sunday Times*; one carried the picture of a soldier comforting an infant victim of war, another showed a scene of civil riot, while the third was a photograph of three greedy-looking businessmen obviously photographed from hiding. Don Tierney had taken the pictures. The frames had a wall to themselves where Don could see them in isolation. They were steady reminders of the standards he had to maintain.

That evening Don was standing in front of the television set, his face glum as he listened to the news commentary and watched stomach-wrenching images of uniformed men running and crouching on shell-wrecked streets, intent on blowing each other to pieces.

At 34 Don had the alert eyes of an old campaigner and the athletic build of a man accustomed to prolonged and strenuous action. He had a face people found interesting, a symmetry of clear-cut features made compelling by the determined, faintly belligerent set of his jaw. As the news film unrolled before him he swirled the wine in his glass, his eyes unblinking as old memories were triggered, familiar instincts touched.

The face of the newscaster came on the screen again, shaking Don from what had been almost a physical reverie. As he reached forward and switched off the set Anne came in from the hallway with Harry Brennan.

'No, straight up, Anne,' Brennan was saying, carefully balancing a coffee tray in one hand, 'that's the truth. I've never eaten better, *anywhere*, than I do here.'

Anne was smiling. 'I don't think Liz would appreciate that much,' she murmured, shaking back her long dark hair as she sat down.

'She'd agree.' Brennan made a soft grunt as he set the tray on the low table. He was a stocky, well-padded man in his fifties, Don's agent and long-time friend. 'One thing about my wife, she knows her limitations.' He turned to Don. 'I was just saying, that was another cracking meal. You're a lucky sod, you know that?'

'Luck's got nothing to do with it,' Don said, grinning. 'She just learns well, that's all.' He crossed to Anne and kissed her cheek. 'She couldn't boil water when I first met her. Taught her everything I know. Isn't that right?'

'Of course,' Anne said lightly, setting out the coffee cups. She glanced at Brennan, 'Humour them. It's the best way, I'm told.'

Standing by the settee, Don became distant again for a moment, the eternal observer, watching his wife and his friend and marvelling at the deep pleasure he could draw from simple domestic events. It was as if all the dangerous, lethal paths he'd trodden had sharpened his need for the ordinary and the low-key. It was supposed to work the opposite way. Life out on the edge, he'd often heard, made you hungry for more of the same – incapable, ever again, of experiencing inner peace. Perhaps it was like that for some people, he thought, smiling faintly as he caught Anne's perfume. For his part, he could relish danger *and* domesticity.

'Black or white, Harry?' Anne asked, holding the percolator over Brennan's cup.

'Black, thanks.' Brennan nodded at the television set, 'How's the world tonight, Don?'

'No change. Still bloody fragile.' Don crossed to the drinks cabinet and opened it. 'Brandy?'

'Silly question,' Brennan said.

'Anne?'

She shook her head. 'No thanks.'

Another of the pleasures, Don thought. Anne's moderation was never censorious, it was a feature of her own nature that implied nothing about other people's. Don poured two large brandies and took them to the table. He handed one to Brennan. 'When will Liz be back?' he asked, maintaining the soothing flow of trivia that had carried them through dinner.

'This weekend, hopefully. It depends on how her sister gets on, of course, but she's on the mend now by all accounts.' Brennan sniffed the brandy. 'Ta. Cheers.' He took a sip and as he did his expression shifted, signalling a change of topic. Brennan was never anywhere for long before he got around to talking business. 'So what time are you off on Friday?' he asked Don.

'Eleven-thirty,' Don murmured without enthusiasm. 'I've got a two-hour wait between planes in Athens. I could do without that.'

Brennan grinned, settling himself into an armchair opposite the settee. 'There, there,' he soothed, 'Not to fret.'

Don wandered across the room and stopped, gazing at the framed magazine covers.

'He'll be fine once he's out there,' Anne said.

'It's not my line,' Don said flatly.

'You signed the contract,' Brennan reminded him.

'In a moment of weakness . . .'

'You'd have been a bloody fool not to. I got you a bloody good deal there.'

Don turned. 'Jack Carver was on today about me covering this latest shooting match for them.'

'Oh no, Don . . .' Anne's delicate features clouded as she stared at her husband. 'Haven't you had enough of war?'

'Who hasn't?' Don said wearily, coming back and standing by the table. 'But there's still a lot of it about. Someone has to cover it. And that's what I'm best at – hard news. Not taking pretty pictures of a Greek island.' He glanced momentarily at Brennan, his eyes faintly accusing.

'But they won't just be pretty pictures, will they?' Anne reasoned. 'They'll be a personal statement, like always.'

'Which is just what the publishers are after,' Brennan said, nodding. 'The four seasons of Rhodes as seen through your viewfinder. All things ancient and modern. From every aspect.'

Don made a pained face. 'Why me?'

'Because,' Brennan told him, 'you did a fair old job on that Cambodia book of yours.'

'That was different,' Don sighed. 'I was there and it seemed like a good idea.' He shook his head. 'I wasn't planning on branching out into travel guides.'

Anne sipped her coffee, smiling at Don. 'It isn't going to be full time, anyway. Just a few weeks here and there over the next twelve months . . .'

'And,' Brennan cut in, 'between times you can take on any news or feature assignments you fancy, can't you?'

'Well, yes,' Don said grudgingly. 'I suppose so.'

Anne raised a finger. 'Preferably ones where you're not likely to get killed, please!'

Don smiled at her and sat down on the settee, putting his arm around her shoulder and nuzzling her hair. 'Would you miss me, then?'

Anne looked at him, her face stiffening. 'Don't, Don! Not even in fun.'

'Sorry love,' he said gently. There were times when he forgot – or chose to overlook – the intensity of his wife's feelings for him. He squeezed Anne's shoulder reassuringly and looked across at Brennan. 'I still think it's a mistake. For me and the publisher both.'

Brenna shook his head firmly. 'Don't you worry about the publishers. They know what they're doing. And it'll be nice for Anne, being out there with you for a while.' He sipped his brandy, looking at Anne. 'Pity you can't go with him on Friday.'

She shrugged. 'I'm only halfway through this Hampstead Building Society Trust job.'

'How's it going?' Brennan asked her.

'Okay. I think. I'm getting through a lot of film. Their PRO seems quite pleased.'

'So he should be,' Don grunted. 'I think, Harry, that it's time the agency invited her in as an associate.' Brennan, a former press photographer, ran a successful photographic agency that listed Don Tierney and a number of other leading photographers among its shareholding clients. 'She's proved her worth, after all,' Don added.

'Good idea,' Brennan said, beaming at Anne. 'Say the word and I'll put you up for it.'

'Really?' Anne looked delighted. She was a person who expected no special generosity from other people.

'Really.'

'Well . . .' Reactive caution took over quickly. Anne shook her head. 'It's a nice thought – and I'm flattered, really I am. But to tell the truth, I'm not sure that one professional photographer in the household isn't more than enough.'

'It's too late,' Don told her, delighting again in the simple, the unmomentous. 'You're getting paid for this Building Trust job, so you're a professional already, aren't you?'

12

Anne made her modest smile. 'Yes, I suppose I am.' To Brennan she said, 'But only part time – as and when I feel like it. You know what I mean.'

'Yes, yes.' Brennan waved her hesitancy aside. 'Think about it. The offer's open.'

'Thanks.'

Brennan raised his glass, smiling broadly at both of them. 'Well,' he said, 'here's to *Tierney's Eye on Rhodes*, eh?'

Much later, when the house had been darkened for the night, Anne and Don went to bed and made love. It was a spontaneous affirmation of their need for each other, a warm joining of bodies that intensified by liquid stages to culminate in a writhing, thrusting frenzy.

Afterwards they lay at peace, arms entwined, panting gently and smiling at one another in the soft light filtering through the bedroom curtains.

'Thank you,' Anne breathed against Don's ear.

'My pleasure.'

'Not exclusively.'

Don's smile widened. 'I hope not.' He kissed her on the mouth. 'I love you.'

'Go on,' Anne murmured. 'I'd never have guessed.' She returned the kiss, then drew back her head. 'Well?'

''Mm?'

'Are you going to keep it to yourself, or are we going to talk about it?'

'About what?' Don was staring at her, puzzled.

'Selling this place and buying a house in the country.'

'It was just a thought I had,' Don said. 'The idea only came to me when I was driving back from . . .' It dawned on him with a shock, as it always did. Spiritual empathy someone had called it. Anne and Don could be miles apart and still it would happen, the miraculous tuning-in of minds. 'My God! It's uncanny, isn't it?'

'Yes it is,' Anne agreed. 'It frightens me, sometimes.'

Don drew her closer for a moment. 'It's very special.'

Anne smiled, rubbing her nose gently on his cheek. 'Well, where shall we look?'

'You wouldn't mind living out of London?'

'Not if that's what you want. Wherever, with you.'

They kissed again, lingeringly, then Don slowly disengaged himself and rolled over on his back. Sometimes he felt too lucky. It was a hangover from childhood when nice times had never lasted long. Yet this had endured, four years so far and still blooming. It astonished him that two people so different in background could mean so much to each other. Anne was the beautiful, sensitive daughter of a diplomat, Don was a lad from Clapham Junction who'd had to sweat and bludgeon to gain every privilege he possessed. Worlds apart, the two of them, yet so immaculately matched that even their brainwaves were compatible. He sighed. At times their closeness troubled him. It took him aside from his ambition, his sense of responsibility – but he wouldn't want it any other way.

'Oh, God,' he moaned.

'What's wrong?'

'I wish I wasn't going away this Friday.'

Anne propped herself on one elbow. 'Harry Brennan will never speak to you again if you don't. Besides, I'm looking forward to the trip.' She poked Don's ribs. 'Anyway,' she said, her voice warm with reassurance, 'you're going to enjoy this assignment, once you get started on it.'

Don was sure she was right. She usually was. But his reluctance to go was stronger, this time, than ever before. Perhaps he was just getting more attached to his wife. There were worse ways to be, he thought, sighing and closing his arms around Anne.

Chapter Two

'Olympic Airways announce the arrival of their flight OA 710 from Athens,' the loudspeaker voice announced. The A300 airbus had landed on time at Rhodes Airport and was taxiing towards dispersal.

Five minutes later the passengers began to disembark. Don Tierney was the last one out. He had a battered camera holdall on his shoulder and he carried a large aluminium camera case with a tripod attached to it. In his other hand he had a carrier bag with his duty-free cigarettes and drinks. He paused at the top of the steps, stretching awkwardly, inhaling the herb-scented air.

Something caught his eye. Years of experience had given him an instinctive curiosity about executive jets. Wars had been started by people who travelled that way; deposed leaders, similarly, were often rescued by those sleek craft. Don was watching one now, taxiing to a secluded corner of the airport. A glossy, champagne-coloured Mercedes limousine was cruising across the tarmac to meet it.

Don shook himself. This wasn't a theatre of war, he reminded himself. This was Rhodes, the place where he was going to take pretty pictures. He moved on down the steps and walked slowly across to the terminal building.

At the head of the luggage conveyor the passengers who had arrived from Athens were milling around in tight groups, anxiously waiting for their bags. Don stood apart from them, content to wait until they'd found their things and gone.

'Mr Tierney?'

Don turned and saw a middle-aged Greek, well-dressed and looking rather fussily self-important.

'Yes?'

'I am Giorgios Nikolaidis.'

Don stared at him blankly.

'Mr Vagianos' representative,' the man said stiffly. 'I am here to meet you and take you to the house.'

'Oh, yes, of course.' Don extended his hand. 'I'm sorry. How do you do.'

'I am very well,' Nikolaidis said, shaking hands as formally as he spoke. 'Welcome to Rhodes.'

'Thank you,' Don murmured. The man reminded him of certain foreign policemen who always bowed before they arrested a European.

'You had a good flight?'

'Fine.'

'I am glad,' Nikolaidis announced, without displaying a trace of gladness. 'Now if you will give me your ticket I will have your luggage put into the car.'

'No, that's all right,' Don assured him. 'I'll grab it when it comes up.'

'Please,' Nikolaidis said firmly. He put out his hand and held it there. With some people, Don thought, there was no point at all in trying to argue. He handed over his ticket.

'Now, if you will please wait over there.' The man pointed to an area where there were some seats, then turned on his heel and shoved his way into the throng, searching for a porter.

Smiling, Don started walking to the seating area. On the way he passed a news stand with Greek and English newspapers on display. He paused, looking at the front page of the previous day's *Daily Mail*. Over a picture of urban carnage he read the headline 'Forty Die in Paris Metro Bomb Horror'. The sub-heading said, 'Terrorists Warn – We Will Strike Again'.

And no doubt they would, Don thought. He'd seen plenty of them and caught their identical whiff of hysteria. His mind shifted towards speculation; where would they be likely to hit next? What was the logical next step for crazy fanatics operating in the centre of Paris?

Again he had to shake himself. *This is Rhodes.*

He put his camera cases and carrier bag on one of the seats. Lighting a cigarette, he strolled over to a large window overlooking the runway and dispersal area. He could see the executive jet again; a few yards from it, facing the other way now, the Mercedes had just collided with an airport motor tug.

Don moved closer to the window. He could see the driver of the car gesticulating at the tug's driver, who was gesticulating back at him. The car's bumper was jammed over the rear of the tug's trailer. No great harm had been done, but it would clearly take some time to separate the vehicles. Already, an Olympic Airways courtesy limousine was speeding across to the scene of the accident.

Don continued to watch, amused, as the driver of the Mercedes went across to have a brief conversation with the driver of the courtesy car, leaving the driver on the tug to go on bawling and waving his arms. The man from the Mercedes was young and lean, dressed in a sober grey lightweight suit and looking, Don thought, very much like a Mormon missionary. After a few moments he was joined by another young man who had been sitting beside him in the car. They could have been twins. After talking earnestly with the driver of the airport limousine they stepped back to the Mercedes.

Don pulled hard on his cigarette, watching closely as the driver and his clone took up bodyguard stances. Two passengers came out of the Mercedes and climbed into the courtesy car. It was a hasty, almost furtive transfer, but the men's faces were visible long enough to register. One was a frowning, bullet-headed, restless-eyed individual with an unmistakably military bearing. When Don saw the second man he felt a mild shock. The austere, humourless face was unmistakable; it was Sir Joseph Marcus, an English industrialist

17

– *The* English industrialist, according to a number of pundits. Marcus headed ACI, the world's largest chemical manufacturing company, and he had just been appointed to chair the new Industrial and Economic Review Committee. According to recent news bulletins and press reports, he was supposed to be spending this weekend at Chequers with the Prime Minister.

One of the escorts got into the limousine and it moved off. Don went back to where his hand luggage was stacked. He was intrigued. What the hell was Marcus doing here, of all places? And why the furtiveness?

This is Rhodes. Don smiled at the automatic reminder flashing from the back of his mind. Yes, he thought, so it was. Rhodes, a place and time apart. Just for once he didn't need to think about shadowy manipulators or try to divine the motives of politicians and warlords. He had his artist's hat on. He was going to be a leisurely pictorialist for a while, instead of cutting time into startling, significant slices.

He stubbed out his cigarette, admitting to himself that he was still intrigued. It wasn't an easy matter to smother his instincts, not when they'd been his companion and guide, not to mention his bread and butter for all these years. A leopard, by contrast, would have found it pretty easy to switch to stripes.

Twenty minutes later Don was sitting beside Nikolaidis in the back of a hired Peugeot 304, travelling through the town and heading for the old city.

It was soothing to watch the passing scene. The Eastern Mediterranean light, Don believed, was the most lucid in the world. Here, on the island home of Helios the Sun God, the fluid, soft shadowed daylight touched stone, brick and glass in a way that enhanced every texture and sheen. The real became more real. Most painters were defeated by the effect; a photographer had a chance of conveying at least some of it accurately.

After a while, Don became aware that Nikolaidis was

looking at him. He was almost glaring. Don raised his eyebrows, inviting a question.

'You are a friend of Mr Vagianos?'

'No,' Don said. 'I've never even met him.'

'Oh.' Nikolaidis looked surprised. 'Then . . .'

Don anticipated him. 'He's a friend of a friend.'

'Ah!' After a small silence Nikolaidis said, 'Mr Vagianos does not usually let any of his property. He is a very wealthy man.'

'Well, that explains why he can afford to lend me his house, doesn't it.'

'Ah!' There was another silence before Nikolaidis spoke again. 'Mr Vagianos does not live in this house I am taking you to, do you understand. It's just one of the many properties he owns here on Rhodes.'

'Yes,' Don said, 'I know. His friend made that clear.'

'Ah!'

Another minute passed. Don stared out of the window, catching sight of a ruined Gothic church, its crumbled stone gilded by centuries of sunlight. It would be something to include in his collection, he thought.

'Mr Vagianos is not on the island at the moment,' Nikolaidis said curtly. 'He is in America. On business. And then he is going to the Far East. He will not be back for several months.'

'Ah!' Don said, continuing to stare out of the window. Nikolaidis glared at him, his lips pursing.

The car was now moving along older, narrower, uneven streets. The architecture became more uniform, an unexceptional style that nevertheless exuded a curious energy. It occurred to Don that Anne had been right, or he suspected she was; there was every chance he would enjoy the assignment. Rhodes could captivate a man.

As they moved steadily through mazed streets intersected by alleyways, Nikolaidis said, 'This is the old city of Rhodes. Here it is always beautiful. Now it is quiet, but in the

19

summer . . .' He made a sour face and shook his head. 'So many people.'

Five minutes later they turned into a square and the driver stopped the car. Nikolaidis made a small sweep of his hand, indicating that they had arrived. When the three of them got out, Nikolaidis said something in Greek to the driver, then went to the boot and opened it. Don looked at him enquiringly.

'From here we must walk,' Nikolaidis explained as he began removing the luggage. 'But it is not far.'

Don moved forward to help, but Nikolaidis seemed determined to carry all the baggage himself. He stood swaying with its weight, prepared to plough on up the narrow street like a pack mule. Don insisted he be allowed to help; finally Nikolaidis surrendered the two camera cases.

'Please to follow me.'

After passing some uniform, white-fronted buildings they came to an old, meticulously restored house. Panting from the exertion of getting there, Nikolaidis unlocked the arched door, opened it and ushered Don inside ahead of him.

The place was small and rather beautiful. Renovations had been carried out with expertise; the woodwork, windows, walls and floors combined the rustic quality of age with the sturdiness of a brand new structure. Beyond another arched entrance at the far end of the hallway was the kitchen. In the cosy, intimate sitting room antique Rhodian furniture had been selected and placed with precision, exactly matching the period and atmosphere of the dwelling.

Antiquity, however, hadn't been allowed to exclude convenience. There was high quality plumbing, electricity, a telephone and air conditioning, all discreetly incorporated. Don was delighted with the house.

'What a great place!' he said, grinning at Nikolaidis, who was gratefully putting down his load.

'It is very old,' he breathed. He switched the lights on and off. 'But it has all the facilities, of course. Mr Vagianos has spent much money on it. It was his father's house.'

'It's beautiful.'

Nikolaidis nodded. 'You will be living here a long time, I understand, Mr Tierney.'

'No,' Don said, 'Just now and then over the next twelve months or so. I'll be coming and going quite a bit.'

'You do not like hotels?'

'No much. And anyway I need a place where I can spread myself.'

Nikolaidis nodded sharply. He was like a rather basic computer, Don thought, needing to get his information in small chunks, lacking the ability to let it accumulate through conversation.

'You are a famous photographer?'

Don shrugged. 'So they tell me.'

'The name means nothing to me.'

'Could be they got it wrong, then,' Don murmured, keeping his face straight.

'And you will be here alone?'

'No, my wife's joining me in a couple of weeks.'

'Ah!'

'And I expect she'll be back from time to time too,' Don added.

'I see.' Nikolaidis made a movement of his mouth that could have been a smile. 'Do you have any questions?'

Don shook his head. 'No, I leave that to you.'

Oblivious to the small joke, Nikolaidis turned towards the door. 'I will let you get settled.' He handed the keys to Don, then took an envelope from his pocket and gave him that, too. 'It is a list of all the things you will need to know about the house.' He walked through the archway to the hallway and Don went with him. At the door Nikolaidis pointed to the envelope. 'My card is there. You will please to call me if you have the need.'

'You've done enough already,' Don assured him.

'Just the same . . .'

'Well, if anything comes up I'll certainly be in touch. Thank you again, Mr Nikolaidis.'

When he was alone Don took his suitcase upstairs and unpacked. In the small, immaculate bathroom he washed quickly then went back downstairs and picked up the phone. He asked the operator for his home number in London then waited, drumming his fingers on the table. When Anne answered he gave her a rapid, almost breathless description of the house. From his tone, she said, it was obvious he was hooked on the place.

'It could happen,' Don said. 'It really could happen.'

'So what are you going to do this evening?' Anne asked him.

'Oh, nothing much. A leisurely dinner by the bay. Read my guide books. Get plastered on a bottle of Castel Danielis . . .'

'Ooh!' Anne squealed. 'I envy you. Order some tzatziki, just for me.'

Don promised he would, then he spent the remainder of the call telling Anne how much he loved her and missed her. Just occasionally, he paused to hear her tell him the same.

Later in the evening, with the scent of oleander hanging rich in the air by the harbour, Don took his meal at a waterside table on the forecourt of a quiet taverna. He ate slowly, listening to the faint bouzouki music, admiring the view across the water and enjoying the closer beauty of the scarlet hibiscus that hedged the taverna's walls. In front of an empty chair beside him there was a bowl of tzatziki and a single carnation standing in a water glass.

Over coffee Don leafed through his guide books and tried, not very hard, to put together a work schedule for himself. The exercise was largely unnecessary, since he never adhered to schedules anyway, but it was a way of reminding himself that he was here to work. Eventually, because the beauty of the evening and its stillness were too seductive, he slid the books aside and simply sat for a while, puffing gently on his cigarette and gazing out over the water.

When his coffee cup was drained to the dark silt on the bottom he nodded to the waiter, who immediately nodded back, smiled, and began adding up the bill.

As Don looked out at the harbour again he noticed a tender moving slowly away from one of the yachts anchored there. He watched, mildly interested, as the boat headed for the shore.

'Your bill, sir.'

'Thanks.' Don took out his wallet.

'The food – it was all right, eh?' The man seemed eager for a compliment.

'Very good,' Don said. He rummaged through the snippets of language in his memory, trying to locate some Greek. '*Kalo. Poli kalo.*'

'Ah!' The waited beamed at him. 'You speak Greek!'

Don grinned at him. 'No, that's about it, I'm afraid. Very *ligo, ligo.*'

The waiter laughed, reaching into his leather purse for change as Don put a banknote on the bill and slid the plate across the table.

'That's all right,' Don said, smiling and shaking his head.

'*Efharisto poli,*' the waiter mumbled and began clearing away the dishes. He hesitated before the untouched bowl. 'The tzatziki – it was no good?'

'Yes, it was very good. That one's not mine.' Don smiled again at the waiter's puzzled face. 'But you can take it away now. It's OK.'

Shrugging, the waiter picked up the bowl and carried it off with the other dishes. Don stood up, taking his cigarettes, lighter and books from the table. As he moved away he glanced down into the harbour again and paused. The motorboat he had seen a minute ago was now alongside a stone jetty, thirty yards down from the taverna. Parked at the top of the steps from the mooring was the Mercedes Don had seen earlier at the airport. Standing beside the car, waiting, were the two Mormon look-alikes, flanking the military-looking man who had accompanied Sir Joseph Marcus.

Don's curiosity was back at full pitch. As he continued to watch, a well-dressed man in his mid-fifties emerged from the tender's day cabin. With the assistance of a sailor he stepped ashore and began climbing the steps.

Don glimpsed the face for only a moment, but it was long enough for him to recognize the man. There probably wasn't a news photographer in the world who couldn't identify him. He was Emric Niedermann, head of the largest private bank in Switzerland and a member of the Board of Governors of the World Bank.

Reaching the Mercedes Niedermann shook hands with the other man, who then hurried him into the back of the car. The bodyguards got into the front and a moment later the car glided away.

Don watched as they disappeared round the curve of the harbour. He was surprised and mystified. Almost against his will, he had to admit that he was deeply intrigued, too.

Chapter Three

The following morning Don was out early, roaming the island in a hired Suzuki jeep. He travelled along the undulating territory encircling the high, rocky centre of the island, through flat-roofed villages and past hillsides shaded by olive trees and cypresses. He drove without thinking, letting the surroundings crowd in on his senses.

To a man who had often struggled an entire day to find one useful picture, Rhodes presented an embarrassment of opportunities. Ancient stone buildings, overgrown with lichen, goaded the eye to find dramatic compositions. The stark white cubes of the village houses made classical counterpoint to the dark-clad women, just as children playing by a dusty road conjured visual metaphors of fleeting youth on a timeless landscape.

There were pictures – great pictures – everywhere Don looked. He photographed village women doing their laundry in the open air and captured a dozen contrasting vistas of shoreline and valley within the space of two hours. Old ladies with their donkeys stood by while he captured them on film, until their superstitious spokeswoman yelled at him in Greek to go away and leave them alone. A solitary tree on a stony slope made a poignant little study; so did the tiny girl who stared sombrely into the Hasselblad's lens as Don took shot after shot.

Rolls of exposed film bulged the pockets of his holdall as he worked steadily through the morning, unaware of time, absorbed completely in the business of capturing memorable images.

Near a wide bay by a roadside shrine hung with votive offerings, he spotted an old one-legged man asleep in the sun, his crude wooden crutch lying across his chest. Nearby, his heavy-laden donkey was patiently cropping the scrubby grass around the shrine. The scene was another small, ready-made masterpiece.

Don parked the jeep well down the road and approached the old man quietly on foot. Focusing rapidly, he took one shot and was about to take another when a helicopter rose sharply from somewhere beyond the edge of the road. Don watched as it circled once then moved away towards the south. The old man slept on, undisturbed by the noise.

He took another shot at the old man, then stowed away his camera out of sight in the jeep and set off in the direction of the retreating helicopter – up a rocky slope beyond which he knew the glittering Mediterranean would be visible. When he reached the ridge, Don was able to survey the sweep of scenery on the other side. The little, white-painted village of Aghios Theodoros lay in a magnificent valley which merited a paragraph or two in all the island's guide books. It was an impressive sight, a natural harmony of abundant vegetation, rocky slopes and sweeping shore. Most striking of all, standing at the valley's edge, was a gaunt castle mound with the Crusader fortress at its top.

Moving closer, caught by the photographic possibilities of the high viewpoint, Don clambered on to a cluster of rocks and looked down into the valley. As he scanned the craggy ramparts of the fortress, letting his eyes wander out beyond it to the sea, he suddenly felt his heart jolt.

Two champagne-coloured limousines were parked on the beach road. Beside the cars five men were standing in a group. Further along there were three other men. A solitary figure was walking towards the cars from the beach, where Don assumed he had just been landed. At that distance no faces were recognizable, but there was enough familiarity about the scene to make Don turn and go haring back to the jeep.

Opening the holdall, he pulled out his 35mm Olympus

camera body and a telephoto lens. He hurried back to the clump of rocks, attaching the lens to the camera as he went.

It was easy enough to screen himself behind a couple of boulders and still have a clear view of what was going on. Don put the camera to his eye and turned the focusing ring, watching the image swim into sharpness.

He recognized the forward trio at once. He panned across the faces of the two bodyguards, centred their military-looking companion in the viewfinder and took a picture. An instant after the shutter had fired, the man moved forward and extended his hand to the figure coming along the beach.

As they met and shook hands, Don realized that each man had unhesitatingly offered his left hand. That incongruity was swiftly dismissed as the camera held on the good-looking, middle-aged face of the newcomer.

'Good God,' Don breathed.

Again, it was someone he recognized – Remo Manzini, a prominent member of the Italian Government. He was also the owner and publisher of several newspapers and magazines. Don pressed the shutter release and wound on the film.

Left-handed greetings were now being exchanged between Manzini and the others waiting by the limousines. It was obvious from their relaxed, cheerful expressions that none of them was a stranger to Manzini.

Don swung his camera back and forth, photographing every face. In fleeting close-up he saw Sir Joseph Marcus and Emric Niedermann. Whatever this was, it was big. And there wasn't a trace of competition for the coverage.

Don worked feverishly, doubling on shots where there might be a chance of camera shake. The curiosity that had been dulled by the morning's work was in complete possession of him now. This was bound to be an exceptional story, he kept thinking. It had to be something cataclysmic. International giants were forgathering on a Greek island, away from the news searchlights. The political and commercial potential of the shots made Don's head sing.

On a second shot of Remo Manzini the film ran out. Don glared at the counter dial, knowing there wouldn't be time to reload.

He glanced down at the beach. The men were getting into the cars. In less than a minute they were driving away. Don kept watching, realizing they were heading for the castle.

He hurried back to the jeep and loaded his equipment in the back. The old man, he noticed absently, was still asleep.

As he started up the engine and swung the vehicle around, Don was making rapid peace with his conscience. It was no betrayal of his assignment, after all, to go after a hot news story when he found one. Harry Brennan had made that clear enough. There was a whole year to photograph Rhodes – more than enough time, if this morning's bag of shots was anything to go on.

Something like guilt persisted. *Why shouldn't I follow this one up?* he asked himself. It was big stuff, after all, it was what he thrived on. And he hadn't pursued it until now – on all the evidence, it had followed him.

Heading for the castle, Don began to realize that it wasn't guilt that was forcing him to justify his actions. There was no occasion for guilt, he was doing his job. What he felt, he finally admitted, was a thin edge of apprehension – perhaps fear.

Which was crazy.

Don had confronted real danger dozens of times. He'd risked his life in civil uprisings, disasters, wars. This was the other news territory, the milieu of political skulduggery, which was light years away from jeopardizing his pelt among violent men and their weaponry.

'Get a grip,' he told himself firmly as he steered the Suzuki along the bumpy, pitted road. The sensation remained, though, a queasy foreboding he had felt in Beirut, Teheran, Cambodia.

Crazy, Don thought. Totally daft.

He gunned the jeep harder, throwing up dust and stones as he swung round on to the straight that led directly to the castle gatehouse. Whatever was bugging him, he decided it couldn't be logical. It had to be an aberration. He smiled. That was it, an aberration. Three uninterrupted hours of taking pretty pictures had knocked his mind off centre.

He pulled up at the barrier and immediately a corpulent, surly-looking man emerged from the gatehouse. He bawled out something harsh in Greek.

'I'm sorry,' Don called back, as pleasantly as he could. 'I don't understand. Do you speak English?'

The man scowled and went back inside the gatehouse, muttering to himself. A moment later a well-dressed, handsome young man emerged and came across to the jeep. He was another Mormon-missionary type.

'Can I help you?' His English was virtually faultless, though too carefully enunciated to be his native tongue.

'I hope so,' Don said. 'Is this the road up to the castle?'

'Yes, it is.'

'Well, I saw the place on my way down into the valley and I'd like to take some photographs of it, if that's OK . . .'

'I'm afraid it's not possible, sir.' The young man sounded genuinely regretful. 'The castle is private property.'

'So I see.' Don nodded at the gatehouse. 'But I'm not a tourist. I'm a professional photographer. I'm doing a book on Rhodes at the moment and . . .'

'I'm sorry.' A trace of firmness had entered the young man's voice. 'I'm afraid you can't go up there.'

Don tried a persuasive smile. 'Just exteriors. A couple of shots close-to. That's all I'm after, I won't get in anybody's way.'

'I've told you.' The young man was looking hard at Don now, his face growing stern. 'The kastello is private property. The owner is in permanent residence. It is his home and he wishes to preserve it as such.' He looked up and pointed. 'There are some magnificent views of it from the mountains.

And from the sea. I'm certain you'll get excellent and very suitable pictures from either position.'

'Well,' Don sighed, 'It doesn't seem I've got much option, does it?'

'None whatever, sir.'

'Ah, well . . .' Don made a small wave and backed the jeep to the side of the road, preparing to turn. As he did, a champagne Mercedes swung into the entrance to the drive. The guard immediately raised the barrier.

As the limousine drew level with the jeep it slowed to a crawl. The rear window slid silently down and a good-looking, grey-haired man leaned forward, looking straight at Don. His features were dispassionate, but there was an intensity in his eyes that Don found disconcerting. They held each other's gaze for the space of a second, then the window slid up again. For just an instant before the Mercedes accelerated away, Don caught the expression on the man's face as he leaned back in his seat. He appeared to be concentrating on something, though with no great effort.

Don remained where he was for a moment, watching as the barrier closed, then he engaged the jeep's forward gear and made a tight turn, moving off the way he had come.

He had gone only a few hundred yards when he was suddenly struck by a violent headache. It was a rending, burning pain that seemed to knife across his skull and tear down into his brain.

At the same instant, thousands of miles away in Hampstead, Anne Tierney had just parked her mini and was about to go into the house. She stopped abruptly, gasping, clapping a hand over her eyes as she staggered across the driveway.

Don steered the jeep to the side of the road and pulled up sharply. Wincing from the pain, groaning, he pressed his hands to his forehead and slumped in the seat. It was like a ball of fire now, consuming his brain, searing into the sockets of his eyes.

And then it was gone. Not an echo of it remained, not even a lingering ache. Don sat up, blinking at the road ahead of him.

In Hampstead Anne was standing by the front door, a surprised expression on her face as she looked about her, panting softly. After a moment she shrugged, unlocked the door and went into the house.

Don had no idea what had happened to him. He lit a cigarette, took a few steadying puffs, then started up the Suzuki again. Perhaps it had been the light, he thought – the sheer intensity of it, the unfamiliar brilliance. The light plus all that critical, non-stop composing and focusing through the camera finder. Whatever it had been, Don didn't want the experience again. He promised himself that he'd pay a visit to an optician. Soon.

Chapter Four

The photographic shop was modern, but there was no clutter of cheap cameras or semi-toy gadgets. The shelves and showcases were stocked with good reliable equipment. There was a display of framed wedding pictures and family portraits, indicating that the proprietor's taste in selecting his stock was backed by a talent for using it.

There was no one around, so Don decided to browse. To one side there was a shelf of books, most of them guides to technique. At the end of the row there were a few expensive hardcover volumes of photographs. Don smiled to himself as he picked one up. The dustjacket showed a Cambodian peasant woman and her child with an Angkor temple in the background. The book was called '*The Faces of Kampuchea: A Journey Through the Kingdom of Angkor with Don Tierney*'.

'You should be proud of that book, Mr Tierney.'

Don turned sharply and saw the proprietor, standing by the door that led to the rear of the shop. He was a soft-paunched, gentle-eyed man with jowls that seemed to lengthen when he smiled.

'There is a picture of you on the cover,' he explained, coming forward. 'And I have seen your face many times in magazines over fine photo features.' He nodded at the thick volume. 'In Greece your book is expensive – but here it has sold very well.'

'I'm glad to hear it,' Don said. 'But it's been out quite a while now. Maybe you should offer this one at a reduced price and get it off your hands.'

The man shook his head gently. 'No,' he murmured, 'I shall keep it. I have my own copy of course, but if you would honour me by signing this one . . .'

'I'm flattered.' Don put the book on the counter and opened it at the title page.

'My name is Seferis,' the man said, handing Don a pen. 'Andreas Seferis. So if you would perhaps write. "To my good friend Andreas, the best photographer on Rhodes", I shall display the book in the window.' His smile broadened. 'The inscription is not entirely a lie – we will, I hope, become good friends and I will not deceive you. I am a pretty good photographer.' He blinked enquiringly at Don. 'Will you do that for me?'

'My pleasure.'

Don started to write in the book, but before he could begin Seferis turned to the front flap and checked the price. He nodded at the dustjacket, then at Don, indicating that he could proceed. Don made the inscription carefully, noticing that Seferis had gone behind the counter, where he took some money from his wallet and stuffed it into the till.

'A man who robs himself,' Seferis explained gravely, 'will rob anyone.'

Don nodded, then made his signature with a flourish and handed over the book. 'There you are, then.'

'I thank you Mr Tierney. I am in your debt.' Seferis read the words carefully then tucked the book away under the counter. Straightening, he spread his hands on the glass top. 'So now, my friend,' he said, beaming; 'what can *I* do for *you*?'

Don reached in his pocket and took out the cassette of black-and-white film he'd shot an hour earlier, up on the rocks overlooking the beach road. 'Do you do your own developing and printing?'

'Certainly,' Seferis said proudly. 'I have a very fine darkroom.'

'Then I'd like you to develop this for me.'

'Certainly.' Seferis took the cassette. 'Develop only?'

'Yes, that's all. For now anyway. I want to check the negs. How soon can you do it?'

'Immediately.' Seferis gestured around the shop. 'As you can see, I am not busy. I will have the negatives ready for you when you return.'

'I've nothing else on,' Don said. 'Mind if I hang around and watch?'

The job took ten minutes. In the darkroom Seferis put the strip of film into a deep tank of fine-grain developer, timed it, then transferred the negatives to a stop bath and finally a fixing solution. A high-speed wash completed the process.

Seferis hung the wet strip on a drying line and drew his rubber-lipped tongs over the negatives, removing the surplus moisture. Don stood close, looking over the man's shoulder, examining the tight-framed portraits he had snatched.

'Good sharp pictures,' Seferis murmured. 'But then naturally that is to be expected, eh?'

Don moved round and unhooked the negatives from the line, holding them to the light, peering at them closely.

'You took them here?'

Preoccupied, satisfied with the exposures, Don said, 'I'd like you to make a good-sized enlargement from each frame. Half plate, say.'

'No problems,' Seferis assured him. 'You would like them today?'

'No.' Don hung the negatives back on the line. 'I'm not in that much of a rush.'

'Tomorrow, then . . .'

'Are you open tomorrow? It's Sunday.'

'From ten o'clock to one o'clock only. I will have them ready for you . . .'

A man's voice interrupted from the shop, calling out in Greek.

'Ah,' Seferis said, 'excuse me.' He opened the door and went through to the shop. After another swift look at the negatives, Don followed him.

A young man was leaning on the counter. He was a year or two younger than Don, though similar to him in height and build. He was clearly not a Greek. His hair was dark blond and his features were delicate, with a slight, pleasant twist to the mouth; a downward tilt at the outer edges of his eyelids gave him a relaxed, easy-going appearance. It was a very British face, Don thought.

Seferis and the newcomer exchanged a few words in Greek, then Seferis turned to go through the doorway to the rear. He stopped when he saw Don standing there.

'Ah, Don!' he exclaimed. 'Two Englishmen together. I must introduce you.' With a grand sweep of the arm he indicated the young man at the counter. 'Here is another good friend of mine, David Bascombe.'

'Hello,' Don said smiling.

Bascombe nodded. 'How do you do.'

Seferis' arm swung proudly towards Don. 'And this is Don Tierney, the very famous photographer. You have heard of him, of course?'

'I very much doubt it,' Don murmured.

'Wrong,' Bascombe said. 'I went to that exhibition of yours last year at the Newbolt Gallery. Very impressive.'

'Don is here to take pictures for a new book on Rhodes,' Seferis explained. His pride sounded almost paternal. 'We are very lucky. It will be magnificent, I think.'

Bascombe nodded. 'I'm sure it will be.'

'Actually,' Don said, coming around the counter, 'I haven't really got started yet. I only arrived yesterday.' Having an ingrained dislike of the limelight, he changed the subject. 'Have you been long on the island?' he asked Bascombe.

'David has come to Rhodes many times,' Seferis cut in. 'He is an expert on our history. And now he lives here in the town.' He turned to the door again. 'Excuse me, I will get those prints for you, David.'

'Into photograph in a big way, are you?' Don asked as Seferis went out.

Bascombe shook his head. 'No, not me. Just the odd

snapshot. But I'm researching a book, and since Andreas has a Xerox machine I occasionally bring in one or two old documents and he copies them for me.'

'You know the island well, do you?'

'Fairly well,' Bascombe said.

Don nodded thoughtfully, taking in the relaxed friendliness of the young man. 'Fancy a drink, do you?'

Fifteen minutes later they were sitting on the pavement verandah of a taverna, sipping Greek coffee and watching the gentle, sunlit bustle on the street. They made natural companions, as Don had suspected; they were easy in each other's company, as if they'd been acquainted for years. They talked idly, and Don noticed that his preoccupation with the mystery at the castle was losing some of its intensity. The atmosphere of Rhodes had a way of diminishing urgency.

'You're a permanent resident now, are you?' Don asked.

'Not really,' Bascombe said. 'Just while I'm on my sabbatical.' He noticed Don's small questioning frown. 'I'm with the History Department of Durham University,' he explained. 'They've given me a year off to do research.'

'You said you were researching a book. What's it about?'

'It's a history of the island from the period of the First Crusade up to the time it was seized by the Knights Hospitallers in 1309.'

'Interesting,' Don murmured, feeling himself instantly out of his depth.

'Well, for me anyway,' Bascombe said, smiling. 'But that's my speciality. Medieval History. It probably bores the arse off you.'

Don laughed. 'To tell you the truth, I've never really got into history. Not even at school.' The confession had been worth making, Don thought. It underlined their intellectual and professional separateness; they had no need to compete with each other.

'Where are you staying?' Bascombe asked.

'In the old city. I've been given the use of a house there.'

'Nice.'

'Yes,' Don agreed, 'it's great. But the old city's a right rabbit warren, isn't it? I'm not sure I'll ever find my way back to the place.'

'Well,' Bascombe said quickly, 'if you tell me the name of the street I'll gladly . . .'

Don smiled. 'I'm joking.'

'I've known it to happen, all the same,' Bascombe said.

'I'm sure,' Don nodded. 'But I think I've got my bearings pretty well fixed.'

They both went silent again for a minute, then Don eased in the question he'd known he would ask, sooner or later. 'Tell me,' he said, 'have you ever been to a place called Aghios Theodoros?'

'Over on the west coast. Yes, often. Why?'

'There's a castle there.'

'The Kastello Aghios Theodoros.'

Don fingered the tiny coffee cup, running the strange memory of that morning. 'I tried to get some shots of it close-to, but I found out it's a no-go area.'

'So I understand,' Bascombe said. 'Didn't used to be, though. At one time anyone could go up there.'

'Who put the ban on?'

'Well, it was unoccupied until five or six years ago . . .'

'And now?'

'A Frenchman lives there. His name's Lavàllière – I see him about here in town from time to time. Not short of a bob or two, by all accounts.'

Don was wondering if it had been Lavallière he'd seen in the limousine, just before that ghastly headache hit him. Just as Bascombe looked so very British, the man in the car had had the appearance and bearing of a high-born Frenchman.

'There's a whole gaggle of them up there,' Bascombe went on. 'And there's others in and out all the time, according to the villagers. Apparently Lavallière does quite a bit of entertaining. It's pretty much open house at the castle all the year round, I gather.'

'Except for photographers, Don grunted. 'What does this Lavallière do for a living?'

Bascombe shrugged. 'I've no idea. But with the kind of money he must have, I don't imagine he has to *do* anything.' A clock inside the taverna chimed and Bascombe looked at his watch. 'I must go. I'm giving an English lesson in ten minutes.'

Don raised his eyebrows.

'Well,' Bascombe said, spreading his hands, 'it all helps. Rhodes isn't as cheap a place to live as it used to be.' He drained his coffee cup and picked up the manilla envelope with his Xerox copies.

'Listen,' Don said, I'm pretty much out on a limb here. All I know about Rhodes is what I've read in the guide books. And it's not the obvious I'm after. I could use someone like you to point me in the right direction and fill in the blanks. Do a little interpreting for me too, maybe. How about it?'

Bascombe looked uncertain. 'I don't know . . .'

'I really would appreciate your help,' Don said. 'For a fee, of course.' Help, not fee, was the persuasive keyword. No decent Englishman of Bascombe's stamp could refuse *help* without his conscience stinging.

'You need someone local, really . . .'

'You're every bit as good, from what Seferis said.'

Bascombe was till resisting. 'My Greek isn't marvellous . . .'

'It's better than mine,' Don said, grinning.

'Well,' Bascombe sighed, standing up. 'Let's talk about it. How about having a meal with me tonight. We'll have a few jars.'

'No.' Don frowned. 'I can't tonight, I'm afraid. I'm tied up. But tomorrow night? Dinner on me?'

'Even better,' Bascombe said. 'I look forward to it.'

They agreed to meet at the taverna around nine o'clock, then Bascombe left. Don watched him hurrying across the street and wondered at the sudden, curious awareness that had gripped him.

Back in the photographic shop, he'd been absolutely sure of his motives; he'd wanted to enlist a guide and interpreter. Detecting the usefulness of a contact like Bascombe had been automatic and Don had gone ahead and made the proposition. But as time was passing – right now, second by second – he was less and less prepared to consider exploiting Bascombe's knowledge or his abilities. In an odd, disquieting way, it felt like an act of treachery to think of the man as anything other than a new and rather precious friend.

Don sighed and stood up. He left a 50-drachma note for the waiter, then stepped into the street and began walking to where the jeep was parked. He was wondering, as he went, how he could explain the sensation to Anne, who shared his instincts more deeply than anyone he'd every known.

In a way it was simple – Bascombe was a natural friend, full stop. But that was like sketchy reporting, it didn't probe below the surface; it was so spare a truth as to be almost a lie. This growing, mounting sense of kinship needed lengthy exploration – but somehow Don didn't want to go into it. The word *sibling* flew into his mind. He rejected it sharply, not wanting to dwell on Bascombe any more. Without knowing why, Don was sure it wasn't the thing to do.

He shook himself and began walking more briskly. This was becoming a very weird day, he thought. Whatever it was – Rhodes, the Mediterranean light, the air – his circuits all seemed to have undergone a disquieting change. And that just wouldn't do. He had to be objective, in full control of himself.

'Work to be done, after all,' he murmured as he clambered into the jeep. He was thinking about those negatives again, getting the bit back firmly between his teeth. He turned the ignition key and the engine throbbed. Those men, that castle – the images aligned in his head like an equation, waiting, *demanding* to be solved.

39

Perhaps, Don thought as he pulled away, the answer would come tonight. He was certainly prepared to work at it. Quite suddenly, the sense of danger came back to hover on the edge of his consciousness. Don gripped the wheel tighter and shrugged. He'd learned, a long time ago, to live with that.

Chapter Five

That night Anne Tierney made a telephone call to Don's number in Rhodes. She stood tapping her fingers nervously on the table for over a minute, the receiver pressed close to her ear. But there was no reply.

Anne hung up, frowning. She had wanted, more than anything, to talk to her husband, to hear his own voice telling her that he was fine.

For an hour Anne had been plagued by a restlessness that had burgeoned, by now, to a keen, heart-thudding anxiety. She had gone through the syndrome many times before, the same pattern of uneasiness, then tension, then an agitation that shimmered into raw fear. It had always been at times when Don was in some danger, occasions when his peril found an unnamed nerve in her and jarred along its length until the emergency was past.

'Where is he?' she asked the blank wall helplessly.

Their sitting room felt hollow. It was cold, it was always cold when they were separated. The whole house became an effigy of itself, lifeless, alien – and never more so than when Don was on a battlefield somewhere, facing unspecified jeopardy.

Anne touched a chair, a treasured vase, the smooth lacquer of a cabinet. Nothing consoled her. The only familiarity she could conjure was in her husband's face, smiling beside hers in a picture frame, radiating his love, underscoring her loneliness and fear.

Anne shuddered, clamping her fingers to her temples, fighting the encroaching panic. *Where is he? What's happening?*

She began to wander around the room, an aimless circuit that dissipated some of the tension. She paused by the television set and glanced at its silent picture. Policemen were wrestling with militants on a protest march; fists and boots were flying, people were being hurt.

Anne switched off the set and strode to the door, then paused and picked up the picture frame. She examined the happy faces, her own and Don's, trying to draw the mood off the picture and into herself. Happiness. Mutual warmth. But the picture did no more than put small tears in her eyes.

She set the frame down carefully. Standing by the doorway, she took a deep breath and told herself, firmly, that she mustn't loose her sense of proportion.

Don isn't at a war. He's on a sunny Greek island. You'll be there with him. Soon.

'Soon,' she whispered, switching out the light.

Undressing for bed, she began to wonder if it had been self-induced, all that panicky fear, the foreboding. Now, after chiding herself, she felt only a steady buzz of tension, no more than was natural for a woman separated from the man she loved. That had been how it started; it was perfectly conceivable that she had used the tension as a springboard to the heights of anxiety and near-terror.

'Hysteria, they call it,' she murmured wryly, getting into bed. She looked at the bedside telephone, wondering if she should try again, then decided against it. She picked up a book from the table and opened it at her place. She couldn't remember much about the story and she had to force herself to make sense of the page, but the exercise was useful. It kept her in control. Or so she hoped.

It had taken Don more than an hour to drive from the old city. The roads towards the west were treacherously pitted; even the bright moonlight conspired to make the journey hazardous. Shadows from fig and olive trees, from boulders and ruins, made counterfeit fissures that had the jeep snaking erratically on the narrow highways, often into real potholes and yard-wide cracks.

Don parked the Suzuki on the road where he had first sighted the castle. He got out, stretched, then slipped his Olympus OMII over his shoulder. He checked that the protective cap was over the zoom lens, then started walking towards the castle mound.

It was another long journey. Since he would have been visible on the road he kept to the stony, shadowed terrain at the side, feeling his way over mounds and through minor, slippery chasms. Twice he lost his footing, smothering his curses as he skidded against bruising rocks and claw-sharp twigs and branches.

The configuration of rocks and vegetation became harder to determine as the road steepened towards the gatehouse. Don moved more and more slowly, protecting his camera with one hand while the other groped ahead of him, locating shrubs and branches to cling to as he pulled himself forward.

Ten yards from the gatehouse he stopped and sat crouched behind a boulder, catching his breath. He could see that the barrier was down; he could also see that the adjacent wall was low enough for him to climb over. He would give himself two minutes before he moved, he decided, even though there was a powerful urge to make straight for the wall. Experience had taught him that there was no point in attacking an obstacle until he had the reserves of wind to overcome it.

Don straightened slowly in the shadows, wiping his hands on his trouser legs. The rule was to think in straight lines and to remember that if he wanted something badly enough, he'd get it. Don wanted this story very, very badly.

He made a dash at the wall, taking no more than seconds to reach it, flatten himself against the brickwork, grip the edge and swing over it.

The road beyond was mercifully smooth and deeply shadowed. Don ran along it, breathing regularly, feeling the ground rise sharply as it wound closer to the rock in a high narrow spiral that brought him, panting again, to the main gate.

Don looked up, daunted for a moment by the height of the battlements. The sharp moonlight highlighted the craggy surface of the wall; looking at it for a few seconds, then testing the first few feet, Don realized he could probably climb to the top. With difficulty.

It took almost ten minutes. Don's hot, rasping breath echoed back at him in hoarse staccato as he spidered his way from foothold to foothold, climbing to the coarse stone with hooked, anxious fingers. A few feet from the top he paused, his lungs labouring. He turned his head and almost let go with fright. A gargoyle, dark and belligerent, jutted a yard from his face. Don closed his eyes and clung tight to the wall, waiting for his heartbeat to calm before he tackled the final stretch.

When he had reached the top he had barely the strength to hoist himself over the battlements. With his camera slung at his back, feeling the stone scrape the skin of his legs and arms, he pulled himself grunting through the space between two massive capstones and dropped down to the courtyard on the far side.

For long, punishing seconds Don lay against the wall, convinced he had done permanent damage to his lungs. His chest felt as if it was on fire. Again he could hear his own echo, a furtive, agonized hissing of air on dry membrane.

But he recovered quickly. The realization that he had made it – that he was *inside* the castle and close to the heart of the enigma – finally brought him to his feet, exhilarated, alert, keen to press on.

He glanced out at the moon-silver water of the bay, taking his breathing pace from the rhythm of the waves. Every nerve and muscle was alert and tuned to his purpose. For one dark instant the sense of danger invaded him. Don ignored it, willed it out of himself as he unslung his camera and wound the strap around his wrist. He took one deep breath, looked carefully around him, then propelled himself down the steps and out across the corner of the courtyard.

* * *

Anne Tierney had fallen asleep. It had been no soft descent, though, no gentle withdrawal. Anne had been pulled down into a vortex of scrambled, kaleidoscopic visions more real and frightening than anything the conscious world had ever inflicted on her. She writhed and twisted on the bed, thumping her fists on the sheets, whining her terror into the darkened bedroom.

She couldn't wake up. Having sought sleep to shield her from foreboding, she was caught in it now, trapped in the dark, miasmal territory of her mind. It was a place inhabited by terrors and atrocities, each one vibrating with the threat of worse to come.

'No, please . . . *No!*'

The tumbling scenario gyrated around her, an unspeakable parading of her fears and revulsions, shot through with hideous warning.

'Please, *please* . . .'

By relentless stages Anne's mind and spirit were being dragged towards the one spectacle she feared most, an enactment of truth she would sooner die than confront. Sweat sheened her body as she moaned and thrashed, digging her fingernails into the skin of her palms.

'Please!' she howled, 'please . . . Don't!'

A pale, dangerous mist lay ahead of her, swirling in folds that enclosed a blackness which was truth, the truth Anne struggled in a frenzy to avoid. The harder she fought, the closer the mist came, unfolding in skeins, baring its dark heart. Anne was suddenly paralysed, unable to struggle any more or turn her head aside. She began screaming, but the sound of it was lost in the roar that erupted suddenly from the hellish presence in front of her.

The door was small, thick and heavily studded. Don threw himself at it and grasped the handle, his eyes wide with fear as he twisted the iron ring left and right. The door stayed tightly shut.

His breath escaped in a shuddering whimper as he tugged and tugged, then realized the door was bolted. With trembling, sweat-smeared fingers he threw back the three bolts and twisted the handle again. The door swung wide.

Don stood in the opening for a second, his camera dangling from his hand. Abject terror spread on his face as he looked behind him, hearing the sound grow, an urgent, angry chatter of something invisible that was coming towards him, pursuing him, meaning him harm.

He began running, panic throwing him forward as he jumped down a flight of steps and almost landed on his knees. The sound, which had dimmed for a second, began to swell again, widening behind him and moving closer as he hared across the courtyard and hurled himself up on to the battlements. For an instant he looked back and saw a shadow, a formless, tumbling mass spilling across the steps and moving towards the wall, the terrible sound moving with it.

Don slipped from the battlements and scrambled crazily down the wall, defying chance and gravity as his fingers clawed the stone and his feet skidded over outcrops of rock and lichen.

Above Don's frantic, scurrying descent, the carved face of the devil Asmodeus glowered malignantly from the main gate. Beyond it, at the window of an unlit room in the castle, a man was gazing into the night, too. He was tall, aristocratic. His face was imposingly ageless with steady, dispassionate eyes. He remained impassive, almost calm, as the turbulent shadow screeched in pursuit across the courtyard and out over the battlements.

Don landed on the road and began running, aware that his hands were bleeding, knowing from the searing pain that his right knee had been twisted. Nothing mattered, no pain or injury – he had to get away.

Jolting fear drove his legs down the winding, dizzying

path, consuming his energy too fast, torturing his heart and lungs. Pain flared in his chest, making Don whimper breathlessly, but his legs moved fast as the horrendous sound filled the air behind him and the stunted roadside vegetation became alive with rustling, angry movement.

Time was being fragmented. One moment Don was struggling over the wall by the gatehouse, then he was halfway along the road from the mound, near-blinded by stinging sweat. After what seemed like no more than seconds, he saw the jeep ahead of him and realized he was on the old country road again.

He forced his legs to carry him, staggering, to the side of the vehicle. His body slumped against the cool metal of the bonnet; he was exhausted and near to collapse.

Then his head snapped up and his eyes widened on a new surge of terror. The second was coming after him again, louder than ever. The undergrowth beneath the trees rippled and shivered as the shadow raced through it towards the jeep.

Don threw himself into the driving seat, dropping the camera beside him. In a frenzy he started the engine and accelerated away, ramming the pedal to the floor. He drove aimlessly, veering from side to side, his face distorted with fear as he slammed the jeep forward through the stark moonlight.

Gradually, he became aware that the sound wasn't behind him any more. He slowed the jeep, braked, then listened. All he could hear was the sound of the engine. With almost uncontrollable fingers he turned off the ignition. The engine died. There was complete, blessed silence.

Relief surged through Don. He folded his arms on the wheel and sobbed into them, washing the terror out of himself. There was nothing in his heart or mind but gratitude, fulsome and overwhelming.

The sound came back with a blast. It was all around him,

deafening, grating his eardrums and entering his skull. Don clamped his hands to his ears and jerked round, staring out at the road. Darker now, dense and agitated, the shadow was advancing on the jeep.

'No . . . Jesus . . . *No!*'

Don saw it close, enveloping the wheels.

'God Jesus . . .'

He flailed his arms around his face, beating back the surreal horde that was starting to engulf him. Screeching, half-insane from the noise and the fear, he switched on the engine and threw it into gear, thrusting the vehicle forward. He steered with one hand, shielding his face with the other as the obscene swarm enshrouded his head.

Something mad happened to the road. It became three road – one going left, one right, one straight ahead. There was no way he could tell which was real. The tyres squealed and Don was nearly thrown from the seat as he steered left then veered back on to the straight path. An instant later the road ran out and became an impassable, choppy terrain of rocks and boulders.

Howling, demented, Don spun the wheel left. The jeep skidded on to soft earth, travelled at speed across twenty yards of open country, then crashed into the side of a derelict farm building. The impact hurled Don through the windscreen and on to the bonnet.

There was an instant's stillness before the fuel tank exploded. Liquid fire jetted into the air and showered down on the jeep, turning it into an inferno. At its crackling, roaring heart Don lay spreadeagled, his eyes wide open. Flames licked along his arms and legs and his hair was ablaze. He was lifeless, his lips drawn back tightly, fixed in the grimace of a final scream.

In Hampstead, Anne Tierney sat upright in her bed, soaked with sweat and trembling violently. She stared at the curtained window, hearing the echo of her own howl. For a moment she was confused, then the dread came down on her in three swift heartbeats, sagging her shoulders and drawing a long, deep moan from her throat.

Chapter Six

A St Christopher medal and an identity disc strung on a silver chain, a wedding ring, penknife, cigarette lighter, wristwatch and keys; the articles of property, pathetic in their isolation, were laid out across Major Lambrinos' desk at Rhodes Police Headquarters. Someone had tried to clean the items, but the scorching and discolouring from the fire were still visible. Anne Tierney sat staring at the objects, her eyes moving across them with the slow, lingering devotion of an acolyte's touch on a rosary.

'These things,' Major Lambrinos said, 'they belong to your husband, yes?'

Beside Anne's chair Harry Brennan stood by, anxiously watching her. She nodded, picking up the medallion and the identity disc, gazing at them.

'Thank you,' Lambrinos murmured. He took a form and put it in front of Anne, laying a pen beside it. 'If you would just sign for them, please.'

Anne stared at the form for a moment, taking in Lambrinos' request. She looked ill.

'Just there,' Lambrinos prompted, pointing to the dotted line at the bottom.

Anne signed the paper and pushed it back across the desk. She began gathering up Don's things and putting them in a plastic bag the police had provided.

Lambrinos cleared his throat. 'You have already been to the mortuary, I understand.'

'Yes,' Anne said without looking up. 'But they wouldn't let me see my husband.'

'He was badly burned, *Kiria*. But since we are now completely satisfied in the matter of identification, we have

50

no reason to cause you any further distress.' Lambrinos picked up a bundle of folded papers and handed them to Brennan. 'Here are the documents authorizing you to remove *Kirios* Tierney's body from Greece.'

As Brennan pocketed the papers Anne slipped the plastic bag into her handbag and stood up. She looked at Lambrinos, absently touching the black silk scarf knotted at her throat.

'You have my very deep sympathy, *Kiria*,' Lambrinos said, sighing heavily. 'But sadly, that does nothing for your pain, does it?'

Anne's voice was small and apprehensive as she said, 'What happened exactly, Major?'

'We do not know for sure. We only know that your husband was driving very fast. Too fast. For some reason, he lost control of the vehicle.'

'But what was he doing out there at that time of night?'

Lambrinos shrugged. 'It was a lovely night. There was a moon. He was perhaps taking some photographs?'

'Yes,' Anne said wanly. 'That's possible, I suppose.'

'Or,' Lambrinos suggested, 'It could be that he had just gone out for a drive.' He looked at Anne gravely. 'It is a question, I fear, that no one can answer.'

Later, Anne and Harry Brennan went to the house Don had been using in the old city. As they entered, leaving the door open behind them, Brennan said, 'I told Nikolaidis I'd drop the keys into his office when we've finished. He said he'd have been happy to meet us here, but he didn't think you'd want a stranger hanging around.'

Anne nodded. 'That was considerate of him.'

'Yes. Right . . .'

Brennan was watching Anne closely. Since they had received the terrible news, she'd maintained a taut, studied control of herself. Here in Rhodes she had shown signs of breaking down. Now, standing in the sitting room with Don's holdall, his Hasselblad camera, the rolls of film and sundry pieces of equipment lying all around, it looked as if

51

her grief might finally swamp her. Anne moved across the room and touched the battered holdall lovingly.

'I wish you'd let me take care of everything out here for you,' Brennan said.

'No.' Her voice was weary as she turned to face him. Her hand trailed away reluctantly from the holdall's scuffed leather. 'It was good of you to suggest it, Harry. I'm grateful for that. I don't know what I'd have done without you.' She looked around the room. 'I had to come. To tidy things up. And to be with him going home. You know what I mean.'

'Sure,' Brennan nodded. 'But we could come back later and do this.'

'I'm OK, truly,' Anne assured him.

Brennan didn't look entirely convinced. 'I'll get the things upstairs packed, then.' He turned towards the door. 'Won't be a second.'

'Harry . . .'

'Yes?'

After a moment's hesitation, Anne said, 'Did I tell you? Saturday night I had a dream. A terrible nightmare. I don't remember any of it now, but when I woke up I knew for sure that something dreadful had happened to Don.'

'Yes,' Brennan said softly. 'You were very close, the pair of you. Closer than most. Don told me once you could even read his mind.'

Anne shook her head. 'No, not really. But from time to time, however far away he was, I could tell for an instant just what he was thinking. And I always knew when he was in any kind of danger. Just like I was part of him.' She frowned. 'That's odd, isn't it?'

'Special,' Brennan said.

Anne made a soft, sad smile. 'That's what Don used to say.'

She turned away, crossed to where the aluminium camera case was lying and put the Hasselblad inside. Brennan watched her for a moment longer then went upstairs. Anne continued packing the odds and ends, moving disconsolately between shelves, tables and drawers, picking up guide books, cigarettes, a light meter and a sample bottle of whisky. As she was putting them into the camera case, David Bascombe walked in from the hallway. He was carrying a bulky white envelope.

Anne swung round, alarmed. 'Who are you?'

'My name's Bascombe.' He took another tentative step forward. 'Mrs Tierney?'

'Yes.'

'I'm sorry if I'm intruding,' Bascombe said awkwardly. 'I – well, I met your husband briefly and I thought I'd look in and . . .'

'Oh,' Anne murmured, nodding. 'I see.'

'I just wanted to say . . . Well, you know.'

'Thank you, Mr Bascombe.'

'I met your husband the day after he arrived.' Bascombe's eyes were pained, replete with sympathy. 'We talked for a bit. We were going to have dinner together on Sunday night. I waited for him of course – he thought I might be able to help him out while he was here. You see I live in the town and I know the island quite well.' He broke off suddenly, blinking back his emotion. 'Such bloody bad luck, Mrs Tierney!' he said angrily. It took a few seconds for him to control his agitation. 'I'm sorry. I'm afraid I'm not very good in this kind of situation. But . . .' He spread his arms helplessly. 'That's what I wanted to say.'

'No apologies,' Anne said, smiling. 'I know exactly what you mean. Thank you for coming.'

Bascombe nodded, turned to leave, then came back, holding out the envelope. 'I nearly forgot. Andreas asked me to give you this.'

Anne took the envelope. 'Andreas?'

'Andreas Seferis. He owns a photographic shop here.

53

Those are some enlargements he made for your husband.'

'Oh, I see.' Anne turned to her handbag. 'There'll be something to pay, then . . .'

'No,' Bascombe said hastily. 'Andreas says there's no charge. It was his pleasure.'

'That's nice of him. Thank him for me, will you?'

'Yes, of course.' Bascombe went to the door. 'Goodbye, then.' He glanced at her briefly before he left. His eyes were still very sad.

'Goodbye, Mr Bascombe.'

Anne gazed down at the envelope for a while then crossed and dropped it into the big camera case.

Brennan came down the stairs carrying Don's suitcase. 'I'll just put this in the taxi.'

As he went out Anne closed the case and the holdall. The stillness of the room was beginning to feel like a presence. She busied her fingers with catches and buckles, wary of succumbing to her imagination.

Brennan came back. 'Give us that, love.' He took the case from her and picked up the holdall. 'Is that the lot, then?'

'Yes,' Anne said quietly, 'that's everything.' She looked around the tidy, quiet room. 'All done.' The finality in her own voice chilled her. She turned sharply and followed Brennan out to the waiting taxi.

The process of healing didn't really begin until after the funeral. Well-intentioned offers of companionship and retreat were gracefully turned down as Anne set about rebuilding her life on her own; friends were fine, they were the adornment of the happy life, but at a time of grief they were like drugs, simply delaying the time when reality had to be faced.

The hardest part, she found, was ignoring the great gap inside her. Having rationalized her loss, she was still left with its devastation, an aching spiritual void where the amputation had taken place. Anne could pace her day, programme it so

54

that she was always occupied, but the emptiness regularly stopped her in her tracks, bewildered and tearful.

She continued to work. Her photographic project for the Hampstead Building Society Trust was two-thirds of the way to completion at the time Don died; now she attacked it at double the pace, fiercely preoccupying herself, establishing her solitary, un-united status.

Four days after the funeral, Anne was standing on a street near her home. She had her camera mounted on its tripod and focused on an old house across the way. It was a straightforward shot, a simple record. Anne framed the building carefully in her viewfinder then made three exposures. Her husband's advice had been always to do that – take one shot according to the meter reading, one under the reading, then one over.

As Anne released the shutter for the third time she looked up. Her breath caught in her throat. There was a mews entrance a little way beyond the old house. Standing there was a man, looking across at her. He was the living, breathing image of Don Tierney.

Anne felt dizzy. She blinked once and he was still there. At that distance it was impossible to be sure, but the resemblance was staggering – he even *stood* like Don, and there was the way his head was turned to her, the precise, familiar angle . . .

A lorry went by, obscuring the man. When it had passed he was no longer there.

Anne stood gazing at the mews for several minutes, unable to move or retrieve herself from the shock, until a policeman stopped and asked her if she was all right.

A week passed. Anne worked on, pursuing the project, filling her days with work and deliberately tiring herself so she could be sure of sleeping at night. The strange sightings went on, too. They were always fleeting, always at a distance; although they were disturbing to her, Anne managed – by an extreme effort of will – to set them aside as features of an aberration, no more than side-effects of her mental and emotional readjustment. Don was dead. The more she told herself that, the less it hurt. Cautiously, Anne began to decide that she was getting over the tragedy.

On Saturday morning she took time out to go shopping. The steady, anonymous bustle of the streets was soothing. Anne moved leisurely from greengrocer's to newsagent's to supermarket, almost enjoying herself. Don had talked often about the mundane times in life, how they held a curious, subliminal value that everybody needed in order to feel complete. He had been right about that, as he had been right about so many things.

Anne stopped by a shop window, looking at nothing in particular, letting her eyes roam over the display. As her gaze moved to the side she caught a reflection from across the street. It was a man – *that* man again, she realized, but nearer now and unmistakably Don's image, even to the clothes he was wearing. Anne spun round and collided with a couple walking past.

'I'm sorry,' she said breathlessly, her eyes scanning the opposite pavement. The man had gone.

All of Anne's emotional barricading began to buckle in that instant. She hadn't imagined what she saw, she couldn't have. No phantom would ever look that solid, and . . .

Her mind shied at the sudden, shocking thought. It was bizarre, self-destructive, it had no place in a sane, reasoning intellect. But it was strong and insistent, demanding to be entertained; nobody could look that much like Don without *being* Don.

That afternoon Harry Brennan called round. After a few minutes of talking about her work and updating Harry on her general well-being, Anne decided to tell him about what she had seen.

Brennan listened patiently, then shook his head slowly. 'It's just not possible, Anne love, is it?'

'But I've told you, it hasn't happened only once. It's too much to be imagination or coincidence – I've seen him half-a-dozen times . . .'

'So there's someone who looks like Don,' Brennan said flatly. 'There's got to be quite a few fellows who do. Have you ever had a really good look at him?'

'No, never,' Anne admitted. 'Just a glimpse.'

Brennan spread his hands. 'There you are then.' He turned and pointed to the drink cupboard. 'You sure you won't?'

'No thanks,' Anne said. Drinking, like immersing herself in self-pity, was something she'd been avoiding. She frowned at the carpet for a minute. 'Harry . . .' she began tentatively.

'What, love?'

'I suppose there's no chance that Don isn't really dead, is there? I mean neither of us ever saw his body, did we?'

'Oh come on, Love.' Brennan's voice was soft and patient. 'There's no doubt about it.'

'Then why do I . . .'

'Because,' Brennan said, 'you want to. It's as simple as that.'

Anne sighed. 'Perhaps you're right. Yet I could swear . . .' She made a helpless gesture. 'And every time I've had the feeling that he was trying to get closer to me – trying to tell me something.'

'You need a rest, girl. Why don't you go away for a few days? Say the word and I'll make all the arrangements for you. Get you booked in somewhere nice – you and Liz both, eh? How about that?'

'I'll think about it,' Anne promised. 'But what if . . .'

'Anne!' Brennan's eyes hardened for an instant, but when he spoke again his voice was gentle. 'It's all in your mind. Don's dead. And there's no way that wishing is going to bring him back.' He kissed Anne's cheek. 'Get a good night's rest. I'll ring you tomorrow.'

Anne nodded, following Brennan across the room and into the hall. She stood by the front door and watched him get into his car, then walked slowly back to the sitting room.

For more than a minute she stood aimlessly in the middle of the floor, feeling the tugs of doubt and certainty. Finally she decided to abandon her fretting and go to bed early, just for a change. She felt very tired.

Anne turned and gave a little gasp. She went completely motionless, staring as the colour drained from her face. Standing in the doorway, only a few feet away, was Don Tierney, looking perfectly real, healthy and rather pensive.

Chapter Seven

'Mrs Tierney's problem was a relatively simple one,' Dr Phillimore said. He was in his room at the nursing-home, sitting with his back to the sunlit window. 'She was deeply in love with her husband. When he was killed in that accident she just couldn't let go of him.'

The decor of the room was modern and relaxing. Harry Brennan sat opposite the doctor at the wide desk, listening, impressed by the quiet certainty in the man's voice.

'It's not that unusual,' Phillimore went on. 'Adjusting suddenly to the death of someone so close to you is never easy. If you're as emotionally vulnerable and as sensitive as Mrs Tierney, then it's even more difficult. She refused to accept it – subconsciously, anyway.'

Brennan nodded. 'So she imagined that he was still around.'

'More than that. She brought him back to her whenever she could.'

'Ghosts?' Brennan said, not troubling to cover his disbelief.

'Most of my patients are haunted by phantoms of one kind or another, Mr Brennan.' Phillimore smiled, his intelligent eyes steady, as confident as his voice. 'If we know anything for certain about the human mind, it's that it is capable of some very strange things. Given the need and the will, under the right circumstances, it can do just about anything – including conjuring up the dead. The mind creates its own reality.'

'Oh, I see.'

'And now you're reassured. Good.' The doctor put his hands flat on the desk. 'But that's only one explanation of the so-called supernatural. As a rationalist and a doctor working in this field, I happen to subscribe to it.'

'Of course.'

Phillimore smiled. 'However,' he said, 'that doesn't necessarily mean it's *the* explanation, does it?'

'I'll settle for that one,' Brennan grunted.

'And fortunately, over the past five weeks so has Mrs Tierney, I think.'

'It was really weird. It got to be that she was seeing Don everywhere, you know. In the house with her, even.'

'Yes,' Dr Phillimore said, 'she told me. And her dilemma was a classic. Emotion versus reason. She's a highly intelligent woman, so however much she wanted to conjure her dead husband, and brought it about, her reason told her it wasn't possible – even though she could see him. Hence her breakdown.'

'But now she's fine.' Brennan's tone suggested he'd like reassurance on the point.

'As far as it's possible to tell.'

Brennan frowned. 'Can't you be more definite?'

'Wouldn't that be nice,' Phillimore said. 'However, I'm satisfied that, as of now, she has everything sufficiently in perspective for me to discharge her. But that's not saying . . .' He shrugged.

'You mean it could happen again?' Brennan looked mildly alarmed.

'Yes, it could. It's unlikely, but it's possible. It depends entirely on how she continues to adjust to her husband's death.' Phillimore looked thoughtful. 'They were obviously very close, the pair of them.'

'Very,' Brennan said. 'They even had some kind of ESP going for them, from time to time.'

'So I understand.'

'Not so much on Don's side, I don't think – but Anne says there were times when she could tell what he was thinking, feeling, even when he was miles away from her.'

60

'And why not?' Phillimore appeared to find no mystery in Anne's ability. 'Two minds finely tuned, both on the same wavelength. One transmitting, the other receiving.' He shook his head. 'I often wonder why some of my colleagues find that so difficult to accept.' He looked at Brennan. 'It's a pity the Tierneys didn't have any children.'

'Anne can't have kids. She told my wife.'

'Yes, it's clear from her medical records. I don't think Mrs Tierney ever fully recovered from that blow. Apart from anything else, children are very useful for channelling all kinds of emotions. Especially at a time like this. Still,' Phillimore added brightly, 'there'll be something else, perhaps. Her work, maybe.'

Brennan looked encouraged. 'That'll help?'

'It could. Depends how important it is to her.'

'Fairly important, I think. She's very good at it.'

'Then encourage her,' Dr Phillimore said. 'See she keeps busy – particularly over the next few months. The important thing is . . .' He was interrupted by a knock at the door. 'Come in.'

The door opened and a nurse led Anne into the room.

'Ah, Mrs Tierney!'

Both men stood up. Anne came towards them; she was pale, Brennan noticed, but she had lost the haggard, troubled look she'd had when she first came to the nursing home.

'I'm all packed and ready to go,' she told Dr Phillimore, then turned to Brennan. 'Hello, Harry.' They embraced warmly then Anne stepped back, shaking her head. 'Driving out all this way,' she said, chiding him gently. 'You shouldn't have bothered. I could have called the local taxi people.'

'No way.' Brennan smiled broadly at her. 'How are you?'

There was the slightest hesitation before she replied. 'Fine.' She glanced towards the doctor. 'Not sorry to be leaving, though.'

'I'm delighted to hear that,' Phillimore assured her.

Brennan had already crossed to the door. 'Where's your case?'

'In the hall.'

Brennan nodded sharply. 'Well come on, then. Let's not hang around.'

Anne turned once again to Dr Phillimore. 'Goodbye,' she said. 'And thank you.' She followed Brennan into the passage, her smile fading.

They walked out through the main door and across the drive to the car. As Brennan loaded Anne's bags into the boot he paused and looked across at the elegant main building.

'Lovely old place,' he murmured, 'isn't it?'

Anne stared up at the windows thoughtfully. 'From the outside,' she said quietly, then got into the car.

It took just over an hour to drive back to Anne's house in Hampstead. A running argument had occupied the last five minutes of the journey; Brennan wanted Anne to come and stay with him and his wife for a few days, but Anne wanted to be left alone at home.

In the sitting room, helping Anne off with her coat, Brennan tried one last time to coax her away from solitude.

'Come and eat with us tonight, at least,' he said.

'No.' Anne's voice was firm. 'Not tonight, thanks, Harry.' She watched the frown spreading on his face. His concern for her was touching and reassuring, but her mind was made up. 'Don't worry, I'm OK. Honest. It's just that tonight I'd rather be on my own.'

'Well.' Brennan shrugged. 'If that's how you feel . . .'

'But tomorrow, though – If you and Liz have nothing else on. I'd like that.'

The compromise seemed to placate Brennan. 'Tomorrow night, then. And that's a promise?'

'That's a promise.'

Anne began to walk around the room, resuming contact with its familiarity. Every few seconds she paused, looking at pictures, lightly caressing ornaments.

'I think you'll find the place is in pretty good nick,' Brennan told her. 'Mrs Butler's been in regularly and Liz has popped in from time to time.'

'I can see that. The place has never been so clean and tidy.'

'You'll probably need to get some food in, though.'

Anne nodded absently. 'I'll nip out to the shops later.'

Brennan folded his hands, watching her. 'Made any plans, have you?'

'Not really.' Anne paused by the settee, shaking her head slowly. 'Not beyond finishing off that job for the Hampstead Building Trust, anyway. That won't take long, I've only got four or five more pictures to take.'

'You hadn't thought any further than that?'

'No.'

'But you'll want to go on working, though,' Brennan insisted, recalling what Dr Phillimore had said. 'I mean I know you won't have to, thank God – not with what Don's left you. But you'll want to carry on with your own photography, won't you?'

'Probably. Just to keep myself occupied.' Anne didn't sound particularly sure.

'Why not join the Agency?' Brennan has stepped closer, trying to infect her with some enthusiasm. 'That's what Don wanted, wasn't it? The only thing that held you back before was . . .'

'That I didn't want to be in competition with him,' Anne said. 'Well, not directly, anyway.'

'Because you know just how talented you are.' Brennan took in the surprised look Anne had shot him. 'Don knew it too, believe me. Anyway, it's a different scene now, isn't it? Just give me the nod and I'll put your name up at the next management meeting.'

'When's that?'

'The week after next.' Brennan smiled at her. 'Well? What do you say?'

Anne thought about it for a few moments, then she nodded. 'Why not? OK, Harry. And thank you.'

'Great!' Brennan looked delighted. 'Consider yourself an associate member as of now. We ought to have a drink on this.'

'What if the other members of the board turn me down?'

'What do you mean, turn you down?' Brennan demanded incredulously. 'They'll all be knocked out by the idea.'

'Just the same,' Anne murmured, reverting to her habitual caution; 'I think I'll wait until the votes have been counted. *Then* we'll celebrate.'

'That's for sure,' Brennan said, glancing at his watch. 'Anyway, I ought to be getting along. I'm playing golf with one of the senior Editors of *Life* this afternoon. And Liz'll be wondering where we've got to.'

'Oh, I'm sorry,' Anne apologized. 'Do you want to ring her?'

'No.' Brennan went to the door and paused there. 'I've got to stop off at the house and pick up my clubs. I'll tell her what's happening then.'

'I hope she won't be too upset.'

'Of course not.' Brennan grinned. 'She'll just be delighted that you're home again and back to . . .' He checked himself abruptly.

'Normal?' Anne prompted.

'Full health. And besides, you're right.' Brennan waved his arm at the pleasant room. 'This is where you belong.'

Anne crossed and stood near the small table by the door. 'Did you know that we were thinking of selling this place and buying somewhere in the country?'

Brennan shook his head, watching as Anne picked up the framed photograph of herself and Don.

'We talked about it the night before Don left for Rhodes. It's what we both wanted.' She stared fixedly at the picture.

'And is it still a possibility?'

'I don't think so,' Anne sighed. 'Not just me, on my own.' Her attention was still riveted on the photograph. 'He was trying to tell me something, you know. I'm sure of that. But he couldn't and now that he's gone . . .' She looked up at Brennan, her eyes narrowing; 'I'll never know what it was, will I?'

Brennan frowned, disturbed by what Anne had said. Anxiety was stirring in him, a trace of doubt planted by Dr Phillimore's own uncertainty.

'Anne, love . . .'

She altered suddenly, smiling brightly at Brennan, the concern and pain instantly gone from her expression. 'I'll see you to the door,' she said, putting the photograph back on the table. 'And do give Liz my love, won't you?'

'Yes, of course,' Brennan said. He went out slowly into the hall, wondering if he should feel reassured.

That night, after more than an hour in bed, Anne found she simply couldn't sleep. She propped herself up on the pillows, switched on the bedside lamp and reached for the alarm clock. It said 1:40. Sighing deeply, she put down the clock again and picked up the bottle of sleeping tablets.

She had the cap half unscrewed before her determination took over. She tightened the cap and put the bottle back on the table.

'The thin edge of a nasty wedge,' she reminded herself, swinging her feet out into her slippers and picking up her dressing gown.

The bland, characterless days in the nursing home had owed a lot of their sameness to the drugs that had been pumped into Anne. It was easy enough, now, to understand how dependence began; being doped wasn't too pleasant but it had a safe, cocooned quality. There came a time when the transition from half-real to stark-real was too harsh to be withstood. It could become better – or certainly seem better – to stay at a constant painless distance from life. That, in

Anne's estimation, was a compromise she couldn't afford. Full awareness, however painful, was the only starting point a person could work from towards fulfilment – even if, as in Anne's case, she had no clear idea what shape fulfilment might take.

She went downstairs to the kitchen and poured herself a glass of milk, then padded through to the sitting room with it.

Sleeplessness, Anne had recently learned, was only a serious problem when it was allowed to frighten the sufferer. The dread of hours spent staring awake was worse than the simple, boring reality. And the dread made sure the condition got worse.

In the nursing home, for more than a week before she had been due for discharge, Anne had stopped taking her sleeping tablets. Instead, she had used the energy she'd derived from the long rest to actively confront her night-time fears. And she had made a stunning discovery; there was no real fear at all, only confusion.

Sipping her milk now, looking across at the picture of herself and Don, she remembered how the simple rationale had come to her. There *were* more wonders in heaven than on earth, it was something she had never doubted – so why, she had asked herself sternly, did she allow her puny, human intellect to dictate that her visions of Don were irrational? Who knew what was irrational?

She had only become ill because she couldn't decide if the sightings were real or imaginary, so the dilemma became simple to set aside. All she had to do was accept, forming no conclusions until there was enough evidence, one way or another, to provide the basis for a firm conclusion.

That had been Anne's guiding principle – it had brought back her self-assurance, or most of it. The staff at the nursing home could think what they liked, they could believe that their regime of rest and drugs and gently persuasive arguing had worked the trick. But Anne knew she had worked it herself.

She glanced across the room suddenly, startled. The curtains by the French windows were billowing, as though they were being disturbed by a breeze.

Anne put down her glass and crossed to the windows. She took a corner of one curtain then hesitated, steeling herself for a shock. She jerked the curtain back. The windows were securely locked and bolted.

Frowning, she released the curtain. She was on the point of turning round when she was seized by the feeling that she was no longer alone in the room. *The doorway!* she thought, feeling her heart begin to thump. *I left the door open . . .*

With an effort she made herself turn, tentative, half-smiling. But there was nothing there.

Anne felt disappointment wash over, trailing quickly into regret as she crossed the room and picked up her glass again. She took a sip and moved over to the fireplace.

God, I could have sworn . . .

She looked down at Don's leather holdhall and aluminium camera case, sitting one on top of the other in the alcove by the fireplace. On an impulse, she picked up the holdall and carried it across to the settee. She put her glass on a table and sat down, opening the bag.

It was inevitable, Anne knew, that nostalgia would continue to well in her. The sight of the bag's contents was especially moving. She knew every item, she'd helped Don to pack them countless times and had watched him use them. The equipment was a formidable symbol of Don's life – of the life they'd had together.

Anne dragged herself away from the sentimental reverie, before it led to the kind of heart-sickness she couldn't cope with. Instead, she took out Don's back-up camera, a battered Olympus, and began checking it with a professional eye. Making sure there was no film in it, she cocked and fired

67

the shutter a couple of times, inspected the lens for dust or scratches and tested the bayonet lens mounting. Satisfied it was in good working order, she put the camera back in the holdall.

It was then that she noticed the sealed white envelope tucked down the side of the bag. She remembered it at once – a man called David Bascombe had given it to her in the old house in Rhodes. Photographs, he'd said, prints someone had made for Don.

Anne took the envelope and broke the seal. The prospect of seeing the few pictures Don had taken on Rhodes was sad, but it had an element of excitement, too. She pulled out the thick sheaf of black-and-white prints and began looking through them.

They weren't at all what she had expected. They were close-ups of men, each and every print, tight-framed shots without enough background to identify where they were taken. She squared the prints and went slowly through them again, squinting at the sharply-focused faces, recognizing none of them.

Anne put the pictures down on the settee and stared at the motionless curtains by the French windows. She was deeply puzzled. And intrigued.

Chapter Eight

Two weeks later, Harry Brennan came round bearing a bottle of champagne and the news that the management committee had accepted Anne as an associate member of the Agency.

'Here's to our new associate,' Brennan said warmly as he raised his glass to Anne in the sitting room.

'Who's still slightly bemused by it all,' Anne said, clinking her glass against Brennan's.

'I don't know why, love.' Brennan sipped his drink and smiled expansively. 'I told you it was a certainty, didn't I? And I was right. Everyone was for it. It was a unanimous decision.'

'Just as long as . . .' Anne frowned for a second. 'Well, they were all good friends of Don's, weren't they?'

'Oh, get off!' Brennan said sharply. 'Sentiment had nothing to do with it.' He gestured with his glass. 'So right, Don was one of them. And they liked him. Maybe some of them even feel they owe him something – but take it from me, there's none of them would think of paying off that debt by voting you into the Agency. Not if you weren't up to standard.'

Brennan paused, seeing the doubt still lingering behind Anne's eyes. He stood in silence for a minute, steadily sipping the champagne, knowing what she was thinking. When he looked at Anne again his face was serious, earnest.

'They're professionals,' he said, 'and bloody hard-nosed where work's concerned. You've been accepted for one reason and one reason only – because you take damn good pictures and they can see the potential in you. And this is just the first step, remember,' he went on, wagging a finger.

'Probationary associate. You've still got to show them they're right. In twelve months' time, if you haven't come up to scratch, they'll be just as unanimous in kicking you out on your arse, believe me.'

Anne studied Brennan's face for a moment, then she smiled. 'Thanks, Harry. I needed to know that.'

'OK.' Brennan was pink and visibly breathless from the rapid-fire delivery. 'Let's not hear any more from you about it, right?' He grinned and raised his glass. 'Cheers!'

'Cheers!'

They both drank from their glasses then Brennan stepped back, openly appraising Anne. 'So how are things? You're looking fabulous.'

'Thank you,' she said with a modest bow of the head.

'Feeling good?'

'Better and better.'

'Knock out! No more . . .?' Brennan moved his hand vaguely to imply his meaning.

'No,' Anne assured him. 'No more ghosts.' She held out her glass and Brennan refilled it.

'And have you finished those photographs for the Building Trust?'

She nodded. 'I dropped the last batch of prints in to their PRO yesterday.'

'Good.' Brennan topped-up his own glass, doing it at eye level, like a pharmacist. 'But you've held on to the negs, I hope.'

'Of course.' At times, Anne thought, Brennan treated her like a child. It didn't offend her, since she knew his intentions were sound.

'Oh,' she said as a thought struck her. 'Talking of photographs, what do you make of these?' She crossed to an armchair where her handbag was lying and picked up the white envelope. 'I meant to bring them with me when I came over to dinner the other night, but I forgot.'

Brennan took the envelope and slid out the bundle of

half-plate enlargements. He stared at the top picture. 'Did you take these?' he asked, shuffling through the rest.

'No, Don must have.'

'Where?'

'Well, on Rhodes, I assume. That man Bascombe gave them to me.'

Brennan looked blank. 'Bascombe?'

'The fellow I told you about – the one who came to the house when we were packing up Don's things.'

Brennan nodded, remembering.

'According to him,' Anne said, 'Don had the enlargements done locally. But why? Do you recognize any of those men?'

'One of two of them,' Brennan grunted. 'Him, for starters.' He handed Anne one of the prints. 'That's Sir Joseph Marcus, big white chief at ACI.'

Anne looked at the picture. 'Yes, of course. His face did ring a bell, but not loud enough. But then he's pretty insignificant-looking, isn't he?'

Brennan found that funny. 'If you're chairman of the second largest company in the world,' he said, 'I reckon it's an advantage to look insignificant these days.' He passed Anne another picture. 'This one doesn't look insignificant, though, does he?'

'You recognize him, too?'

'He's Remo Manzini. Another bloody millionaire. He's also a member of the Italian Government. A lot of people in the know are predicting he'll be the next Prime Minister of Italy, no less.'

'What was he doing on Rhodes?'

'A good question,' Brennan answered. 'And with Joseph Marcus. It doesn't fit.'

Anne pointed to the military-looking man in the picture, shaking hands with Manzini. 'Who's that?'

'No idea.' Brennan squinted at the picture again. 'Some kraut flunkey or other, from the look of him. Can't you just see him in a nice pair of shiny jackboots?' He began leafing through the prints again and stopped at another familiar face. 'Well, well. Curiouser and curiouser. Mr Money himself.' He handed the print to Anne. 'Emric Niedermann.'

The name meant nothing to Anne. 'What does he do?'

Brennan pantomimed high astonishment. 'What does Emric Niedermann do?' he laughed. 'You're obviously not a reader of the *Financial Times*, girl.'

'No,' Anne agreed. 'Pink's never been my favourite colour.'

'Well, how about *Time*? They did a cover story on him two or three weeks ago. He's Niedermann's Bank, the largest private bank in Switzerland. For an encore he does a very good impersonation of one of the governors of the World Bank.' Brennan shook his head at the picture. 'He's bloody high-powered.' He leafed through the remaining prints. 'Can't place any of the others, I'm afraid. Not off the cuff.' He began to put the sheaf back in the envelope, then stopped, looking at Anne. 'There's no way Don could've taken these pictures in Rhodes, love.'

'Why not?'

'Because when a group like this gets together for a chinwag, the whole world knows about it. And a lot of people start trembling.' Brennan thought for a moment. 'I'll tell you what, Don could've taken them at that international conference he covered in Philadelphia last year.'

'But why have them printed up in Rhodes?'

Brennan shrugged. 'Maybe he mislaid this roll at the time. Then when he got to Rhodes he found it in his camera bag, wondered what the hell was on it and popped in into this . . .' He peered at the name on the envelope; 'Mr Seferis, got him to develop it and pull off some half-plates. Mystery solved.'

'I'm not so sure,' Anne murmured.

'There's no other explanation, is there?' Brennan took the prints from Anne, added them to the others and slipped them all back in the envelope.

'No, you're probably right.' Anne took back the envelope and tossed it on the chair again. When she turned back, she noticed Brennan was watching her cautiously.

'By the way,' he said casually, 'About Rhodes – what are your feelings?'

'I didn't see much of the place.'

'You know what I mean.'

Anne blinked at him. 'I'm not sure I do.'

Brennan ran his tongue thoughtfully along the inside of his cheek, then he said, 'Would you consider going back there to . . . Well, sort of pick up on what Don was doing?'

Anne looked stunned. 'You're not serious, Harry . . .'

'Yes I am. But it's just a thought. And if it's not on as far as you're concerned, we'll give it the elbow. But I had lunch last week with the publisher who was planning on bringing out *Tierney's Eye on Rhodes* and he thinks it's a great idea.'

Anne shook her head. 'I couldn't.'

'Why not?'

'Well,' her eyes wandered to the framed magazine covers on the opposite wall. 'I'm just not good enough.'

'That's crap and you know it,' Brennan snapped, his cheeks colouring. 'All right, so you're not Don Tierney. But no one's asking for facsimiles. *Your* viewpoint, in your own style. It would be your book – and a sort of memorial in its way, wouldn't it?'

Anne looked at him steadily, trying to accommodate the idea. 'It could be, I suppose . . .'

'The best kind.'

Anne moved to the window and gazed out for a while. Brennan said nothing, letting her think the proposition out. Finally, without turning she said, 'If I did the book, I'd want to include the pictures Don took of the island – those Hasselblad films we brought back. And his name would have to be on the book, too.' Her voice went a little sad. 'It wouldn't be mine. It would be ours.'

73

Brennan nodded gently. 'That would be no problem.' He smiled at Anne as she turned to face him. 'Well,' he asked her coaxingly, 'what do you say?'

The table, covered with a spotless, dazzling white damask cloth, was situated at one corner of the open terrace on the castle's north wall. The view of the sea and the Rhodes countryside was panoramic, uninterrupted. One man, Raoul Lavallière, sat at the table clutching his white napkin as a servant cleared the luncheon dishes and the silver.

As the servant moved away Lavallière remained motionless, his eyes fixed on the line where sea and sky merged. He was handsome, silver-haired, and an ageless face that was unquestionably aristocratic. His clothing was as immaculate and studied as his bearing; when he moved his head a slow fraction towards the eastern skyline, one broadcloth shirtcuff slid an inch along the edge of the table, maintaining the symmetry of his position.

The servant came back with a tray. He set out a small plate, a fruit knife, a bowl of fruit and a crystal wine glass, which he half-filled from a bottle of red wine. Wordlessly, he set down the bottle and withdrew.

Lavallière sipped his wine, savoured it, sipped again and put down the glass. He looked at the fruit bowl for a moment, then reached out for a grape. His sleeve brushed against the wine glass, toppling it.

Frowning, his eyes unsettled, Lavallière stared at the spreading scarlet stain, watching it begin to trickle over the edge of the tablecloth. It was as if he were reading something.

His face remained disturbed as he looked up slowly and gazed out across the sea to the north, narrowing his eyes at the shimmering horizon.

Chapter Nine

A week after deciding to take up Brennan's proposition Anne left London, taking with her the same equipment Don had used.

Before Harry Brennan saw her off on the plane to Athens, he explained that Costas Vagianos would be sending his man Nikolaidis to meet her at Rhodes, just as he had met Don. Also, the house in the old city was at Anne's disposal, if she decided she wanted to use it.

The first leg of the flight took three hours. After transferring to an Olympic A300 Airbus at Athens, Anne arrived in Rhodes just after seven o'clock local time. Twenty-five minutes later she was in the old house again, putting her hand baggage in the bedroom. Before going downstairs she paused by the window, inhaling the curiously scented air and watching the play of evening light on the flowers.

In the sitting room, Mr Nikolaidis was testily drawing a finger along the ledge above the fireplace. He had found dust. With an irritated, petulant hiss of breath he took the folded handkerchief from his breast pocket and began rubbing at the ledge with it. Hearing Anne's footsteps on the stairs he jammed the handkerchief into his trouser pocket and turned to face her as she came through the archway from the hall.

'I love that little roof garden,' she said, smiling brightly and looking around her. 'What a delightful house this is.'

'Your husband liked it too, I think,' Nikolaidis said stiffly.

'Yes, he did. Very much. He told me about it on the telephone the day he arrived. I was looking forward to seeing it – but then when I did, it didn't really register . . .'

'Of course not,' Nikolaidis said sympathetically. 'I understand. So you will be staying here, yes?'

At first Anne had wondered if she would, but now she had no doubts. 'Yes, please.'

'In that case,' Nikolaidis said, 'Mr Vagianos has instructed me to tell you that the house is at your disposal for as long as you require it.' He took the keys from his pocket and handed them to Anne.

'That's very kind.'

'Mr Vagianos and Mr Harry . . .' Nikolaidis frowned, trying to remember.

'Brennan?'

'Ah, yes, Mr Harry Brennan – they are good friends.'

'Obviously.'

Nikolaidis nodded sombrely. 'In Greece, friendship is a debt. Calling on that debt does not weaken the friendship. It strengthens it. So by staying here, you are doing both gentlemen a favour, Mrs Tierney.'

'What a nice thought,' Anne said. And a refreshingly unselfish one, she thought. She was sure, already, that she was going to love being here.

'So.' Nikolaidis rubbed his hands briskly, glancing round the room with a little frown. 'I will now go and speak to the woman who is paid to clean the house. There is dust and there should not be. Tomorrow she will come again.'

'No, really,' Anne protested, 'please don't bother. I'm quite happy to . . .'

'Please. It is her job and she must do it correctly.' Nikolaidis nodded curtly and moved into the hall. Anne went with him. He paused by the suitcases and camera bags. 'May I help you with these?'

'No, that's OK, thanks. I can manage.'

'Very well.' At the front door Nikolaidis paused and looked at Anne rather awkwardly. 'Mrs Tierney, I regret that your husband and I did not start off well together.' He made a spread-fingered gesture towards himself. 'I think he found me too correct. And perhaps even a joke.'

Anne opened her mouth to protest but Nikolaidis raised a hand gently to silence her.

'He was not alone in this opinion. And it is my fault, I fear.' A small flash of regret creased the corners of his eyes. 'Sadly, such is my nature that I do not always reach people as I would wish. And for me, in a foreign language, it is even more difficult.' He smiled briefly, his eyes remaining regretful. 'I want you to know, however, that your husband's death was a great shock to me. I felt no small sadness because of it.'

'Thank you, Mr Nikolaidis.' Anne held out her hand to him; after a moment's hesitation he took it with enthusiasm. 'We've made a better start, I think,' Anne said.

'Yes we have. And I am glad. I hope that you will find peace here, and that when you leave you will have many happier memories of Rhodes.' He took a card from his pocket, then bowing slightly he handed it to Anne. 'My card. Please telephone me if I can be of assistance to you in any way.' Nikolaidis bowed again. '*Harika poli.*' He turned, pulled open the door and left the house. Anne watched him walk away down the narrow street, then she closed the door and went back to the sitting room.

It was even better to stand in the house alone, taking her time to examine and admire the quality of the place, the layout of its furnishings. She could imagine how much Don would have come to enjoy it here; it was the kind of dwelling that encouraged familiarity and affection.

After a closer inspection of the pictures and ornaments, Anne picked up the telephone receiver and listened. It was connected. She put it back, crossed to the fireplace and took down the small ikon from the shelf. Its dull-glinting amber patina had caught her eye from across the room. It was a beautiful, finely-wrought miniature fresco. The Madonna's face was overlaid with a tracery of fine cracks, the respectable marks of age on the ancient varnish. Anne ran her fingers across the surface, enjoying the texture, marvelling quietly at the special beauty that could only come from antiquity.

Then, very gradually, the movement of her hand slowed until it was motionless, poised over the ikon. The feeling was starting to wash over her again, the certainty that there was another presence in the room.

Part fearful, part expectant, Anne turned by slow degrees, still clutching the ikon, until she was looking at the arched opening to the hall. There was nothing there.

The anti-climax was becoming familiar. Like the anticipation it was an amalgam of feelings, a mingling of relief, disappointment and puzzlement.

Anne put the ikon back on the shelf; as she did so, she reminded herself of the formula, the procedure for remaining sane and undisturbed. *Accept, simply accept. Don't chase answers.*

She turned from the fireplace, deciding she should unpack right away. Keeping herself occupied was another indispensable aid to the balanced state of mind.

On the counter of Mr Seferis' photographic shop there was a glass case with a solitary book inside. It was the copy of *The Faces of Kampuchea* which Don Tierney had signed for him. The book was propped open at the inscription. Behind it and to one side, there was a card-mounted newscutting, showing a picture of Don over an account of his death. In the front of the case was a bunch of artificial flowers.

Seferis was standing behind the counter, thumbing through the sheaf of black-and-white enlargements, his jowls undulating as he slowly shook his head. He raised his eyes and looked at Anne, who was standing opposite him.

'I regret I cannot help you, Mrs Tierney.' He frowned at the pictures one more time. 'No, I am sorry. When I developed them I thought most possibly they were taken here on Rhodes, but Don did not say.' He handed back the prints. 'There is nothing in them to make me sure.' He tilted his head, studying Anne's face. 'Is it important to you to know?'

'No,' Anne said lightly, 'not that important. I just couldn't place them and they really ought to be filed.' She put the prints back in the envelope and moved away from the counter. 'Thank you, Mr Seferis.'

'Anything,' he assured her. 'Any time, Mrs Tierney.' With an attempt at modest pride he added, 'Don was my friend, you know.'

Anne nodded at the glass case. 'So I see.'

'A simple monument. You do not object, I hope?'

'Of course not.'

'I am so glad.' Seferis stepped over to the case and pointed. 'Please – read what Don wrote in his book for me.'

Anne peered at the familiar handwriting. '"To my good friend Andreas". . .'

'That is my name.'

'Yes,' Anne murmured; 'I rather gathered . . . "The best photographer on Rhodes".'

'I told him,' Seferis sighed, '"Don, that is too much", I said. But he insisted.'

'He obviously thought very highly of you,' Anne observed, simultaneously wondering how Don could have known the man long enough to establish a friendship.

Seferis slapped a hand to one flabby cheek. 'Such a tragedy!' he moaned, rolling his eyes. 'What a loss to photography. And to you an even greater loss, of course.'

Feeling rather embarrassed, Anne nodded as graciously as she could. 'Yes. Well, thank you again, Mr Seferis.'

Hastily, Seferis came out from behind the counter and escorted Anne to the door. 'You arrived yesterday?' he enquired, swinging the door open.

'Yesterday evening.'

'And you will be staying for some time.'

'A month or two,' Anne told him. 'Maybe longer.'

'Well, as Don was my friend so I hope it will be with us.'

He stepped aside to let Anne out. 'I am at your service. At any time. But on Sundays only from ten o'clock to one o'clock.'

Anne smiled her farewell, thought for a moment, then turned right and walked slowly away. It was an arbitrary decision, since she had no engagements to keep or schedules to obey. The morning was warm and sunny so she decided, as she strolled along the pavement, that she would spend an hour or so wandering around the new town, acclimatizing herself, getting to know the layout and perhaps spotting a promising restaurant or two.

She had been walking for five minutes, enjoying the reflected warmth from the white-fronted shops and tavernas, when she was distracted by a man's voice, somewhere behind her.

'Excuse me . . .'

Anne stopped and turned. A young man was coming across the street towards her at a trot. She didn't immediately recognize his face.

'It's Mrs Tierney, isn't it?'

Anne stared at him.

'David Bascombe,' he said, stopping in front of her. 'Remember?'

At approximately the moment Anne recognized Bascombe, a man called Dietrich von Reitz was approaching the study of Raoul Lavallière in the Crusader Castle at Aghios Theodoros.

Von Reitz was a shaven-headed man of military bearing with incisive, restless eyes. He marched stiffly along the stone corridor, stopped by the study door and squared the sheaf of papers he was carrying. He then looked sternly to left and right before he tapped the door and went inside.

The room was large and austere. The few pieces of furniture were of the same period as the castle itself – medieval chairs, a side table and a pair of tall, stout wooden candelabra. Only the large, magnificently carved desk by the far wall was of a later period; its three telephones and the reading lamp struck an incongruously modern note. Beyond the desk a large tapestry, depicting Templar Knights defending a castle in the Holy Land, covered almost the entire wall.

Lavallière was sitting behind the desk reading a thick, closely-typed report. He appeared to be engrossed. Von Reitz stood a few feet away. He looked worried.

Eventually Lavallière looked up, faintly irritated at the intrusion.

'I apologize for disturbing you, *Maître*,' von Reitz said, stepping closer to the desk. 'But I have just received the lists of names of those people who arrived yesterday by air and sea.' He separated the sheet from the bundle under his arm. 'There is one name which I felt I should bring to your attention immediately.' He placed the list in front of Lavallière and pointed to the name. 'Mrs Anne Tierney.'

Lavallière stared hard at the page then looked up, staring off towards the window. 'His wife,' he murmured.

'You think so?' Von Reitz said, pursing his lips with teutonic primness.

Lavallière glanced at him disdainfully. 'I have been expecting her arrival.'

'Why is she here?'

'I'm not certain why.' Lavallière looked across to the window again. 'That is something we must find out.'

The immediate pain of Don's death had made it difficult for Anne, at their first meeting, to be more than civil to David Bascombe. Now, with natural perspectives at least superficially restored, she found him friendly, easy-going and interesting. They walked for over an hour together in the sunshine, David acting as guide and historian, Anne absorbed in what she was being shown and told. Eventually they stopped for coffee at a taverna by the harbour. Neither one was aware that this was the place where Don had eaten

81

dinner on his first night in Rhodes.

As they sipped their coffee, Bascombe told Anne how he had met Don, and about the tentative business proposition that had been made.

'I can see why Don wanted you to help him,' Anne said. 'Speaking Greek and knowing the island the way you do – were you going to agree?'

'We never got around to talking about it. I probably would've agreed, though. Just for the fun of it.' He grinned. 'It would have made a welcome change from Byzantine Rhodes.'

'When's your book going to be published?'

'Oh . . .' Bascombe shrugged. 'Not for ages yet. Autumn next year, at the earliest. The following spring, more likely.'

'It sounds fascinating,' Anne said, meaning it.

'Well maybe, if you're into that period of history.'

'How's it coming?'

'I haven't started the writing part yet. I've still got quite a bit of research to do.'

'And that's taking up all your time, I suppose?' There was a clear line of intent in Anne's questions; she didn't care if it showed, since it wasn't devious.

'Well, it keeps me occupied,' Bascombe said.

'So.' Anne hesitated for a moment. 'There's no chance of you doing the same for me as you were going to do for Don, then?'

Bascombe studied her candidly, then smiled. 'I'm glad you asked. I was trying to get up the nerve to suggest it.'

'I'd be very grateful,' Anne assured him. 'Whenever you can. For the first couple of weeks anyway, just until I get my bearings. And only if you're sure it won't interfere with your work too much.' Anne put down her cup, adopting a more businesslike tone. 'Whatever you and Don had agreed about . . .'

'He was going to pay for dinner.'

Anne smiled. 'Well, I think I might be able to top that.'

'I'd rather you didn't,' Bascombe said quietly.

They held each other's eyes briefly, then Anne picked up her cup and sipped from it, breaking the moment. 'We'll work something out,' she said. 'When could we make a start, Mr Bascombe?'

'Mr Bascombe!' He laughed, shaking his head. 'David, please.'

'Of course,' Anne said, lowering her eyes.

'And you're . . .?'

'Anne.'

'With or without an "e"?'

'With.' It was the simplest kind of personal scrutiny, but Anne felt her face growing warm.

'Right.' Bascombe folded his arms, looking pleased. 'How about tomorrow morning then, Anne?'

She was surprised. 'So soon?'

'Is that too soon for you?'

'No,' she said hastily, 'the sooner the better. But haven't you got things planned for tomorrow?'

'Nothing I can't switch to another time.' There was no trace of the reluctance he had shown when Don Tierney had asked for his help. 'Tomorrow's fine.'

'Great.' Anne felt a nice surge of enthusiasm. 'Tomorrow then. This afternoon I'll fix myself up with some transport.'

Bascombe put up a hand. 'No need. We can use my car. It's a bit of a wreck, but it goes.'

Anne thanked him for that, but pointed out she would need a car of her own.

'Even so,' Bascombe said, 'you shouldn't hire one before you have to. Here in town it's a hell of a sight cheaper to use taxis. And where you're living in the old city, it's far easier to walk everywhere.'

Anne considered it. 'Yes,' she said finally, 'I suppose you're right. All those narrow streets.'

'And come the tourist season,' Bascombe pointed out, 'vehicles are banned from going in there – for most of the day, anyway. So save yourself the hassle. And a fair bit of money as well. Hire a car when you have to, but meantime . . .'

'You've convinced me. We'll use yours. Thanks. But . . .' Anne made an attempt at looking stubborn; 'I pay for the petrol.'

'At Greek prices,' Bascombe said candidly, 'I won't let my pride stand in the way of that suggestion.'

Anne hadn't heard him. She was staring at a chair a few yards away. An Olympus camera was hanging over the back; the strap was the same kind Don had used on his cameras. The man sitting in the chair was built like Don. Even with his back to Anne, he bore a resemblance that was startling – the hair, the shoulders, even the clothes were the same as those Don had worn when he was working.

'Is something the matter?' Bascombe asked.

The man was turning his head in Anne's direction. She was transfixed.

Bascombe was becoming worried. Anne had gone pale. 'What is it?'

The man looked over his shoulder. His face was nothing like Don's. He waved to someone and Anne went on staring. A woman joined the man. They shook hands and she sat down at the table. They launched immediately into an animated conversation.

Anne returned her attention to Bascombe. She looked drawn, rather ill.

'You all right?'

'Yes,' she said, passing a hand across her forehead. 'I'm fine. It's just that for a minute . . .' She glanced at the other table again.

Bascombe leaned across the table. 'Are you really OK?'

She nodded. 'I'm sorry. Forgive me.' She smiled weakly. 'Where were we?' She noticed that Bascombe was still gazing at her; he looked genuinely concerned. 'Post trauma reaction, that's all,' Anne said, feeling some explanation was in order.

84

'According to Dr Phillimore, anyway.'

'Dr Phillimore?'

'I had a breakdown shortly after Don was killed. I was out of my mind for a while. Or so they said.'

'And were you?'

Anne stared at her hands, pale on the table top. 'I'm not sure,' she said.

Chapter Ten

For two days Anne and David Bascombe roamed the island in Bascombe's ancient Volkswagen beetle. It was a time of intense, continuous activity which David found enjoyable, if rather exhausting. His companion's energy, he observed to himself, was relentless. Like Don, Anne tended to see photographic possibilities everywhere; no hill or mountain road was too steep to climb in search of fresh pictorial material, no scrubby countryside too rough to tramp across for the sake of a good viewpoint.

People tended to predominate in Anne's photographs. At the mountain village of Embonas she photographed a wedding, an impromptu series of shots aimed at contrasting the shy happiness of the couple with the exuberant high spirits of their guests. Two old men playing tavli under the sheltering arms of a tree at Kritina provided classical unselfconscious character studies. On the road between Eleoussa and Arhipoli David stopped the car so that Anne could shoot two rolls of film on a river bank where, oblivious to the camera, peasant women were washing the bright-coloured rugs they would sell to the summer tourists. A mile further down the road a solitary old woman, laden with olive branches to fodder her donkeys, provided another unforgettable shot.

Everywhere Anne and David went, from Platania to Arhangelos, from Malonas all the way north to Afandou, the extrovert village children made natural subjects, while the older people, the animals and the sun-drenched landscape produced automatic compositions that Anne recorded with calm, unhurried professionalism.

By the afternoon of the second day they had begun

working their way around the coastline. Anne had decided from the outset, that a general survey of the island would make the best beginning to the project. From a careful study of the hundreds of pictures she was collecting, there would emerge what Don had called a thematic mainline, a pictorial essence of the island's character; from that she would be able to take her lead for further pictures, building steadily towards the final selection.

At one o'clock David suggested they turn off the main road at Faliraki, where there was a long beautiful stretch of beach and an excellent place where they could eat. The day before, Anne's enthusiasm had infected them both so intensely that they had forgotten to have lunch. Today David was determined that wouldn't happen.

They sat on the sunny forecourt of the Dimitrias Faliraki Restaurant and were waited on by the proprietor, a smiling, curly-haired man called George Galatas. As they ate their seafood luncheon, washed down with generous glasses of crisp, dry Lindos wine, David silently revised his original impression of his companion.

His first evaluation of her – beautiful, intelligent, fetchingly shy – had been modified by his knowledge of her bereavement. David had thought that Anne's restrained manner was a temporary offshoot of her loss and her recent illness; now, having seen her thoroughly preoccupied by work, he knew that it was an inborn trait. She was a naturally graceful girl whose self-containment and modesty would have made her deeply desirable to him – given different, less overshadowed circumstances. As it was, David was content – and, he believed, rather privileged – to accompany her around Rhodes, enjoying her presence, helping her.

For the rest of the afternoon they travelled along the east coast, going as far south as Malona Bay before the light began to fail. With several dozen more shots in the bag they drove back to the old city and decided, on the spot, to have dinner at a taverna near Anne's house.

Neither one of them was aware, as they sat outside enjoying their meal, that they were being watched from a champagne-coloured Mercedes parked a few yards away. They had been just as unaware, earlier that day and throughout the previous day, that the same limousine had shadowed them steadily wherever they went, and that the same two young men, pleasant-faced and smartly dressed, had been watching them just as intently as they did now.

The following morning, as Anne came downstairs in her dressing gown, she found a letter on the rug by the front door. There was no stamp on the envelope, which was of high-quality vellum with Anne's name written on the front in elegant italic script. She opened it and took out an engraved invitation card.

RAOUL LAVALLIÈRE REQUESTS THE PLEASURE
OF MRS ANNE TIERNEY'S COMPANY
AT A SOIRÉE TO BE HELD AT
THE KASTELLO AGHIOS THEODOROS
FROM 6 TO 8 : 30 P.M. ON WEDNESDAY 9TH MARCH,
1983.

An hour later, bathed and dressed, Anne brought coffee to David Bascombe who was sitting at the table on the roof garden. He had arrived fifteen minutes before and was closely studying a road map of the island.

'Black or white?'

'Black please,' David said absently, then looked up. 'I thought we'd drive out to Plantania this morning, then maybe go on down to Lindos.'

'OK,' Anne said, pouring the coffee. 'What about that place where the old potter lives – the one you told me about?'

'It's on our way.' David started refolding the map.

'Good.' Anne set down his coffee and picked up the

invitation card. 'Does the name Raoul Lavallière mean anything to you?'

David nodded. 'That's for sure. Why?' He glanced up and saw the card. 'Oh. So you've been invited to the presence too, have you? Mine arrived this morning. Much to my surprise.' He took the card from Anne and studied it. 'I wonder what we've done to be so honoured. As far as I know, no one on the island has ever been inside King Raoul's castle – certainly not since he took the place over, anyway.'

Anne took back the card, frowning at it. 'So, as you say, why us?' She looked at David. 'And who else?'

'God knows. Maybe this soirée's an open day for all us proles. I doubt it, though. By all accounts, that would be a bit out of character for Lavallière.' He grinned at Anne. 'We'll just have to wait and see, won't we?'

'You're going, then?'

David rolled his eyes. 'You must be joking! I wouldn't miss it for the world. Quite apart from natural curiosity, the Kastello has to be one of the finest examples of a Crusader fortress outside the Middle East.'

Anne sat down slowly, tapping the card with her fingers. 'Who is this man? What's he doing on Rhodes?'

'Funny thing,' David murmured, 'that's what Don asked me. He was very interested in Monsieur Lavallière.'

'Really?'

'Hardly surprising. Lavallière's one of our local characters. And very intriguing.' David sipped his coffee. 'Let's hope he turns out to be worth all the speculation, eh?'

Just after six o'clock on the evening of March 9th, the old Volkswagen drove up to the gatehouse at the Kastello Aghios Theodoros. Without hesitation or even a trace of curiosity, the attendant raised the barrier and allowed David Bascombe to pass through.

David drove up the twisting road to the main gate and

through to the deserted courtyard beyond. He braked, switched off the engine and glanced across to Anne. In her stylish short evening dress she looked rather too smart for her transport.

'Not exactly bustling, is it,' David murmured.

Anne peered through the window. 'Somebody's coming.'

A smartly-dressed young man stepped up to the side of the car and opened Anne's door. He helped her out, stood back a pace and made a small bow. 'Good evening, Mrs Tierney.' He glanced across at David, who was climbing out on the other side. 'Good evening, sir.' He waved his hand towards the castle's main entrance. 'Please follow me.'

As they went through the door they could hear the sound of delicate, well-modulated music.

'Monastic,' Anne whispered to David.

'Huh?'

'The atmosphere.' She looked at him and smiled. He was wearing his best business-meeting suit which made him look, Anne thought, like a rather uncomfortable solicitor.

They were taken along a passage and led down a flight of steps into a reception hall.

'If you would just wait here,' the young man said, bowing again and going to the door. Instead of leaving the room, he positioned himself to one side of the doorway, his hands folded in front of him as if he were on guard.

'Well, what about this, then?' Anne whispered, looking around the hall.

'Incredible,' David murmured. 'Must be almost exactly the way it was originally.'

The room was wide and high-ceilinged with a stone-flagged floor. At one end there was a long high table with four gold goblets standing on it in a row. Fascinated, David crossed and picked up one of the goblets, turning it in his hands, examining the fine hand-chasing.

Anne was staring at a painting in a framed wooden panel. It showed a thirteenth-century Knight Crusader dressed in full body armour, with a red cross on his white surcoat and and identical cross on his shield.

'Who's he?' Anne whispered.

'No idea,' David whispered back.

'He's my kinsman,' a clear voice announced from the doorway. 'Tibald de Montrefort.'

Startled, Anne spun round and saw a tall, handsome man in a white dinner jacket standing halfway down the steps. In the instant Anne turned to him his face seemed to register shock and disbelief, but it cleared swiftly like a shadow as he smiled, continuing down the stairs and crossing with his hand outstretched.

'I am Raoul Lavallière.' His rich, softly-accented voice was undoubtedly French. 'Good evening, Mrs Tierney.' He shook Anne's hand, his eyes fixed intently on her face, then he turned and shook hands with David. 'Mr Bascombe.'

Feeling rather bewildered, Anne glanced up at the painting again. Although the man was bearded and his hair was fairer, he bore an uncanny resemblance to Lavallière.

'Le Comte de Montrefort was once master of this castle,' Lavallière was telling David. 'Did you know that?'

'Really?' David was genuinely surprised. 'No, I didn't know.'

Lavallière turned to Anne. 'I'm so glad you were able to come – both for the pleasure of your company, and for the opportunity it provides me of personally expressing my sincere condolences on the tragic death of your husband.'

'That's very kind of you.'

Turning back to David, Lavallière said, 'With your special interest, Mr Bascombe, I considered that it was high time you visited the Kastello, too.' He smiled warmly. 'You will find it interesting, I think.'

'It's fascinating,' David said, nodding. 'Magnificently restored.'

'Thank you.'

Anne was frowning at Lavallière. 'Did you meet my

husband while he was on the island?'

'Sadly, no. I had hoped that we might – here, over dinner one night perhaps. But unfortunately that was not to be. I have always been such a great admirer of his work. Particularly his war coverage.' Lavallière sighed. 'He captured such telling and poignant moments with his photographs. Each one of them an indictment of our stupidity. And many of them clearly taken at considerable risk to himself. He was a very brave man, I think.'

'Yes,' Anne said huskily, 'he was.'

Lavallière brightened. 'So now, with my thanks for this private moment with you, let us put away the past, eh? Shall we join the others?' He offered Anne his arm and escorted her to the door. David followed them.

'Tell me something, Monsieur Lavallière,' Anne said. 'How did . . .'

'You are too beautiful to go unnoticed, Mrs Tierney, and Rhodes is not a big island. So word reached me.'

Anne was a little dumbfounded. She had known people to anticipate a question before, but never that well.

They walked along a short passage and turned into the main hall. It was warm, light and colourful. There was an attractively arranged buffet at one end; in the centre three musicians on a small dais were playing something by Albinoni, while the other guests – no more than two dozen of them and none of them Greek – stood around in pairs and groups, sipping their drinks and talking quietly. The women, Anne noticed, were mostly in their twenties, good-looking and very fashionably dressed. The older men were well-groomed and distinguished, while the younger ones were all, without exception, extremely handsome.

Lavallière beckoned to one of the men who were circulating with drinks. He came over immediately and held out his tray to Anne.

'I'm sure you will find the Chablis very much to your taste, Mrs Tierney,' Lavallière said. 'Seventy-six was a fine vintage.' An aide approached as Anne was taking a glass. He stood at a respectful distance and nodded to Lavallière. 'Excuse me.' Lavallière went across to speak to the man.

David was gazing around the room, looking rather uncomfortable. 'It didn't say anything on the invitation about dressing up, did it?' he murmured to Anne.

'Don't worry about it.'

'Oh, I won't. No point. This is the only suit I've go to my name.' He smiled. 'Well, shall we mingle?'

'Why not?'

For the next hour they moved among the other guests, learning nothing in particular about them, indulging in light, inconsequential talk about the island, its weather, this gathering and how pleasant everything was. Anne felt, at times, as if she were up against a barrier, an obstacle to real conversation that was so skilfully erected that its dimensions and limits couldn't be defined.

Nevertheless, the evening *was* pleasant, as everyone kept saying. As the sun began to set, Anne wandered to one of the embrasured windows and looked out at the sea. The gold light dusted her face as she watched the peaceful, almost mesmeric movement of the waves. The wine had softened her, making her aware of the subtle rhythm of the water as it lapped on the shore. For the first time in many weeks Anne began to feel thoroughly at one with herself.

'You're not eating, Mrs Tierney?'

She turned and saw Lavallière standing beside her. 'David . . . Mr Bascombe's getting something for me.'

'Ah! Good.'

'I was just admiring the sunset.'

'Yes.' Lavallière looked out through the window. 'It's beautiful, isn't it?'

Anne was studying his face. 'Have you lived here long, Monsieur Lavallière?'

He shook his head. 'Five years only. Until then my home was in Lebanon. Near Sidon.'

'In another castle?' Anne asked him, smiling.

'Certainly. Even older than this one. But . . .' He shrugged. 'Regrettably the situation in the Middle East forced me to move from there.'

'And you prefer Rhodes to France?'

'Yes, I do. I have not lived in France for many years.' He looked closely at Anne, the sunset reflecting rich bronze in his eyes. 'And you? Do you like this island?'

Anne nodded. 'More and more, as I travel round it. It has an atmosphere all of its own.'

'Which cannot be easy to convey with a camera.'

'No,' Anne admitted, 'it isn't. But that's what Don wanted to do.'

'And now you have taken over that task from him.'

'No.' Anne shook her head firmly. 'I'm just standing in, that's all. I won't be able to match what he would've done. But it seemed a pity to leave the job unfinished.'

'I agree.' Lavallière glanced aside at a man walking towards them. 'Ah!' he called out. 'Von Reitz.'

Dietrich von Reitz came and stood beside them, smiling cautiously. Anne found his face immediately familiar, but she couldn't place it for the moment.

'Forgive me, *Maître*,' von Reitz said, his accent clipped and precise. 'I would have joined you earlier, but there were some matters I had to attend to.'

Lavallière nodded. 'Of course. Mrs Tierney, may I introduce Dietrich von Reitz. He is a business associate of mine. Mrs Tierney.'

Von Reitz gave Anne a curt, teutonic bow. 'How do you do.'

'How do you do.' As Anne took his hand she almost remembered where she had seen his face. It was a fleeting certainty that escaped before she had time to acknowledge it. Anne smiled to cover the small confusion, but the moment of recognition had registered with Lavallière. He fixed his eyes sharply on Anne for a moment, then looked at von Reitz.

'I am seriously considering giving Mrs Tierney the view from here.'

Anne laughed. 'And do you live in this lovely castle too, Herr von Reitz?'

'Yes. I have that privilege.'

Anne spotted David Bascombe over by the door. He was wandering around aimlessly with a plate in each hand. 'Will you excuse me, please, gentlemen?' She pointed. 'Mr Bascombe's looking for me. And he has food!'

'Of course,' Lavallière said. 'And I hope you enjoy it.' As Anne moved away he stood watching her for a moment, then turned to von Reitz. 'There are photographs,' he murmured. 'And negatives.'

Von Reitz nodded, his face expressionless.

'But she is not to be harmed,' Lavallière said, looking across at Anne again. 'That is unnecessary.'

Anne and David got back to the house in the old city just after nine. They went inside and while Anne made coffe they talked over the evening together. Anne kept coming back to the resemblance between Lavallière and the man in the painting.

'It's not all that surprising,' David said as they carried their cups into the sitting room. 'Lavallière said de Montrefort was an ancestor of his, didn't he? It may be a direct line, in which case . . .'

'Even so,' Anne insisted. 'The resemblance is uncanny.'

'What interests me more,' David said, 'is that de Montrefort was clearly a Knight of the Temple.'

'Why's that so interesting?'

'The Knights on Rhodes were all members of the Order of Saint John of Jerusalem. Hospitallers.'

Anne sat down, looking frankly puzzled.

'You know,' David said patiently, sitting down opposite her. 'Saint John's Ambulance and all that. Football matches and open-air pop concerts, God help 'em. Only in those

95

days, they were the lot who patched up the wounded when the other Crusaders had got through belting hell out of the infidel.'

Anne nodded, beginning to understand.

'And when the Saracens finally kicked all the Knights out of the Holy Land,' David went on, 'the Hospitallers grabbed this place. They were very jealous of their rights here and they protected them. There may have been a few Templars around from time to time, but as far as I know there's no record of one of them ever holding a castle on the island. And yet . . .' David shook his head.

'What?'

'I've seen the name de Montrefort somewhere very recently.'

'During your research, probably,' Anne suggested.

David nodded. 'Has to have been. But I'm damned if I can remember where or in what context.' He sipped his coffee, thinking. 'Mind you, it wouldn't have had any relevance for me. I'm dealing with the history of Rhodes up until the Hospitallers moved in on the place in 1309. De Montrefort wouldn't have come on the scene until after that – and then he couldn't have been around for long.'

'Why's that?'

'In 1312 the Templars were all excommunicated,' David said. 'The ones who hadn't already been burnt at the stake, that is.'

'Charming.'

'That's the way practical problems were handled in those days.'

'And things haven't changed all that much, have they?' Anne observed dryly.

David laughed and sat back in his chair. 'So what do you think of friend Lavallière?'

'He's charming.'

David made a face. 'Bit too smooth for me. What about the rest of them?'

96

'Well, you were right. There wasn't a local in sight, as far as I could tell.'

'Not one. And they weren't exactly open with their chat.'

'Who do you think they are?'

David shrugged. 'Some of Lavallière's rich cronies, I imagine. From what I've heard, there's always at least a dozen of them in residence up there.'

'All looked after by those clean-cut young men,' Anne murmured.

David drained his cup and put it down. 'Yes, there were a good few of them about, weren't there? Lavallière seems to have surrounded himself with them.' He narrowed his eyes. 'Do you think maybe he's . . .'

'No, I don't,' Anne said firmly. 'In fact I'm sure he's not.'

'And your certainty's based on what?' David asked teasingly.

'The way he looked at me.' Anne changed the subject quickly. 'Does he have many visitors, do you know?'

'Dozens, apparently – according to what I've been told in the village, anyway.'

'Yes, well . . .' The face of Dietrich von Reitz was hovering in Anne's mind again, the association becoming clearer now. 'A man like Lavallière, with his kind of money, he'd know a lot of people, wouldn't he? Politicians, bankers, people like that.'

'For sure,' David said flatly. 'Raoul Lavallière probably knows God.'

Late that night Lavallière sat in his study at the castle, examining a wooden tryptych standing on his desk. The lamp cast a hard yellow light on the ancient pictures; the outer panels depicted idyllic, idealized pastoral scenes, but the one in the centre was a head-and-shoulders portrait of a woman.

The artist's brushwork, the clothes of his subject and the style of her hair all indicated that the picture had been painted in the late thirteenth century. Lavallière stared at it intently, breathing softly through parted lips.

The woman's name, Agnes Beauvoir, was inscribed on a decorative scroll at the bottom of the portrait. She was beautiful and the painter had depicted her with a wide-eyed, almost impossible innocence. Aound her neck she wore a gold chain on which hung a single diamond in the shape of a tear drop.

A sigh, barely inaudible, escaped Lavallière as he gazed at the picture. The painted face gazed back, timeless in its beauty. Except for a few tiny variations of detail and expression, the woman in the portrait could have been Anne Tierney.

Chapter Eleven

As Anne lay in bed the following night, drifting into sleep, her fading consciousness stubbornly re-ran the thoughts that had occupied her for most of the evening. There was excitement – her first batch of colour proofs were due back by air from London the following day – and there was confusion. She had finally become certain where she had seen Dietrich von Reitz before, and one of the half-plate prints made by Mr Seferis had confirmed it; there was no doubt that the man shaking hands with Remo Manzini was von Reitz.

So what did it mean? The question churned around, answerless, as the small excitement about the proofs clamoured for prominence.

Sleep finally closed in on her, making smoky dreams of her uneasy curiosity. She saw the German's face, smiling at first, then darkening to a scowl as he extended a hand in treacherous friendship. And wasn't it his left hand? The image faded, making way for others as Anne sank deeper into unconsciousness.

Downstairs, someone had entered the house. Soundlessly he walked into the sitting room and crossed to the writing desk. He opened the drawer and removed the envelope with the enlargements and negatives. Taking care to make no sound he closed the drawer, then left the house again, closing the front door softly.

Later, in the early light of morning, Raoul Lavallière stood by the fireplace in his study, watching the prints and the acetate negatives burn. He was still gazing at the ashes when von Reitz came in and put a bulging document folder on the desk.

'I now have a complete dossier on Mrs Tierney, *Maître*, he said. 'I will leave it here for you.' He cleared his throat. 'It would seem that recently she had some kind of mental breakdown.'

Lavallière went on staring at the flames. 'I know,' he said quietly.

At midday Anne was in the cargo office at Rhodes airport. She had just collected a packet of proofs and was arranging the despatch of another box of films. With the formalties attended to, the Greek official behind the counter handed her the air waybill.

'Thank you. Do you have any idea when that packet will get to London?'

The man shrugged and looked at the clock. 'Who can say? God willing, it will be some time today.'

'Thanks. That's close enough.' Anne picked up her proofs and left.

On the way home in the taxi, the temptation to open the packet of proofs was all but overwhelming. But Anne resisted. She wanted to do it in the house, where she could lay them out and make a frank assessment of her very first shots for the book.

The trip seemed endless. Anne tried to remember what was on the pictures, feeling the swift evaporation of the certainty she'd had when she took them. Perhaps her meter readings had been wrong – meters *did* go haywire sometimes. And focusing; she hadn't alway used the screen magnifier, even though she knew she should have, so the sharpness of some key shots might be out. Then there was always the possibility of camera shake . . .

By the time she got home Anne was so anxious to see the pictures she practically ran into the sitting room. She threw her handbag down on a chair, tore open the packet and pulled out the wad of prints. She began running through

100

them, a nervous preliminary check to make sure there were no real disasters.

She stopped suddenly, frowning. Squaring the bundle again, she began to look through the pictures more slowly. They were her shots all right, but some of them were wrong. They weren't what she had taken.

Anne took a deep, steadying breath and looked again. On several shots there was a man with his back to the camera, a man who hadn't been there when Anne took the photographs. At first he was a distant figure, but as she went on flipping through the prints, throwing them on the table one by one, he got closer. And on each successive picture he was turning his head a little more towards the camera.

Anne stared at the top picture of the pile on the table. Her hands were shaking. There was something terribly familiar about the man, something her mind was recoiling from. But she had to go on.

In the next four prints he was almost on top of the camera. Anne began shuddering in disbelief as she looked at the final shot. The man was facing the camera and smiling. And he was unmistakably Don Tierney.

Chapter Twelve

David Bascombe was standing by the sitting-room window, thumbing through the colour proofs, when Dr Mavros came puffing down the stairs.

'I have suggested that she take a sedative and rest for a while,'Mavros said, coming across the room. 'But she insists that is unnecessary.'

'I feel a bit of a fool.' David put the pictures on the window ledge. 'I really oughtn't to have troubled you. I'm sorry about that, doctor.'

Mavros waved the apology aside with a pudgy hand. 'If, as you say, she was hysterical when you arrived here . . .'

'Well, close enough.'

'Then you did the right thing. And I am not very far away, am I?'

'Even so.'

Mavros looked towards the stairs, then back at David. 'What caused her to become so upset? Do you know?"

'She didn't say anything to you?'

'Very little,' Mavros grunted. 'She merely protested that there is nothing wrong with her, and suggested that perhaps you over-reacted to an emotional moment brought on by lack of sleep and concern about her work.'

'Well . . .' David shrugged. 'That has to be what it was all about, then. But she was in quite a state.'

'And she would not say why?'

'She was too overwrought.'

Mavros was nodding. 'And what did *you* think was the cause of her distress?'

David glanced at the pictures for a moment, then shook

his head. 'I had no idea. But I do know she's been through a pretty rough time lately.' He told Mavros about Anne's bereavement.

'Ah, yes, of course! I had been trying to decide why the name Tierney was familiar to me. The English photographer who crashed his car, yes?'

'That's right. A couple of months back.'

'I read about it in the paper.' Mavros gave Don a confident little nod. 'There I think we have the answer. I would say that in the tragedy lies the true explanation of what happened here today.'

David nodded expectantly. He had known the doctor for some time and was aware that the old man never said more than he had to.

'Cruelly,' Mavros said, 'grief often does such things to us. In our need to overcome it, we foolishly believe that we have. Then we discover, months or even years later, that it is still lying in ambush for us, somewhere in our desolation.'

David nodded again, encouraging Mavros to continue.

'A memory cunningly triggered by some small thing, the sight or sound of something once shared – that is all that is needed to rekindle anguish and resurrect despair.' Mavros smiled rather sadly. 'We Greeks know that well and we admit freely to the pain it causes. But you Northern Europeans are all too often shamed by it, so you pretend to be nothing more than overtired.'

Mavros buttoned his jacket, preparing to leave. 'You are assisting Mrs Tierney with her work, did you say?'

'Yes,' David replied. 'For the time being, anyway.'

'But clearly you are also her friend.'

'Of course.' David paused, then added, 'At least I hope that's the way she sees it.'

'I am sure she does.' Mavros started moving towards the front door. 'Speak firmly to her, as a friend, about overdoing things. But say nothing more. In that way you will save her embarrassment.'

103

David went to the door and opened it. 'Thank you for coming, Dr Mavros.'

'Please. I am only sorry that Mrs Tierney is suffering from something which I cannot cure.' He paused outside the door. 'You have not entirely abandoned your research I hope, Mr Bascombe.'

'No way,' David assured him. 'Just taking a breather from it, that's all.'

'I am glad to hear that, because I am very much looking forward to reading your book. I hope you have not forgotten you promised to send me a copy when it is published.'

'I haven't forgotten.'

'Good.' Dr Mavros moved away, waving. 'So, *andio*.'

'*Andio*.'

David closed the door and went back to the sitting room. He crossed to the window and picked up the photographs again, going through them slowly.

He could find nothing, nothing at all to explain what had happened. They were just pictures. He had been there when Anne took them. They were excellent, well-composed studies, a credit to her talent. But there was nothing, as far as David could see, to make her wail and tremble the way she had as he came in and saw her standing there, her eyes wide and terrified, staring at the pictures.

Lavallière was re-reading the dossier that von Reitz had prepared for him. The thick folder contained photographs, dozens of closely-typed pages of personal information and copies of Anne's medical records. As he was studying the photostats of old hospital reports there was a knock at the door. Lavallière closed the dossier and pushed it to one side.

'Come.'

Dietrich von Reitz came in carrying a red leather folder. He closed the door and crossed to the desk, where he removed a stapled document from the folder and put it in front of Lavallière.

'This has just arrived by courier from Berne, *Maître*. It is the report of the South African arms purchases in Europe which you asked Chevalier Niedermann to prepare for you.'

Lavallière casually scanned the first page and nodded. 'Acknowledge receipt by Telex.'

'Yes, *Maître*.' Von Reitz took another sheaf of paper from the folder and handed it across. 'And this is a complete list of those who will be in attendance on the twenty-fifty, with finalized details of their travel arrangements. Only Chevalier Ortega will not be with us.'

Lavallière looked up, frowning.

'On doctor's orders,' von Reitz explained. 'He is unable to make the journey. I have had it confirmed.'

'Very well, if you are satisfied. It is not essential that he attend on this occasion.' Lavallière stood up, crossed to the window and gazed out at the sea. Von Reitz continued to hover by the desk. After a minute Lavallière turned and looked at him.

'Is there something else?'

'Yes, *Maître*.' Von Reitz coughed delicately. 'The Tierney woman.'

'What about her?'

'She is a threat.'

Lavallière stared at him coldly. 'Is that an established fact or an opinion?'

'An opinion, naturally,' von Reitz said. 'But it is one I hold very strongly.'

'In which way is she a threat – in your opinion?'

'If she puts names to any of those faces . . .'

'She has already identified some of them.' Lavallière smiled thinly. 'Including you, von Reitz, since I introduced you.'

Von Reitz seemed alarmed at that. 'In that case she is an even greater danger. With her background she will know many journalists. If she dropped even as much as a hint to any of them and aroused their curiosity, it would jeopardize everything you have achieved, *Maître*. It would not be easy to explain away the presence of many of those who were here.'

'Any more that it would be easy to convince anyone that such a gathering ever took place.' Lavallière turned and looked out of the window again. 'And where is her proof? The photographs her husband took have been destroyed. So have the negatives. Besides, she is not even sure that they were taken here on Rhodes.'

Von Reitz still looked deeply troubled.

'The fact that you appeared in some of the pictures,' Lavallière went on, 'is certainly not sufficient to place them with any degree of certainty. After all you are a widely travelled man, Colonel, are you not?'

'But should she decide for any reason that this *is* where they were taken – well then, surely, even without the photographs her word alone could be enough to excite interest.'

'Ordinarily, perhaps,' Lavallière said, 'but not now. Recently she has been confused. So much so as to require treatment in a clinic. And today . . .' He turned and faced von Reitz. 'Today she is even more confused and I doubt if even those closest to her would give much credence to anything she told them. In any case, I assure you, she is far too preoccupied to give the matter any further thought.'

'Nevertheless,' von Reitz insisted, 'as a precaution, do you not think that it would be advisable to . . .'

'No! I do not!' Lavallière said sharply. 'She poses no threat to me.' He became thoughtful for a moment. 'Once, perhaps. But certainly not now.' He glared at von Reitz, his eyes a stern warning. 'I have already told you, she is not to be harmed. So do not be tempted – either to protect your own interests or out of a mistaken concern for mine. Is that understood?'

'Yes, *Maître*,' von Reitz said quietly. 'It is understood.'

'I hope so. Now you may leave.'

When he was alone again Lavallière sat down at the desk. He gazed up at the wooden tryptych and gazed at the face of the woman in the centre panel. After a moment he sighed and set it down again, carefully.

Anne was standing by the fireplace with the bundle of colour proofs in her hand. David was by the sideboard, looking at the framed photograph of Anne and Don.

'You shouldn't have called the doctor,' Anne said. 'I asked you not to.' She seemed perfectly calm as she spoke, as if the emotional eruption hadn't occurred.

'You had me worried,' David murmured, still looking at the photograph.

'Momentary shock, that's all,' Anne sighed. 'Thanks for not saying anything to him, though.'

David looked at her. 'He seemed satisfied with his diagnosis.'

'An hysterical outburst.'

'Something like that.'

Anne looked down at the prints for a moment, then glanced at David. 'You think I'm off my head, don't you?'

'No.' He smiled at her reassuringly. 'Over imaginative, perhaps – and susceptible. Just now, especially.'

'Imagination's got nothing to do with it,' she said firmly. 'When I opened the packet and looked through these proofs Don was in them. I promise you, I didn't imagine it. I wasn't even thinking about him at the time.' She put the pictures down. 'He hasn't been on my mind nearly so much lately. Not like in the early days. Anyway, it wasn't that kind of image. It was *real*. As real as you are to me now.' She stabbed a finger at the pictures. 'He was there.'

'But Anne, think about it. He can't have been, can he?'

'I saw him,' she said adamantly.

David nodded to the photographs. 'And now?'

107

Anne shook her head impatiently. 'But I didn't imagine it. He was there. Not a shadow – a living human being. Just like before, only on film.'

'Before?' David looked puzzled.

'Oh, yes, of course.' Anne looked at him balefully. 'I haven't told you about that, have I?'

'Not a word.'

'I nearly told you that day when we met up again. Only it seemed like it was all in the past then, so there wasn't really any reason. But this has happened before. I've seen Don several times since he was killed.'

David wasn't hiding his concern for her. 'Do you want to talk about it? Will that help?'

Anne thought for a moment, then she nodded. 'Yes I think I'd like to.' She glanced through the window at the sunlit street. 'Do you mind if we go out somewhere? I could use the fresh air.'

They went together to the wall surrounding the old city and took the stairway to the top, where there was a path. As they strolled along the wall Anne told David about the first sighting in Hampstead, and the subsequent occasions when she had either seen Don or felt his presence.

'It got so I couldn't handle it. I began to think maybe I was cracking up. So when Harry Brennan took me to see Doctor Phillimore and he suggested I go into the nursing home for a while, it seemed the bright thing to do.'

David was nodding, strolling along easily at her side. 'And?'

'Phillimore explained it all away. As best he could.'

'And while you were in there – did you see your husband again?'

'No. And I haven't since, until today.' She stopped for a moment, letting the soft breeze ruffle her hair. 'And I *did* see him.'

'Yes,' David said quietly, 'I'm quite sure now you did. Just like the other times.'

Anne's eyes searched his face. 'I'm back where I started, you mean. Is that what you think?' She smiled at the helpless expression on his face. 'Silly question. Of course you do. It's the only rational answer, isn't it?'

David put up his hand, almost touching her shoulder, then withdrew it again. 'I – I honestly don't know what to say. I'm just not qualified. I wish to hell I could help in some way.'

Anne was still looking at him, reading his sincerity. 'Yes,' she said, 'I believe that. And I'm grateful.'

'For what it's worth,' David said hesitantly, 'my advice is that you . . .'

'Go back home and see Phillimore again,' Anne cut in, nodding. 'Yes, that would be the sensible thing to do. And if I thought for one minute that what's been happening was brought on by some kind of neurosis. But you see I don't. I never did, really.'

She turned abruptly and crossed to the battlements, resting her arms on the rough stone and gazing out over the city.

David watched her for a few moments, then came and stood beside her. 'Are you saying that you honestly believe Don is . . . well, haunting you?'

'Yes, if that's the right word for it. Although I'm not sure it is.' She turned to David. 'I certainly don't expect you to accept the idea.'

'You were certainly very much in love with one another. I accept that.'

Anne nodded. 'No one can imagine how close we were. Don and I shared everything, including our thoughts. Even when we were miles apart.' She shivered a little, even though the day was warm. 'I've tried to make myself accept, without forming any conclusions. But I'm not sure that's working. The feeling I get when I sense him or see him is too – too certain, David. Right from the moment I woke up from that terrible nightmare and knew that he was dead, even then I felt he was there in the room with me.'

109

'Anne, love!' David frowned at her, troubled by the bright, almost fanatical intensity of her eyes. 'You can't go on believing this. You mustn't.'

'I can,' she said firmly. 'And I do.'

'You're just tormenting yourself.'

Anne shook her head. 'Not being sure, that was the only torment. But now I am. Quite sure I'm sane and certain sure that I did see Don in London, and that he was on those photographs when I looked at them.' She began walking again and David followed her. 'Thinking about it,' she said musingly, 'that makes sense, too. When I saw Don back home, it was always on familiar ground, somewhere we had in common. Here, the only part of our lives we've ever shared is photography. And I'm using his cameras.'

'Oh, come on, for God's sake!' David was suddenly exasperated. 'You're an intelligent human being, but you're talking nonsense. What you're suggesting just isn't possible. And even if it were, *why?* Ask yourself that. What does he want from you?'

'I think he's trying to tell me something,' Anne said without hesitating. 'And I believe he will, eventually.'

David stared at her, disarmed by the calm simplicity of her reply. 'You're prepared to leave it at that?'

'What choice do I have?'

David sighed. 'And meanwhile?'

'I've got a job to do,' Anne said. 'With or without your help.' They paused by the wall again and Anne put her hand on David's. 'I'll quite understand . . .' Realizing what she had done, she withdrew her hand sharply. 'Either way, I'd rather not talk about it any more. Please.'

She turned from the battlements and walked slowly away along the path. David watched her. He was worried for her, not at all certain what he could do. After a minute he caught up and fell in step beside her.

'If you'd like,' he said, as casually as he could, 'I thought maybe this afternoon we could drive out to . . .'

'No, not this afternoon, David. Tomorrow. Is that all right with you?'

'Of course, whatever you say.'

'I've nothing special on. I just want to be alone for a while.' She saw David's uneasy little frown. 'I'll be all right. And you do understand, don't you?'

'Sure. I understand.'

'I'm sorry to mess you around.'

'No problem,' David assured her. 'Only now I don't have any excuse for not shutting myself away in the museum.' He walked on for a few paces then stopped abruptly. 'Anne. Let go.'

She looked at him patiently, then nodded. 'I will. When I have to. When there's nothing to hold on to any more.'

Chapter Thirteen

Later that afternoon, as David Bascombe was settling to his research at the museum, Anne went into the new town and rented herself a car.

She was being less than impulsive. The motivation had grown in her steadily, up on the old city wall, and now she was following an instinct that she chose to believe had been planted in her.

First, Anne drove to Embonas, the mountain village where she had photographed the wedding. She parked the car, took Don's Olympus OMII from the back and set off on foot.

There was no scheme, no professional structured plan of approach. She simply went from place to place, street to street, taking pictures aimlessly, with no regard for composition.

After half an hour she went back to the car, reloaded the camera with fresh film, and drove off, heading for a fishing village where she had also taken a number of pictures a few days before.

As the day wore on Anne visited Arhangelos, Kritina, Eleoussa and Platania, all of them places where she had taken pictures earlier. At each location she followed the same procedure as before, shooting randomly, not caring about the framing or even the subject matter.

Finally, she drove to the spot where Don's jeep had crashed. She parked the car a few yards away and walked across to the derelict building.

She stood motionless, yards from the point of final impact, staring at the faint scorch marks on the stonework. As silent testimony it was explicit enough. The ground towards the building was churned and pitted; where the fire had been there was a huge, ragged oval of blackened ground clotted with chunks of melted rubber.

Even so it was curiously peaceful, Anne thought. The only sound came from the movement of the grass and leaves as the wind passed over them. The sun was diffuse and gentle, warming her, making it almost impossible to believe she was standing by the scene of that hideous cataclysm.

By degrees, the familiar feeling began to enclose Anne, the certainty that there was a separate presence, another person standing somewhere behind her. She let the sensation grow, filling her with its certainty, then she turned slowly, the same happy expectation mingling, as before, with apprehension and a trace of fear.

She almost jumped with the shock. Raoul Lavallière was standing a few yards away, by the roadside. His Mercedes limousine was parked behind him and one of the young aides was holding the door. In the midst of her confusion, Anne had time to wonder why she hadn't heard the car arrive.

'Monsieur Lavallière?'

'Good afternoon, Mrs Tierney.' He came across to Anne slowly, his eyes fixed on her. 'I was on my way back to the Kastello and saw you here.' He smiled. 'Are you well?'

Anne moistened her lips. 'I'm fine, thanks. And you?'

Lavallière inclined his head, replying with a single, slow nod. 'And I am delighted to meet you again.' He pointed to the camera slung over Anne's shoulder. 'You have been taking more photographs, I see.'

'Not seriously today. Just looking.'

Lavallière nodded, then glanced across at the ruined building. 'I am intruding. How thoughtless. This is where your husband had his tragic accident, is it not?'

'Yes.'

'Lavallière sighed. 'Forgive me.'

'Please,' Anne said hastily, 'I was about to go anyway. I was passing, so I just thought I'd spend a few moments here.'

'I understand.'

Anne turned and together they began walking in the direction of her car. As they reached a clump of large rocks littering the way Lavallière offered Anne his hand. She took it.

As his fingers closed around hers she experienced a sudden, electrifying thrill, a surge of physical arousal that halted her, staring dazedly at the tall Frenchman, her breath catching in her throat.

Lavallière returned her look, his eyes calm, confident.

With an effort Anne managed to take her hand from his and continue walking without his help. Her knees trembled and once she almost tripped, but finally she made it to the road.

She paused a few feet from the car. She felt weak, her flesh and nerves reverberating in the wake of the onslaught.

Lavallière stood for a moment, looking at her. 'We will meet again,' he said. 'I am sure of it. So, *au revoir*.'

Anne swallowed hard. 'Goodbye.'

Smiling disarmingly, Lavallière paused and said, 'Whatever you were looking for, Mrs Tierney, you will find it. I am certain of that, too.'

Perplexed, Anne returned the smile. Lavallière walked back to his car and she climbed into hers, taking a deep, shaky breath before she started the engine and drove off. As she passed she saw Lavallière standing by his limousine, watching her intently.

The drive back to the new town was slow and erratic; three times Anne took a wrong turning, adding miles to the journey as she distractedly tried to understand what had happened to her. Admitting that it *had* happened was difficult enough. Not since Don's death had she felt the least tremor of sexuality in herself. That had died at the instant he had – as completely, she'd believed, as the withering of a once opulent, dazzling flower.

But now this. To think of it made her cheeks flush. It was

so often true that reality lacked the colour and vibrance of imagination, but what had happened to Anne the moment she touched Lavallière's hand was so devastating, so rich and complex, that now it defied the efforts of memory to conjure even half its power.

Even her shame, she realized, was secondary to her amazement. She had never thought herself capable of physical awareness on that scale. And it had happened without the slightest of preliminaries.

As she got within sight of the town, another perplexity surfaced. *Whatever you were looking for, Mrs Tierney, you will find it.* She could still hear his voice and see his assured, confident smile as he said it.

What had he meant?

Anne stopped the car opposite Mr Seferis' photographic shop. She stayed behind the wheel for a few minutes, drumming her fingers absently on the rim, trying to see a pattern in the whole puzzling matrix of the day. Finally, her head aching with the effort to draw sense from imponderables, she stepped out on to the pavement, her legs still shaky as she reached in to take the bag of films from the back seat.

After three and a half hours of studying in the museum library, David Bascombe decided to finish for the day. He tidied the books on the table and stood up, putting on his jacket. As he was pocketing his notebook and pen the librarian, Stavros Kaloudis, came tiptoeing into the room. He was a man of about sixty, bespectacled and distracted-looking, dressed neatly in a carefully preserved dark suit.

'Ah, you are leaving, *Kyrie* Bascombe. I came in to see how it is going with you.'

'Not a lot of progress, I'm afraid,' David said, piling some of the books and walking to the shelves with them. 'I haven't really been able to concentrate this afternoon. Not on the political implications of Rhodian sea power in 200 B.C., anyway.'

Kaloudis nodded sympathetically. 'You have given yourself a great task with this history of yours. So much reading, so much thought.' He wrung his hands, another small mark of sympathy. 'It is not always easy, eh?'

'Well, not today.'

Kaloudis went to the table and began re-rolling a map and a drawing of an ancient warship. 'I will return these to the archives, shall I?'

David nodded, sliding the books on to a shelf. 'Thank you, *Kyrie* Kaloudis. I'd be grateful.'

Kaloudis paused, noticing a book lying beside the map. It was a nineteenth-century French volume by the Abbé Monory, entitled *L'Histoire de L'Ordre St Jean de Hierusalem*. He picked up the book and opened it. 'I would not have thought,' he said, 'that Abbé Monory had much to say about the period of our history in which you are interested at the moment.'

'No,' David agreed, coming back to the table, 'you're right. I was checking on something else. I knew I'd come across a reference to Tibald de Montrefort somewhere fairly recently – probably when I was digging out material for that piece I did for *History Today*.'

'De Montrefort?' Kaloudis was looking blank.

'Doesn't that name mean anything to you?'

Kaloudis shook his head, glancing at the title of the book again. 'He was one of the Knights of Saint John?'

'No. That's what's interesting. At least, according to the portrait of him up at the Kastello Aghios Theodoros, he wasn't. In the painting he's depicted as a Templar.'

'You have been inside the Kastello?' Kaloudis was looking impressed now.

'Briefly,' David nodded.

The librarian's expression shifted towards awe. 'The Frenchman, Lavallière – you are a friend of his?'

'Friend would be stretching it a bit,' David said. 'Just an acquaintance. I've only met him once.'

116

'Even so, he must think most highly of you to invite you to the Kastello.' Kaloudis gestured to the book. 'Did you find the reference.'

'Only the engraving of de Montrefort.' David took the book and leafed through it. He found the illustration and showed it to Kaloudis. 'The Abbé hardly mentions him in the text, except to say that the Grand Master of the Hospitallers hailed him as "our brother in Christ".'

Kaloudis nodded, still looking impressed.

'He's mentioned briefly here, too, in Bishop Greystoke's book.' David picked up another volume, slim and leather-bound, thumbing the pages until he located the reference. 'Here we are. He's on about tithes and taxes and he quotes from one letter that was written, allegedly, by one of the Hospitaller Commanders in 1320.' David cleared his throat and read from the page; '". . . a punitive impost which, had it been put into effect, would have undoubtedly found favour with many among us, principally Tibald de Montrefort and those others of the Ninth Tongue."'

'But the Hospitallers,' Kaloudis pointed out, 'were divided into only eight tongues – according to the language of the country from which they came. There was no ninth tongue.'

'Exactly,' David said, putting the book down again. 'But then, we all know how suspect that old fraud Greystoke is as an historian. Most of the time he even gets his dates wrong. So his book isn't very helpful.' He gazed around at the stacked shelves. 'I can't find anything else here about de Montrefort or the castle.'

Between them, the two men took the remainder of the books from the table and carried them to the shelves.

'Sadly,' Kaloudis murmured as he slid the volumes into their places, 'we have very little here in the museum concerning the island's occupation by the Knights. There are few artefacts and even less written material, I regret to say.'

'Yes, sad,' David agreed.

'Shameful, when you think how important a part the

Knights played in our past. But then, we Greeks seem only to be interested in our classical history – obsessed with it, in my opinion, often to the exclusion of much else which should be preserved. There *are* on Rhodes, however, some documents from that period which are not catalogued in the library.'

'Really?' David paused with a book halfway to the shelf.

'Yes. Those which were discovered by the Turks when they took the island from the Hospitallers. But they are of little importance, and most of them exist as copies elsewhere.'

'I hadn't heard about those.'

Kaloudis looked pleased to have added, however slightly, to David's knowledge. 'They were kept in the vaults of the Turkish library here in the city until 1974,' he said. 'But then, when Cyprus was invaded, they were removed for safe keeping.'

'And you have them here now?'

Kaloudis nodded. 'Still unpacked. I doubt if there is anything among them which would add greatly to your knowledge of the Kastello Aghios Theodoros. However, it is always possible. If you wish,' he added generously, 'I will gladly make them available to you.'

'I'd certainly like to take a look at them some time,' David said. 'Just out of general interest.' He stepped away from the shelves, preparing to leave. 'As far as de Montrefort's concerned – well, like you say, there's probably not much point. And I was just amusing myself, anyway. Whiling away the time.' He smiled at Kaloudis. 'It's really not that important.'

As Andreas Seferis came through from the darkroom he found Anne standing by the counter, gazing at Don's book in the glass case. She looked up sharply, her face anxious.

'Are they ready?'

'Most of them,' Seferis said.

Anne nodded, then warily she asked, 'Are they all right?'

'Truthfully, I haven't examined them closely.' Seferis shrugged. 'They will be OK. But not my best work, of course. I wish that had been possible. However, at such speed . . . '

'No, I didn't mean that,' Anne said hastily. 'I'm sure you've done a marvellous job. I'm most grateful to you for having them printed up so quickly.'

'I told you,' Seferis reminded her grandly, 'any time. If I can be of service to you as I was to your husband – my good friend Don – then it is a pleasure for me.' He spread his hands, the gesture of a man used to accommodating the foibles of others. 'It was the same with him. Everything in a rush. Wait, I will get those which are done for you.'

Seferis went off to the back of the shop and was back a minute later, clutching a bundle of black-and-white enlargements.

'There are two more which I must put in the drier,' he apologized. 'But that will take a few minutes only.'

Anne almost snatched the pictures from him. She riffled through them hurriedly, seeing the bland and unimaginative images, searching each one for a trace of the inexplicable. But they were no more than rather superior snapshots, devoid of any mystery.

Seferis frowned at her, reading the disappointment on her face. 'They are not how you wanted them, Mrs Tierney?'

Anne mumbled something, some reassurance that seemed to placate Seferis as she turned with the pictures in her hand and left the shop.

Later, at home, she went through the prints again; as before, she found nothing extraordinary. She dropped them beside the colour proofs on the sideboard and tried to still the shifting, half-formed sense of desolation that was dogging her. In the nursing home she had known this feeling often and had even pinned a name on it; spiritual exclusion. Things were happening to her, none of them within the boundaries of her understanding. Anne had known the same depressing bewilderment as a child, trying to find answers

119

that the adult world stubbornly kept from her.

That's exactly how it is, she thought. *I'm like a child who knows what's happening, but who can't be told how or why.*

She went to the portable tape machine and put in a cassette. Music rarely diverted her, but it could always make her low moments more bearable. The opening strains of the Bruch Violin Concerto swelled from the speakers; Anne sighed, picked up the colour proofs and sat down with them, fanning them across her lap.

The telephone rang, startling her. Anne put aside the proofs, got up and turned down the volume of the music before picking up the receiver.

'Hello? Oh, hello David.' She was instantly pleased to hear his voice. More and more, David Bascombe seemed to represent the only stable factor in her existence.

'So how are you feeling?' he asked her.

'I'm fine. A little bit down, maybe, but I'm all right . . .'

'I was wondering if you'd like to join me for dinner.'

She frowned at the mouthpiece. 'I was planning to eat here.' She couldn't be sure if she wanted to go out or not.

'It's somewhere special,' David said.

'Well . . .'

'Oh, come on,' he coaxed. 'It'll do you good. I promise you, you'll enjoy yourself.'

Anne smiled weakly. 'All right then.' It was soothing just to give in, without putting herself to the effort of a real decision. And besides, she badly needed some diversion. 'What time will you pick me up, David?'

Chapter Fourteen

Dinner, it transpired, was to be at the home of one of David's friends. That much was a surprise, but to Anne the big surprise was the friend – not, as she'd suspected, some fusty academic, but a beautiful Greek woman called Ismini Christoyannis. She was a slender person in her mid-thirties with light golden hair and a smiling, animated face. She made Anne welcome immediately.

'You have a beautiful home,' Anne told her, looking admiringly around the sitting room.

'You like it?'

'Very much.' The place exuded charm, Anne thought. The furniture had been selected with care and imagination, and as with Anne's own home in England, the paintings and ornaments disclosed a great deal about the owner's tastes.

'I'm glad it pleases you,' Ismini said. 'But do not encourage me, or I will not be able to resist taking you on a tour of the whole house.'

'I hope you will. Have you lived here long?'

Ismini nodded. 'I was born in this house. Each time I leave it I promise myself that it will be the last.'

'Are you away a great deal?'

'Ismini spends most of her time in Athens,' David explained, coming across from the drinks trolley with a glass for each of the women. 'When she's not jetting around the world, that is. She's usually only here at weekends.'

'Sadly,' Ismini said. 'But this time for one whole month – to be lazy in.' She raised her glass. '*Yammas*.'

They toasted each other, then Ismini turned to Anne and said, 'In the days I have been back this time, David has often spoken about you. You live in London, he tells me.'

'Hampstead.'

'Near the heath?' Ismini asked, surprising Anne.

'Not far away. You know Hampstead?'

'Quite well. I spent three years in London.'

That solved a small mystery for Anne, who had been wondering how Ismini had learned to speak English so well. 'Did you enjoy your time there?'

'Very much, and I have been back many times since.'

'I'm hungry,' David interrupted. 'What are we eating tonight?'

Ismini laughed. 'We are having many things. Do you like Greek food, Anne?'

'Yes, I do.'

'Good.' Ismini looked at David. 'So then, I think all that needs to be done now is for you to make one of your special salads.'

'If you insist,' he said, rubbing his hands.

'Insist!' Ismini turned to Anne, her eyes wide. 'It is he who insists. According to David, we Greeks do not know how to make a good salad.'

David nodded. 'It's true. There's a hell of a sight more to it than just chopping up tomatoes and cucumbers and sprinkling them with feta cheese.' He wagged a professorial finger. 'Making a good salad requires a great deal of imagination. It's an art.'

'Then we will eat as soon as you have produced another masterpiece,' Ismini said, putting down her glass. 'Come, I will show you the things I have bought, in the hope that they will inspire you.' She flashed a smile at Anne. 'Make yourself comfortable, I shall only be a moment.'

Anne watched Ismini and David go off to the kitchen, then she turned and made a slow tour of the room, her habitual practice in new places. The momentary embarrassment she'd felt when she arrived was dispelled now. She was sure she wasn't invading any special intimacy – on the contrary, Anne felt she was being made welcome to a bright, open friendship.

'He is happy,' Ismini said, coming back through from the kitchen. 'It would seem that I thought to buy all the right ingredients.'

'You indulge him,' Anne said.

'Of course,' Ismini said. 'He is a very dear friend.'

Anne was continuing her slow circuit of the room. 'Have you known each other long?' she asked lightly.

'Yes.' Ismini picked up her glass and sipped from it. 'For more than two years now. We met on the plane from Athens. I was returning for the weekend and David was on holiday from the university. He was on his way over to do some research.'

Anne turned, facing Ismini. 'He seems to be very much at home here. On Rhodes, I mean.'

'He makes many visits. And he comes back whenever he can. He is in love, you see.' Ismini smiled as Anne blinked at her. 'With the island. So, you could not have a better guide, could you? As I could not have a better friend – we are lucky, you and I, to share his friendship.' Ismini nodded at Anne's glass. 'Would you like another drink?'

'Thanks.' As Ismini went to the drinks trolley Anne turned and gazed at the crammed bookshelves along one wall. 'So many books,' she murmured.

'Learned texts,' Ismini said over her shoulder. 'Most of them, anyway. Some of them not so learned, I regret to say, but it is necessary that I read them just the same.'

'For your work?'

'To keep up to date.'

Anne was peering at the spines, trying to make sense of the titles. 'What do you do?' she asked.

Ismini turned with two fresh drinks in her hands. 'Didn't David tell you?' she held out a glass to Anne. 'I am a psychiatrist.'

Anne's instant surprise billowed swiftly into anger. 'I see.' She glared at Ismini, ignoring the drink. 'No, David didn't tell me that.' She stamped across to the side table and reached for her handbag. 'Undoubtedly because he knows that if he *had* told me I wouldn't be here.'

Ismini looked genuinely bewildered. 'Why?'

'Oh, come on now!' Anne hissed, 'You're not going to pretend he hasn't said anything about me – hasn't told you about what happened this morning, for instance. About everything that's been happening since my husband was killed.' She was trembling. 'That's why I'm here, isn't it?' she demanded. 'Well thank you, but I thought I'd made it clear to David. I don't need a psychiatrist.'

'No,' Ismini agreed calmly, 'it is quite possible that you do not. And it is that possibility which interests me.' She moved closer to Anne. 'Of course David told me. He is worried about you. Worried *for* you.'

'For my sanity, you mean . . .'

'Do not blame him for that. Be grateful for his concern.'

Anne shook her head. 'So he asked you if he could bring me here. So that you could look me over.'

'No,' Ismini said firmly, 'he did not ask me that. I asked him.' She paused, her eyes steady and sincere. 'What he said intrigued me. I thought that perhaps I might be able to help you in some way.'

'Well I'm afraid you can't. I'm not looking for treatment.'

'Good. Because I am not offering it.' Ismini smiled. 'I would never do so until I was convinced that it was necessary.'

Anne frowned. 'And you're not?'

'No.' Ismini held out the glass again. After a moment's hesitation Anne took it.

'You don't think that it's all in my mind?'

'Oh, it's entirely possible that everything you have experienced is the result of an obsessional hysteria,' Ismini said.

'And that was my initial diagnosis. But now that I've met you, my professional opinion is that it's unlikely.'

Anne had relinquished her grip on her handbag. 'I didn't imagine it all. Is that what you're saying?'

'I am saying that it is unlikely,' Ismini explained. 'For one thing, you are obviously psychic. You are maybe even a sensitive.'

'I assume you got that from David, did you? That weird sort of ESP I had with Don?'

'Really?' Ismini looked intrigued. 'That's very interesting – but no, as a matter of fact David didn't mention that.'

'Then how can you tell?'

Ismini smiled gently. 'There is an English expression, is there not – "It takes one to know one"?'

'You!' Anne looked astonished.

'Yes,' Ismini said. 'You are surprised?'

'Somewhat.' Anne studied the other woman's face. 'Are you trying to humour me?'

'Why should I do that?'

'For my peace of mind.'

'But you know that I am not, don't you?' Ismini's eyes widened a fraction, locking on to Anne's.

For an instant Anne felt dizzy, as if the room were shifting in two directions at once. Then, abruptly, the movement was inside her, right at the core of her mind. Her own mental images were being probed and displaced. She felt compelled to keep her eyes on Ismini's and as she went on staring the compulsion swelled, forcing her to vocalize what she was seeing.

'You were just a child,' she murmured. 'It was on your birthday. You were eight years old.'

Ismini relaxed, smiling at Anne. 'You see?'

Anne was amazed. 'And that's the answer?'

'You have suspected it for some time.'

Anne gulped from her glass then stood gazing at Ismini,

shaking her head slowly. 'But why me? And why now?'

'It is an ability we all have,' Ismini said lightly. 'To one degree or another. Most people reject it as something which is alien to them, and so that seventh sense withers. In you, though, it has always been stronger than in most people. Now you call on it because you have a need to.'

'It's frightening.'

Casually, as if she were passing on an ordinary reminiscence, Ismini explained how she had discovered her own psychic ability. The first time it had disturbed her deeply; it had distressed her parents even more. The second occurrence led her father to believe that his daughter's mind was unbalanced. Ismini began to believe it herself.

'I was a child growing up here, on Rodos, which is still not the most enlightened place in the world. So I fought against it, consciously denying it to myself.'

As time passed, she went on, she had more psychic experiences and they began to torment her. But she stopped telling anyone about them. Out of fear and ignorance she would lie when her family asked what was wrong. For the remainder of her childhood and for some years after, Ismini went on lying to other people and refusing to admit to herself that she possessed the seventh sense.

'Which is why, when I qualified as a doctor, I decided to specialize in clinical psychiatry.'

'What did you hope to achieve?'

'A better understanding of mental illness,' Ismini said. 'And through that, perhaps, a knowledge of the phenomena which people so often attribute to psychosis, simply because they are afraid of them.' She smiled wryly. 'At best, they are dismissed as eccentric aberrations.'

'Like seeing ghosts.'

'Among many other things.'

Anne nodded. 'And have you made much progress?'

'We all have. Telepathy and extra-sensory perception are accepted much more widely now. Psychokinesis, too. At least they are admitted as factors to be taken into consideration with other aspects of human psychology. That is great progress.' Ismini sighed. 'There is still a long way to go, however. And very little evidence to work on. Most of the psychiatric disturbances I deal with are just that – some kind of malfunction in the normal mental processes.'

Anne nodded, but rather warily. 'That doesn't apply to me?'

'No,' Ismini assured her. 'I am convinced of it now. As you are.'

'So what do I do about the way I am?'

'There is nothing you can do. Only come to terms with it.'

'It's difficult to accept.' Anne frowned at her half-empty glass. 'I mean, I could read Don's thoughts, and I could always sense when he was in danger. But I've never known anything like what's happened lately . . .'

'You have never lost anyone so close to you before,' Ismini pointed out.

'That's true.' Anne looked up. 'Are you married?'

'I was.'

'Oh, I'm sorry. Do you miss him?'

'On occasions,' Ismini said. 'But we have not entirely lost contact.' She saw Anne's enquiring look and read the question in it. Ismini shook her head. 'He is a lawyer in Athens. We are divorced.'

Anne smiled sheepishly. 'I see. Do you have children?'

'No. I regret that.'

'So do I.' Anne was used to understating what she really felt, which was a great deal more than regret. 'Don and I would have both liked a family. But . . .' She shrugged. 'Apparently I can't have any.'

'Ah. Yes, that is sad.'

The mood between them had softened to a point where Anne felt she could make her apologies. 'I'm sorry I got a bit uptight with you,' she murmured.

'It is understandable. Am I forgiven for having David bring you here tonight?'

'Yes, of course. At least I've got official confirmation now that I'm not going crazy. What will you tell David?'

'Jus that,' Ismini promised. 'And I'll try to make him understand.'

David came in from the kitchen, rubbing his hands again. 'Right,' he said breezily, 'we can eat whenever you like. The salad's a work of genius and I've opened the wine.'

'Shall we then?' Ismini asked Anne.

'Certainly.' Anne grinned. 'If only to award marks to the salad.'

As they moved towards the door Ismini asked David if he was going to the carnival the following day.

'Yes. I thought Anne ought to see it.'

'What carnival?' Anne asked.

'At Arhangelos. It's an annual affair. You might get some good shots there.'

'More than likely.' Anne looked at Ismini. 'Are you going?'

'Probably. Why don't we all go together, the three of us?'

For an instant the eyes of the two women met and held. There was a momentary surge in Anne, a sense of unity. She'd almost forgotten how good that could feel.

Late that night, the stillness of Anne's house in the old city was broken by the opening strains of Bruch's violin concerto.

Anne came awake suddenly. She sat up, craning her neck towards the door. After a moment she realized it was the tape recorder downstairs.

Someone's playing the machine!

With the realization came the familiar, half-uneasy certainty that all she need do was go down there. She only had to get herself out of bed and down those stairs. Anne had no doubt who she would see.

She pushed back the covers and crept to the door. Her

heart was thumping and her hand trembled as she pulled open the door and heard the music swell around her.

Don loved that concerto.

She went down the stairs slowly, scarcely breathing. The music was so loud now it engulfed her. At the bottom she stood for a long moment, tensing herself, trying to edge aside the fear and accept what was in the sitting room. The conviction in her was stronger now than it had ever been. He was in there.

She stepped through the arched doorway, smiling tentatively, accepting, *wanting*.

'Don?'

Anne looked around the half-dark room. The music pounded on and the recorder's dials blinked brightly from the table. She looked in every corner, along each wall, slowly, carefully.

There was no one else in the room. It seemed impossible. This time she had been certain.

Confused and disappointed, she crossed and switched off the tape machine. The silence merged instantly with the terrible hollow inside her, deepening it. Anne suddenly wanted to scream her frustration, bang her fists on the walls and let out all her pain in one screeching, hammering torrent. But she did no more, finally, than sink down on the arm of her settee and cry into her hands.

Chapter Fifteen

The hot, dusty streets of Arhangelos were crammed with revellers. Tables laden with food and bottles of wine crowded the pavements outside shops, tavernas and bars. There was music everywhere, loud and raucous, blaring from loudspeakers, radios and village bands. Spontaneous dancing seemed to break out every few minutes as the bright-costumed men, women and children whirled and stamped wholeheartedly in the energetic business of enjoying themselves.

A fancy-dress parade was moving slowly down the main street. Ismini Christoyannis and David Bascombe were standing by the roadside, watching, as Anne took photographs on the other side of the street. As the bright procession went past David glanced as Ismini.

'Did she tell you what happened last night?' he asked.

'Yes,' Ismini said, frowning. 'It must have been terrible for her.'

She had been watching Anne since they arrived in the village. It was as if there was an article of personal discipline demanding that, no matter what the pressure, Anne must pretend she was all right. But the pretence was showing. She was strained, edgy, taking her photographs mechanically and non-stop, as if she was using the exercise to distract herself. When she had told Ismini about the episode with the tape machine, Anne had looked dark-eyed and very troubled; she still looked that way. The feverish activity with the camera was window-dressing, as much for Anne's own benefit, Ismini believed, as for anyone else's.

A donkey cart full of masked, banner-waving children came by, catching Ismini's attention. At the same instant Anne stepped back into the mouth of a narrow alley to allow a crowd of revellers to go past. Absently, she turned and looked down the passageway. At the far end there was a beautiful old chapel, rising sunlit from the shadows.

Anne stepped further into the alley and took a picture of the chapel. She took a few steps closer and photgraphed it again. As she turned to go back to the street she noticed an open gateway on her left. It led into a small yard. In the centre, surrounded by ancient, work-worn baking implements, there was a traditional Rhodian bread oven. In spite of her mood, Anne could see the photographic possibilities at once.

She stepped into the yard, moving to one side of the oven, choosing her viewpoint. She raised the camera slowly to her eye.

Out on the street, Ismini suddenly realized that Anne was no longer there. Without thinking, impelled by a warning she couldn't define, she pushed through the crowd in front of her and lunged across the street, her eyes darting left and right.

'Anne? *Anne!*'

The light in the yard was just right, a slanting, gold-tinged luminance that brought out the pitted texture of the old oven and threw a framing pattern of shadows on the ground. With the camera pressed to her eye Anne slowly turned the focusing ring, bringing the scene into sharpness. The view-finder image was immaculate. Anne pressed the shutter release, trapping the picture.

Ismini was standing in the mouth of the alley, looking along its shadowed length. The feeling in her was more powerful now, a dark imperative, goading her forward. She began walking briskly down the alley.

Anne moved to where some old farm implements were leaning against a corner of the yard. Again, the combination of textures and shadows created a striking, harmonious composition. Anne took up her viewpoint, raised the camera and focused.

The sound of the carnival was suddenly gone. There had been no warning, no premonitory shift in her awareness. In total silence Anne was staring into her viewfinder, seeing Don Tierney standing beside the farm implements. He was smiling at her.

Anne lowered the camera. He was still there. The sun made the same play of light and shade on his face and clothes as it did on everything else. He was real. Anne stood transfixed, staring.

'Anne, my love.' He put out his arms to her.

Ismini came to the gateway of the yard as Anne took a step forward. '*Anne!*'

Distracted for an instant, Anne turned her head and saw Ismini. She looked at the corner again. Don was no longer there. The sound of the carnival came rushing back.

Ismini ran across the yard and closed her arms around Anne.

'It was Don. He was *here*. He spoke to me.'

Ismini nodded, drawing Anne closer.

'You saw him?' Anne's eyes searched Ismini's face. 'Did you hear him?'

'No,' Ismini breathed. 'But there was something here.' She glanced around the yard. 'A presence of some kind. I felt it.'

A desperate wail broke sharp in Anne's throat. 'It was Don,' she moaned. 'It was him! Oh, Ismini!' She buried her face in the soft wool of the other woman's cloak. 'Help me, *help* me! Please!' She looked up, her face streaked with tears. 'What is it? What is he trying to tell me?'

That evening David Bascombe brought Anne to Ismini's house. As Ismini closed the curtains, Anne sat down on the settee. David stood opposite, staring at her. She was pale and drawn, like someone trapped in an illness that had already taken too much of her strength.

'Are you all right?' David asked her.

Anne nodded.

'And are you sure this is what you want?'

'Quite sure.'

As Ismini came across from the windows David drew her aside. 'I'll wait in the car,' he murmured.

Ismini shook her head. 'It is not necessary.'

'I think Anne would prefer it.' He sounded cold, rather distant. 'Anyway, this isn't really my scene.'

'And you do not approve.'

'I just hope you know what you're doing. I know she asked for your help, but isn't there any other way?'

'Don't worry,' Ismini said.

David shrugged and looked across at Anne. 'See you later.' He crossed to the doorway. 'Give me a call when you're done, Ismini,' he grunted, going out and closing the door behind him.

Ismini sat down on the settee beside Anne. 'Are you ready?' she asked quietly.

Anne looked at her a little uncertainly. 'Now?'
'Unless you would rather wait . . .'

Anne shook her head.

'Remember though,' Ismini said, 'I can promise nothing.'

'I understand that.'

'So then.' Ismini took Anne's hands in hers.

Anne frowned. 'Shouldn't we . . .'

'Sit at the table? No, we do not need to do that. And the lights do not have to be turned out, either.'

'I see.' Anne cleared her throat nervously. 'What do you want me to do?'

'Think of your husband. Bring a picture of him into your mind and try to hold it there for me.'

Slowly, with her eyes wide open, Anne began to conjure the picture layer by layer, strengthening it, the image of Don Tierney as she had seen him that afternoon. As the detail and colour gained intensity Anne's breathing became fast and shallow. She began to whimper softly as the picture took dominance in her mind and quenched the other, fainter images.

Ismini closed her eyes, holding tightly to Anne's hands. She concentrated, her jaw hardening as she strove to take the image across into her own awareness.

'Help me to him, Anne . . .' Ismini's voice spoke in Anne's head, telepathed there with ringing clarity.

The picture kept slipping out of focus. Anne strained to hold it, to sharpen its lines.

'Together, Anne . . . Together. Help me . . .'

As one side of the picture became clear the other faded into softness. Holding it all was becoming too much of an effort. Anne strove, grunting, to bring it whole and clear to the front of her mind, to the place where Ismini could receive it.

'I cannot do it without you . . .'

'I'm trying!' Anne's desperate, frantic voice sang through Ismini's mind as the image fluttered weakly behind it. 'I'm trying!'

Both women had their eyes shut now, clenching them in the taut, wrenching struggle to make the picture cross the linking path between their minds.

'There is something,' Ismini's transmitted voice panted. 'There is . . . A barrier . . . I cannot do it – I cannot reach . . .'

'You can! You must!' Anne's voice was a command; wrung fiercely from her desperation. She had the picture now, was holding it, ready to have it taken across. 'You *can*! You're almost there . . . Believe me. I know it. I know it!'

Outside there was the sound of a sudden wind approaching from the south east, a low roaring in the air that swooped abruptly and burst on the house in a savage hurricane. Leaves were ripped from the trees. Snapped branches slammed against the windows as the turbulent air screamed across stone and ploughed up chunks of earth. David Bascombe was in his car, parked in the front drive. He struggled to get

134

out, but the force of the wind kept the door rammed shut.

Inside, the entire house was shaking. Ornaments, pictures and books slid across tables and crashed down from shelves. The windows bulged inwards, rattling, twisting their ancient joists and sending tremors along the walls. As the wind screeched the two women held tightly to each other's hands, each one's voice howling within the other's head.

'Something between us . . . I cannot . . . Something stopping – I can't . . .'

'You can! Please!' The picture of Don was fading, only a shadow remained, thin, indistinct. 'Please try . . . You're nearly there! Don! *Don!*'

'Not possible. Something too strong . . . Too strong. I cannot!'

With a sharp, pained cry Ismini jerked her hands away from Anne's. The link was broken instantly. At the same instant the storm subsided and quickly died away.

Anne opened her eyes slowly, as if she were coming out of a sleep. She sat watching anxiously as Ismini, exhausted, struggled back out of her trance.

'Are you OK?' Anne whispered, touching Ismini's cheek.

Ismini nooded weakly. 'I'm sorry.'

'Was it my fault?'

'No. You gave me the image I needed.' Ismini stared at Anne, her eyes troubled. 'I could not make contact. There was something . . .' Perplexed, she shook her head. 'It was very strange.'

'It almost happened,' Anne said soothingly. 'It will next time.'

Later, when David had come back inside and was breathlessly telling them about the storm, Anne watched Ismini gradually reassemble her faculties. Now it was she who looked ill.

'It was quite incredible,' David was saying. 'A real freak wind. It seemed to come whooshing up from Lindos. I've never seen anything like it. Not on Rhodes.'

135

Too exhausted to repond to David's story, Ismini stood up and moved towards the door. Anne followed her. David, gathering what was happening, buttoned his jacket and moved out into the hall with them.

'Are you sure you won't change your mind?' Ismini still looked deeply troubled. She had asked Anne to move in with her for a time but Anne had declined. 'It would be a pleasure. And there is more than enough room for both of us. You could move in tomorrow . . .'

'I appreciate the offer,' Anne said. 'But I'm really very happy where I am. Honestly.'

'Well,' Ismini sighed, 'I shall leave the invitation open. You will be welcome – any time.'

Anne smiled. 'I know. Thank you.'

At the front door, Anne impulsively kissed Ismini on the cheek. 'I'm very grateful.' She hesitated, then said, 'We'll try again, won't we?'

'Perhaps,' Ismini said wearily. 'We will see.' Anne's disappointment was instantly visible. Ismini smiled and nodded resignedly. 'If that is what you wish.'

Anne returned the smile and walked off towards the Volkswagen. David stepped close to Ismini.

'What happened in there tonight?'

'I'm not sure,' Ismini said quietly. 'But I am worried, David. Deeply worried.' She glanced at the car. 'For her.'

Ismini stood by the open door long after Anne and David had gone. She was holding an image that no one had transferred to her, a picture of Anne Tierney being slowly encircled by darkness, a thick fog of evil so dense that no one would ever penetrate it.

Finally, Ismini had to pull herself away from the depressing vision. As she turned, she saw the destruction in her garden and wondered, vaguely, what sort of wind could be savage enough to do that.

*   *   *

At fourteen minutes past midnight Anne stirred in her bed and opened her eyes. She blinked twice, raising her head a fraction from the pillow. She knew she was awake, dream and reality were too distinct in their sensations for her to be mistaken. But the room was altered.

It had the appearance of a child's dream grotto. Everything was where it should be, but the light was soft and rose coloured, misty, merging to pale blue at the ceiling. *Alice in Wonderland*, Anne thought; the room might have been a setting from the film she had loved since childhood.

She pinched her arm, checking, and got the authentic tactile sensation of consciousness. She was definitely awake, but she was awake in a shimmering fantasy.

And then she saw him, standing by the silver-bright window. Don. There was no doubt at all. He was smiling at her. Anne sat up, startled, breathless.

'Anne!' He came towards her, holding out his arms.

'Don! Oh, Don . . .'

With his arms still outstretched he came and sat on the bed. Anne let him enclose her in a tight, warm embrace. A *real* embrace; he was there, he was flesh and he was breathing. Anne blinked back her tears and stared at his face, touched it, put her lips on his and felt the beloved, unmistakable pliancy of her husband's mouth.

'Darling, dearest Don . . .'

His embrace loosened and he pushed the bedclothes aside. Anne lay back, delirious with the familiarity of every movement, tingling with the joy of his body pressing along the length of her own.

'I love you, love you . . . '

The slow mingling of their limbs brought forward an eagerness in her that revived, to perfection, the zest she had always felt in their lovemaking. Anne spread her thighs without hesitation and let herself respond to the rhythm of his body.

'You're here,' she moaned against his neck. 'You're with me. At last . . .'

The current of physical need drove her hips, sharpening the intensity of her pleasure. Reason, logic, doubt – they were nothing. This joining of bodies transcended every other reality. She groaned softly and pressed her body closer to his.

With his face an inch from the pillow, breathing open-mouthed and easily, Raoul Lavallière smiled as he drove himself harder against Anne's willing, joyfully enclosing warmth.

Chapter Sixteen

At mid-morning the following day, Ismini went to the sports stadium. She stood by the top row of tiered seats and watched the athletes running round the track in the sweltering heat. Some were exercising with more style and energy than others. One, in particular, didn't look at all professional. He was in a faded tracksuit and was jogging rather casually around the bend in Ismini's direction She waited a minute then slowly descended the steps, arriving at the trackside as the jogger was going by.

'Good morning,' she called out.

David Bascombe stopped, recognized her and came across. 'Hello, love,' he panted. 'Excuse the sweat.' He kissed her on the cheek. 'I didn't know you were into this kind of thing.' He glanced at her feet. 'Can't be easy in those shoes.'

'I called at your house,' Ismini explained. 'Your landlord told me you had come up here.'

David picked up his towel from the bench. 'Twice a week, if I can.'

'A healthy mind in a healthy body,' Ismini said, smiling.

'God!' David put on a stricken face. 'That sounds boring. I might give this up.' He began towelling his face. 'Something urgent, was it?'

'Probably.' Ismini's smile had faded.

'Trouble?'

Ismini sat down on the bench. 'Have you seen Anne today?'

'No. She told me not to bother picking her up.'

'Have you spoken to her?'

David shook his head. 'Not this morning. Why?'

'I called her and we had coffee together, earlier.' She frowned as David sat down beside her. 'How was she when you drove her home last night?'

David thought for a moment. 'She was OK, I think. A bit quiet. But that's understandable.' He looked at Ismini. 'Did something happen after I dropped her off?'

'She says not,' Ismini sighed.

'Only you don't believe her?'

'I'm not sure I do.' They spent half an hour at a smart café that morning, and throughout the time they were there Anne had behaved almost coolly towards Ismini. The closeness of the previous night seemed to have vanished.

'I thought you two had some kind of special empathy going for you,' Don said. 'Like being able to read each other's minds, even.'

'We have,' Ismini said. 'And we can. But Anne was fighting me this morning. Deliberately shutting me out.'

David looked surprised. 'Why would she do that?'

'To protect herself, perhaps.'

'From you?'

'Oh, I don't know.' Ismini gazed out across the track. 'From my reaction, maybe. And from the consequences of it.'

'But you're not working against her.'

'No, of course not.' Ismini turned to David. 'But something or someone is.' Her face was earnest, concerned. 'And that is why we did not succeed in establishing a link with her husband. Some force prevented it. Which is why I am worried for her.' Ismini's eyes were grave with certainty. 'Anne is at risk, David.'

'What kind of risk?' He looked sceptical. 'From where? Donald Tierney?'

'Perhaps,' Ismini said. 'Or from someone who is using him.'

She stared at the track again, recalling how Anne had

140

behaved earlier – politely and with modest reserve, answering questions evasively and closing her mind like a clamp around something she didn't want to share. Something that could possibly destroy her.

For the hour between noon and one o'clock Anne took pictures in the village of Aghios Theodoros, a picturesque, sloping settlement dominated by the mound of the Kastello. She photographed the church, the beautiful white houses with their hand-carved doors and shutters, the mosaic-inlaid pathways and the quaint shops. She worked differently today, moving serenely from place to place, enjoying the sense of accomplishment as she steadily blended art with craft to gather her pictures.

On a steep, quiet street she stopped suddenly, halfway through making an exposure. She turned and saw Raoul Lavallière, standing at the top of a narrow flight of steps.

'Good morning.' Anne said brightly.

Lavallière smiled. 'Welcome to the village of Aghios Theodoros, Mrs Tierney.' He came down the steps. 'You have not been here before, I think.'

'No. It's beautiful, isn't it?'

'Very.' With his eyes fixed on hers, Lavallière took Anne's hand and kissed it.

Anne almost gasped, feeling the same sudden, erotic surge as before. She was held by it, possessed, staring dumbly at Lavallière's calm, smiling face. After a moment he released her hand.

'You were not, I hope, going to leave without calling on me.'

Anne recovered her poise with an effort. Bewildered again by what had happened to her, she forced a smile and said, 'I didn't want to disturb you.' She moistened her lips. 'I thought about it, though. To ask you if I could take some photographs inside the castle.'

'But of course you may,' Lavallière said grandly. 'You are always welcome there.' He waved his arm towards the castle mound. 'Shall we go?'

Anne blinked at him. 'Now?'

'If you have finished here. And if you will do me the honour. There is a path. It is a pleasant walk.'

'My car's parked in the square,' Anne said.

'Then you will give me the keys and I will send someone for it.'

Resistance was the furthest impulse from Anne's mind. She was vaguely aware that her mind, in fact, was capable of holding very little at present, apart from her confusion.

She followed Lavallière along a narrow passageway and out on to a sunlit street at the other end. As they started to walk down the gentle slope two men from the village, approaching from the opposite direction, stood aside to let them pass. They paid bowing respect to the tall Frenchman as he walked by.

'*Kalimera*, *Kyrie*,' they mumbled in unison.

'*Kalimera*.' The faintest smile curled Lavallière's lips as he acknowledged them. Walking at his side, Anne began to feel like an adornment of his grandeur.

As they made their way through the village, everyone they passed, even the children, made gestures of homage. Outside a small house, an old woman struggled out of her chair at the sight of Lavallière. She shuffled across to him, seized his hand and kissed it.

'*Chronia polla*, she croaked fervently.

Lavallière placed his other hand on her head, as though he were granting a benediction. Anne looked on, fascinated.

'*Episis*,' Lavallière intoned softly. The old woman hobbled back to her chair.

When they were further along the road Anne asked Lavallière what the old woman had said.

'She wished me many years,' he replied. 'She is grateful for a small service I was able to do her family.'

'That was kind of you.'

Lavallière shook his head. 'You flatter me, Mrs Tierney. Kindness has nothing to do with it. It was an obligation.'

Anne looked up at him questioningly.

'My kinsman, de Montrefort, held the castle of Saint Theodore. The people of this village were his people. They served him well.'

'And now you live in the castle . . .'

'And the debt has been renewed,' Lavallière said, nodding.

As they continued on through the village Anne was increasingly aware of her companion's stature among these people. They didn't simply respect him, it seemed. They adored him. There wasn't one head that failed to turn and show smiling subservience. Anne had noticed a similar, in some cases identical regard among the guests at the soirée. That degree of eminence, coupled to the almost unthinkably potent effect he had on her, made it impossible for Anne to form a balanced appraisal of Raoul Lavallière – there was simply no one, in her experience, to whom he could be compared.

When they had reached the castle, Lavallière took Anne to the north-facing battlements and told her that she was at liberty to make her way down through the castle from there, photographing whatever she wished. He excused himself and left her to carry on.

Later, Dietrich von Reitz joined Lavallière on the flight of steps overlooking the central courtyard, where Anne was engrossed in taking her pictures. For a few moments von Reitz said nothing; he stood beside his master, his face troubled and brooding as he observed the way Lavallière's eyes remained fixed on his visitor.

Finally von Reitz spoke up. 'Is this wise, *Maître*?' he asked nervously.

Lavallière continued to watch Anne. 'What harm is she doing?'

'None, while she remains in the courtyard. But what if she

143

asks to photograph the interior?'

'If she wishes to,' Lavallière murmured, 'then she will have my permission, Colonel.'

Von Reitz stiffened. 'Without restriction?'

'We have nothing to hide. There is no one of any consequence in residence. Our special guests do not arrive until Saturday evening.'

'I would remind you, *Maître,*' von Reitz said, shifting his feet, 'that her husband also took photographs in the castle.'

'And they were destroyed when he was killed.'

'There were others, though, which she has seen . . .'

'But which also no longer exist.'

'Nevertheless.' Von Reitz sighed restlessly, glancing down at Anne again. 'We still do not know how much of an impression they made on her. Being here today might well refresh her memory of them and rekindle her curiosity.'

Anne took her final shot in the courtyard and turned, approaching the steps.

'You worry needlessly,' Lavallière said, looking at Von Reitz. 'I have told you already, she has forgotten about those photographs.'

Von Reitz stared at him. 'Are you certain of that?'

'Absolutely certain. She hasn't missed them and she doesn't even think about them any more.' He smiled thinly. 'She now has something of much more importance on her mind.'

Anne was coming up the steps. Both men turned to face her as she reached the top.

'Good afternoon, Herr von Reitz,' she said.

Von Reitz bowed stiffly. 'Good morning, Mrs Tierney.' With barely a trace of cordiality he added, 'It is good to see you again.' He turned to Lavallière. 'Excuse me.' He performed another sharp bow then turned and walked smartly away from them.

Lavallière beamed at Anne. 'Is there anything else you would like to see which interests you as a photographer?'

'I think I've got enough,' she told him. 'For today, anyway. I mustn't make a nuisance of myself.'

'In no way are you a nuisance,' he assured her. 'Nor could you be. But if you have finished for now, then we can have lunch.'

'Oh . . .' Anne was taken aback. 'That's very good of you, but I wasn't expecting . . .'

'Perhaps not,' Lavallière observed smoothly, 'but I am.'

He pointed across to the courtyard to where a white-covered table, laid for two, had been set up in the shade. Beside it was a heated serving trolley, laden with food and attended by a manservant. A little closer to the table, one of the handsome young aides was standing by.

'*Soles aux crêpes* is a favourite of yours, I think,' Lavallière said quietly.

Anne stared at him blankly, bewildered again.

David Bascombe had decided to skip lunch. Food invariably made him sleepy if he was obliged to exercise his intellect afterwards. Since his research had been neglected lately, he'd decided that the most fitting procedure, following a stimulating hour at the stadium, was to go to the museum and get on with the groundwork for his book.

He had been reading for over an hour when the museum librarian, Mr Kaloudis, came into the room. His arms were piled high with documents.

'Here they are, *Kyrie*,' he grunted, bringing his load to the table. 'There are more, but I think you would prefer not to have so many at one time.'

Mystified, David hastily cleared a space on the table then helped Kaloudis to put the material down. There were scrolls, bundles of folded parchment, manuscript folios and parchment sheets in leather binders. David picked up one of the manuscripts, glanced at it, then stared enquiringly at Kaloudis.

'They are some of the documents which were in the

Turkish library,' Kaloudis explained, 'the ones I said I would make available to you – to help in your search for information on the Kastello Aghios Theodoros and the Knight Templar de Montrefort.'

'Ah, yes, of course.' David had forgotten about them. 'Thank you, this is very kind of you, *Kyrie* Kaloudis.' He stared at the mound on the table. 'I hope you didn't go to a lot of trouble on my account. It was only a casual enquiry.'

Kaloudis' face stiffened. 'I see.'

'I did say that at the time, didn't I?'

'Possibly,' Kaloudis murmured. 'But without sufficient strees, perhaps.' He nodded curtly at the documents. 'Had you made that absolutely clear to me, then I would certainly not have . . .'

'Well, no, casual's not the right word,' David cut in hastily, making amends. 'What I mean is, there was no urgency about it.'

'You said you would be interested to see them,' Kaloudis pointed out huffily.

'Yes indeed. I am. Very interested – and I'm very grateful. It's just that I know how busy you are and I'd hate to think that I'd imposed on your time.'

'When I say that I will do something,' Kaloudis announced primly, 'I make every effort to do so with speed. It is an attempt on my part to discourage the slander that we Greeks are . . . How is the expression? Ah, yes . . .' A look of distaste soured his face; '"Long on promises but short on delivery."'

David feigned astonishment. 'Who says that?'

'There are those who do,' the librarian mumbled, folding his hands. 'It is said mischievously.'

'Well!' David managed to look appalled. 'It certainly doesn't apply in this museum. Particularly not in the library.' In an attempt to further mollify Kaloudis he added, casually, 'I was only saying to the Minister when I was last in

Athens, how impressed I've always been with the dedication and efficiency I've found here.'

It worked. Kaloudis wasn't simply mollified, he was disarmed. 'You said that? To the Minister?'

'Well, I thought I'd let him know how I felt. For what it's worth. He seemed quite pleased.'

'As I am, that you have such an opinion,' Kaloudis gushed. 'But then, I am confident that you did not imagine for a single moment,' he raced on, wringing his hands, 'that I considered that you, *Kyrie* Bascombe who, if I may so, I have always looked on as a fellow Rhodian in all but birth, have ever subscribed . . .'

'Of course not,' David said. 'And I do appreciate you digging these out for me.'

Kaloudis made a dismissive gesture. 'They are mostly day books, accounts, inventories of stores, minor records of one kind or another. But who knows, you may find one or two references to the Kastello which will be helpful to you.' He smiled. 'I will leave you to study them.'

As Kaloudis went to the door David sat down behind the pile of documents. He picked up a scroll and was about to unroll it when the librarian paused with the door half open.

'Ah, *Kyrie* Bascombe,' he said tentatively, 'if you should perhaps learn anything from the documents which you feel is worthy of passing on to your friend, *Kyrie* Lavallière when next you visit him, you might possibly mention to him that I was of some service to you in this matter.'

David nodded. 'I'll make a point of it.'

'Not that I wish to advance myself with him, of course . . .'

'Of course not.'

'Merely to gain his respect for the museum, you understand.'

'I understand.'

'Of course you do,' Kaloudis said. 'But then, as I said, you are almost Greek.' He nodded respectfully and went out.

David smothered a laugh as he sat back and gazed at the heap of ancient documents. Since the trouble had been taken, he thought, he might as well go through them. He opened the scroll he was holding and began examining it.

It was slow, dull work. After twenty minutes of inventories, minor land transfers and trading accounts, David decided he would eat after all. Perhaps a little drowsiness would soften the boredom.

He sent out for a sandwich and a bottle of beer. When they arrived he uncapped the beer bottle, took a long swig from it then drew another of the bound volumes towards him and riffled through it. It contained over a hundred parchment sheets, many of them badly faded. David laid the bundle flat and examined the title page.

It was printed in Turkish, French and English; under the heading *Ahment-Hafuz Library*, *Rhodes*, it read *Miscellaneous Inventories, Lading Bills, Receipts and Calendars Relevant to the Sovereign Military and Hospitaller Order of St John of Jerusalem, Rhodes, 1300–1350.*

David yawned and began going through the document page by page, locating nothing among the lists and columns of figures to merit anything more than casual attention. He paused to bite into his sandwich, then began turning several pages at a time, finding more of the same dreary, uninformative material.

He was on the point of abandoning the volume when, in the middle of what looked like a commonplace inventory, he found a block of meticulously-written text in a small, secretive hand. David peered closely at it. It was in French, and it appeared to be continued from the previous page.

Mildly intrigued, he turned to the beginning of the text and began reading it, chewing absently on his sandwich.

'I, Philibert de Belabre, Novice of the Sovereign Military and Hospitaller Order of Saint John of Jerusalem, in defiance of the edicts of the Grand Master, the Sacred Council and the Pilier of the Tongue of Auvergne and Marshall of the Order, do set down for posterity these events which took place within the castle of Saint Theodore in the Grand Priory of Rhodes in the year of Our Lord one thousand, three hundred and seventeen in the interests of truth, for the betterment of knowledge and secure in the consolation of the absolution granted me by my confessor . . .'

As David read on, his surprise and fascination mounted. He scanned the text practically without blinking. Finally, he became so engrossed that he even forgot about his sandwich and the remainder of his beer.

Anne found luncheon on the castle terrace delightful. The grandeur and opulence of her surroundings were matched superbly by the quality of the food and wine. The cooling breeze, the attentiveness of the staff – most of all, the conversation of Lavallière, served to enrich the occasion and make it memorable. Anne couldn't recall when she had last enjoyed a meal so much.

Towards the end of the main course, Lavallière set down his cutlery, picked up his wine glass and twirled it thoughtfully. After a moment he leaned towards Anne. 'Would you marry again?' he asked her.

'No,' she replied without hesitating. Then she saw the way Lavallière was looking at her. The reply clearly hadn't convinced him. She shrugged. 'Who knows? Perhaps, in time.'

'I think it would be a pity if you did not.'

'Why?'

'So much of your life is still ahead of you,' he said. 'You should not allow this tragedy to prevent you living it to the full.' He sipped his wine, savouring it. 'You have a great deal to bring to marriage. Beauty, talent, tenderness. And, with the right partner, there would be much you could take from marriage to fill your needs.'

'Not just mine,' Anne said quietly. She was momentarily held by Lavallière's gaze. 'His too, hopefully.'

'That is not the question.'

With some effort, Anne returned her attention to her plate and began eating again. Lavallière did the same.

A moment later Anne said, 'I'd certainly never remarry while Don is so close to me.' She felt compelled to make the point. 'You may not believe this, but there are times when I imagine I reach out and touch him.' Reticence had modified her disclosure; she hoped, suddenly, that Lavallière wouldn't ask her to enlarge on what she meant.

'You find consolation in feeling that he is near, do you?'

'Some,' Anne said. 'But little peace of mind. That is why I tried to reach him.'

Lavallière's head snapped up. 'Reach him?'

'Yes. You'll probably think I'm being stupid – even irresponsible. But recently I met a woman here on Rhodes. Ismini Christoyannis. She's . . .'

'A medium,' Lavallière interrupted, so quietly he might have been speaking to himself.

'I think she prefers to be called a sensitive.'

Lavallière shrugged away the difference. 'Has she helped you?'

Anne told him about the previous evening's attempt to contact Don. 'She nearly succeeded, I'm convinced of that. Next time, perhaps.'

Lavallière was staring at her. 'When is the next time to be?'

'I'm not sure at the moment,' Anne said. 'Something's happened since. Something so very real, and yet it can't have been. But I wouldn't want to risk . . .' She cut off suddenly, wondering why she had mentioned it at all. Something about Lavallière – not simply his gaze or the appearance of him, but his entire aura – seemed to break down her ability to hold things back. She smiled foolishly and shrugged. 'I just don't know,' she said lamely, concentrating on her plate again.

Lavallière stared at her for several seconds before he took up his own knife and fork and resumed eating.

After lunch Anne was escorted through the castle gateway by her host. He walked with her towards the spot where her car was parked, at the head of the driveway to the valley road.

'Thank you again for that magnificent lunch,' Anne said. 'And for letting me photograph the castle.'

'I am sorry you have to leave,' Lavallière said.

'I'm afraid I must. I've got to get some films off to London and do some shopping.'

They paused by the side of the car.

'You will come again?' Lavallière asked.

'Yes, I'd like to.'

'On Friday night, perhaps? We are having a diversion – a masquerade.' He smiled. '*Un petit bal moderne.* Your friend, Mr Bascombe, would also be welcome. As your escort.'

'Well, I'm not sure . . .' Anne stammered. It was rather short notice.

'Please.' Lavallière's eyes were compelling, almost insistent. 'You will enjoy it, I promise you.'

'David may not be free on Friday night . . .'

'Then come on your own if he is not. At nine o'clock?'

Anne hesitated, but only briefly. She nodded. 'Thank you.' She got into the car and started the engine. 'Is it a celebration?' she asked, leaning out.

'Of course.'

Anne looked pleased. 'What will we be celebrating?'

'You will decide that, Mrs Tierney,' Lavallière said, inclining his head. 'On Friday.'

Puzzled, Anne smiled nevertheless and waved, then drove off towards the gatehouse.

Von Reitz, who had been watching from the gateway,

came across and stood beside his master. Lavallière was still staring at the driveway. 'There is a woman called Christoyannis on the island,' he murmured. 'Ismini Christoyannis. I want her address.'

Later that afternoon, in the midst of her shopping, Anne stopped outside a lingerie shop in the new town and looked at a diaphanous nightdress that was displayed in the window. On a sudden impulse she decided to buy it.

At that same moment, a short distance away, Ismini was turning her car into the driveway of her house. A champagne-coloured Mercedes limousine was parked on the opposite side of the road.

As Ismini's car slowed to negotiate the turn, the rear window of the Mercedes glided silently down. Raoul Lavallière leaned forward and gazed out.

Ismini was compelled to turn her head. She saw Lavallière and their eyes locked momentarily. She frowned at the intensity of the man's stare; after a moment he leaned back with a look of light concentration and the window glided up again. The limousine moved off. Puzzled, Ismini continued on up the drive and parked the car at the top. She got out, unlocked the front door and went into the house.

The headache struck her just as she reached the sitting-room. The pain was searing. Ismini staggered, scarcely able to see as the slicing agony put zigzagging sparks across her vision and tore at the inside of her skull. She tripped, blundered into a chair and slumped down on the arm of it, her hands clamped to her temples. The pain swelled, burning, threatening to tear open her head as she hunched in on herself, too breathless to scream.

It vanished as swiftly as it had come. Ismini looked up, uncomprehending, absently checking her pulse. Myriad clinical possibilities tumbled through her mind. She rejected all of them.

For a long time she remained where she was, dazed, staring at the rug. Whatever it had been, whatever the cause, she was wise enough to know that the answer didn't lie in any medical book.

Chapter Seventeen

Ismini was on the settee, nursing a half-finished drink. Anne was standing by the window, watching the fast-failing light on the garden outside. Both women were listening – or half listening – as David gave them an excited rundown on his discovery at the museum library that afternoon.

Ismini's small preoccupation was with Anne, whose own preoccupation was a mystery. In the manner of the trained psychiatrist, Ismini had already evaluated Anne's behaviour in organized, summary form: politely attentive but withdrawn; measureably tense; impatient, as if keen to abandon this social get-together and be away to other, more important business. There was nothing pathological about any of that, except when it was viewed in the light of the previous evening's events. Anne had become a relative stranger.

Experience was telling Ismini that she mustn't say anything, even though she dearly wanted to. Anne was making a considerable effort to cover her feelings, but she couldn't quite control her restlessness; in that state, whatever its cause, she wasn't likely to respond kindly to well-intentioned prying. Ismini, therefore, sat quietly listening to David giving him as much of her attention as she could, while Anne stood twitching by the window.

'It confirms that Tibald de Montrefort *was* a Templar,' David was saying enthusiastically. 'And it also explains what he was doing on Rhodes. He was on the run.'

'From what?' Ismini asked.

'The Inquisition.'

'Smart fellow,' Anne murmured.

Ismini leaned forward, forcing her attention on the subject. 'Had he committed some crime?'

'All the Templars had, according to the Pope and King Philip of France,' David said. 'By the time de Montrefort and his cronies turned up here, most of the Order were in prison, or had been tortured to death or put to the stake.'

The specific crime of the Templars, David explained, was that they had become too rich and powerful. There were other accusations aimed at the Order – Devil worship, carnal vices – but it was their dangerous power and their influence that became their downfall. They were a threat which more powerful and influential men decided not to tolerate any longer. In 1312 they were suppressed by the Council of Vienne.

'Sorry,' David said suddenly, checking his flow. 'I'm running on a bit, aren't I?' He sat back in the armchair, shaking his head. 'It's just that the portrait Anne and I saw up at the Kastello didn't make any sense, until today. And the story behind it is fascinating. What's more,' he said, his face lighting with boyish glee, 'it's never been published anywhere, as far as I know.'

'So,' Ismini said, 'it is something of a *coup* for you, no?'

'A minor one.' David held up his empty glass. 'May I have another?'

With a fresh drink and Ismini's encouragement, David went back to his story. 'If this young novice, Philibert de Belabre, hadn't secretly written the whole thing down, we'd still be none the wiser.'

Anne frowned at him. 'He was taking a bit of a risk, wasn't he?'

'Right,' David said. 'Life imprisonment, or maybe even the chop.'

'Why did he do it, then?' Ismini asked.

'To satisfy his ego. It's plain from the way he tells it that he was very proud of the part he played in getting rid of de Montrefort and his lot. But I reckon that the Grand Master and the other bigwigs among the Hospitallers would have gone to any lengths to keep what happened under wraps.'

David paused to sip his drink. He frowned at it, decided it wasn't right and took it back to the trolley for more water.

'Well come on, then!' Anne complained, interested now in spite of herself. 'You're not going to leave it there, surely.'

'I don't want to bore you,' David said teasingly.

'You know very well you are not teasing us,' Ismini chided. 'Is he, Anne?'

'Come on,' Anne ordered him. 'Finish the story.'

David came back slowly to his chair and sat down on the arm. 'Well,' he said, 'none of the Orders was above reproach – it was fairly common knowledge, even in those days. But apparently de Montrefort had really got the goods on the Hospitallers.'

If what de Montrefort knew ever got out, David explained, then not even Pope Clement could have gone on turning a blind eye to the activities of the Knights of St John on Rhodes. It was easy, therefore, for de Montrefort to blackmail the Grand Master of the Hospitallers into giving himself and his fellow knights sanctuary at the Kastello Aghios Theodoros.

'You're destroying all my illusions about knights in shining armour,' Anne said.

'Not before time, then,' David grinned. 'Anyway, everything went smoothly for a while, until the Hospitallers began to suspect that de Montrefort and the Templars living in the castle were into the full black magic bit.'

Anne moved closer, listening intently now.

'There were even those who believed that de Montrefort had sold his soul to the Devil long before he became a Templar. There was a lot of talk about throwing the Templars off the island, but the Grand Master of the Hospitallers didn't buy that idea – de Montrefort had too much of a hold on him. Even when the Templars were dissolved by the Pope, the Grand Master still wouldn't act against the ones he was harbouring.'

David paused to take a drink from his glass.

'Go on,' Anne urged him. The story was all the more vivid for her now that she had lunched with de Montrefort's kinsman in the very castle where it had all happened.

'In 1317,' David continued, 'word finally got back to the Hospitallers that there was proof, beyond any doubt, that shortly before he fled to Rhodes, de Montrefort had murdered his mistress – a woman called Agnes Beauvoir.'

'Why?' Ismini asked.

'According to local gossip, it was because she'd told him she was carrying his child. Some years earlier, a soothsayer had prophesied to de Montrefort that his destruction would be brought about by the flowering of his own seed.'

'And he believed it?' Anne said.

'It would seem so. Well, this was all too much for the Hospitallers. Not only was de Montrefort a murderer, but his victim was a Beauvoir. The Beauvoir family had close ties with the Order.'

Anne was nodding, encouraging David. 'So what did they do?'

'The Grand Master still wouldn't take any direct action against the Templars,' David said. 'However, he conveniently looked the other way one night when a dozen of his Hospitallers, young Belabre among them, went to the castle to dine with the Templars. During the meal, a couple of the Hospitallers secretly opened the gates and let in three hundred of their fellow knights. Between them, they systematically slaughtered everyone in the place. Including de Montrefort.'

'So much for the prophecy,' Anne murmured.

David nodded, then went on to explain that if the Hospitallers had left it there they would have been in the clear. They had done no more than clean out a nest of heretics and execute a wanted murderer. But their zeal overshot the bounds of political discretion; they murdered

157

half the villagers of Aghios Theodoros as well, women and children among them. The Hospitallers' position was indefensible.

'So the Grand Master, threatening hellfire and worse, put the lid on it all very firmly. It had never happened. There had never been any Templars on the island. There had been no attack and the villagers had died during a minor outbreak of the plague. That, he hoped, would be the end of it.' David stood up as he rounded off the tale. 'And it would have been, if young Belabre hadn't fancied himself as an historian.'

The two women were silent for a moment, then Ismini nodded. 'You are right, David, it is a fascinating story.'

'There has to be a professorship in it for you,' Anne said. 'At least.'

David laughed. 'I very much doubt it. It's not that earth-shattering. I'll settle for a few quid for an article in *History Today*.'

Ismini got up and put her glass on the table. 'I think we should go,' she said to David. They had a dinner appointment with a mutual friend.

David drained his glass and as Ismini crossed to the other side of the room he moved close to Anne. 'Are you OK?' he asked her quietly.

'Yes,' she assured him. 'Just a bit tired, that's all.'

'Then you mustn't be too late getting home.'

'No, you're right.' Anne moved to the door, picking up her handbag on the way.

'Are you going to tell Monsieur Lavallière what you have discovered?' Ismini asked David as Anne went through the doorway ahead of them.

'I might.'

'Did you get on well with him?'

David shrugged. 'He's all right. Not really a man's man, though. But with those looks and his money he's got to be a wow with the women. Especially if they're into Mercedes limousines.'

Reaching for the light switch, Ismini frowned at him.

'Although,' David added, 'those eyes of his would turn me off. They look straight through you, don't they?' He suddenly realized what he'd said. 'Sorry, I'd forgotten – you've never met him, have you?'

Ismini was frowning. 'I am not sure,' she said. 'I think I may have. This afternoon.'

Shortly before midnight Anne went to her bedroom, undressed and put on the nightdress she had bought that afternoon.

She stood for a minute before the mirror, gauging the effect. The garment's near-transparency was subtle, making her body visible only where it touched her. Anne had never worn anything quite like it before. It wouldn't have been appropriate, somehow. This was a fantasy nightdress, giving her body a dreamlike, ethereal appearance. In the circumstances, she reflected, it was now entirely appropriate.

She sat down at the dressing table and brushed her long dark hair, then she dabbed perfume on either side of her neck, preparing herself with the subdued excitement of a bride on honeymoon.

When she had finished at the dressing table she stood up and put out the overhead light. She climbed into bed, propped herself on the pillows, then switched off the bedside lamp.

The room was lit only by the moon, its light falling in pale shafts through the unshuttered window. Anne sat back against the pillows, her hands folded, waiting.

At midnight Raoul Lavallière sat at his desk, holding the tryptych, gazing at the picture of Agnes Beauvoir. He remained motionless for several minutes, then he slowly set the tryptych down again and opened a drawer in the desk. He removed a jewel case, set it down and opened it. Inside

159

was a gold chain with a single, tear-shaped diamond pendant.

Lavallière took the pendant carefully from the case and held it up before him, staring at it thoughtfully.

Anne had fallen asleep, still propped against the pillows. The moonlight had shifted a fraction, spilling on to the foot of the bed. The room was silent, peaceful.

'Anne.'

She stirred, then her eyes opened slowly. The room was changed again, misty pink and pale, luminous blue. She saw Don Tierney step out of the shadows by the door and come towards the bed. He was smiling.

'Don, darling . . .'

He reached into his pocket and removed a diamond pendant. Still smiling, he held it out to Anne. She opened her arms to him, welcoming him into her bed.

Very early next morning, as the sun was rising over the island, Anne woke from a deep, contented sleep. She remained as she was for a while, lying curled on her side, recollecting what had happened – or what had seemed to happen.

Smiling, she sat up, looking at the disturbed and rumpled bedclothes beside her. Then she saw the spark of light from the night table. The pendant.

She stared at it without blinking, sure that if she lost sight of it for an instant, it would no longer be there.

But it remained. Cautiously, Anne leaned across and picked it up. The diamond winked rainbow flashes at her. Understanding came in a rush. The pendant had been part of the dream, yet it was here, solid, an undeniable presence. *It was real*. So none of it could have been a dream.

Propelled on a delirious surge of joy, Anne leapt out of bed and threw on her clothes. In less than five minutes she was running through the front door, smiling radiantly as she jumped into the car and drove off.

The mood was almost holy, a fervent elevation of her spirit that carried her forward on pure impulse, heading for a secluded cove she had photographed a few days before.

She drove down on to the beach. Braking hard near the water's edge she switched off the engine and got out.

For a long minute she stood staring out across the sea. It was suddenly and urgently important to her, *imperative*, that she totally erase the mourning, the doubt, the timid refusal to accept another and higher reality. The act had to be symbolic. Her joy had to be permitted free reign.

Anne kicked off her shoes and began walking across the beach towards the sea. As her step quickened she unbuttoned her dress and let it fall on the sand. Close to the edge she pulled off the rest of her clothes and began running, naked and enraptured, until the water closed around her and she began swimming into the morning tide, happier than she had been in her entire life.

Chapter Eighteen

The main hall at the castle was transformed into a superior discotheque for the evening. The conversion had been executed with great imagination and flair; concealed strobe lighting played across surreal decorations on the walls and ceiling which altered perspectives and threw back their own reflections on the people gathered for the masked ball. At one end of the hall there was a bar, well-manned and serving champagne exclusively. The music, almost as surreal as the glittering decor, was a clever blending of the tolerable and the outrageous, issuing powerfully from concealed speakers.

There were about thirty guests, all of them in evening dress. The women wore silver and gold eye masks, the men full-face adornments covered in silver or gold foil. The men's masks were skilful creations, sculpted to resemble prominent historical and contemporary figures. Napoleon, Caesar, Robespierre, Beethoven and Hitler rubbed shoulders with Mick Jagger, Elvis Presley, John Travolta and Richard Nixon. Even Lavallière's young aides were masked, all of them identically as fawns, complete with embryonic antlers.

Anne and David Bascombe took one pace into the hall and stopped, daunted by the noise and the exotically bizarre surroundings. Anne was wearing a short evening dress, perfectly styled for her height and figure. David was in his one and only suit.

'Well,' David murmured, 'at least you're garbed for the event.' He smiled at Anne, fingering his lapel in comic self-mockery. He leaned closer to her, eyeing the tear-shaped pendant at her throat. 'That's lovely.'

'Thank you,' she said. 'Don gave it to me.'

162

Raoul Lavallière came forward to greet them. He was wearing a white dinner jacket, but no mask. He smiled, his eyes fixed for a moment on Anne's pendant.

'Mrs Tierney.' He bowed, then he took her hand and kissed it.

Once again a deep, warm thrill surged through Anne. The contact, fortunately, was only momentary and she was able to recover herself without showing that anything had happened.

'To be fair,' Lavallière said, 'I am not certain that I should allow you to proceed any further. You will be the envy and outrage of every other woman here tonight.'

'I sincerely hope so,' Anne said, smiling.

Lavallière nodded to David. 'Good evening Mr Bascombe. I am delighted to see you again.'

'You've made one or two changes,' David observed, looking around the hall.

'For tonight only, I can assure you. Do you approve?'

David smiled. 'A couple of drinks and I expect it'll grow on me.'

Lavallière turned and took an attractive eye mask from a table by the door. 'Permit me,' he said to Anne, and placed it over her eyes. He picked up another one, a full-face creation, and offered it to David.

'No, not for me, thanks. I'll stick with the one I'm wearing. Like you.'

Lavallière made a small frown. 'The idea of another identity does not attract you?'

'Not really,' David said. 'Anyway, everyone would know who I am. I'm underdressed, as usual.' He turned to Anne, indicating the busy dancing area. In a Liverpool accent he said, 'You dancin'?'

Mimicking the accent perfectly, Anne said, 'Who's askin'?'

'I'm askin'.'

'I'm dancin'.' Anne smiled at Lavallière and in her normal

voice she said, 'Will you excuse me?'

'Of course,' he replied. 'Enjoy yourselves.'

As the couple went down among the throng in the centre of the hall, Lavallière remained by the great door, watching them.

The evening passed quickly. The champagne, the music and the dancing combined to cancel the normal awareness of minutes and hours; to David, mild intoxication and foot-weariness were the only indications that the night must be wearing on.

After one particularly strenuous bout of dancing, he took a break with Anne by the side of the dance floor, where he stood sipping his drink and surreptitiously marvelling at how fresh she still looked. They had been standing there only a couple of minutes when an attractive and rather drunk brunette came forward from the throng and put out both her arms to David.

Embarrassed, David shook his head at the woman. 'No thanks. I'm sitting this one out.'

Either she didn't understand, or she wasn't prepared to be turned down. She made a pouting mouth, stretched her arms out even further and beckoned him urgently with twitching fingers.

David patted his right thigh and winced at her. 'Got a bad leg, love.'

Clearly exasperated, the woman grabbed David's hand and started dragging him on to the floor. He made a panicky, wild-eyed plea to Anne.

'You dancing?' she called out to him.

'Who's asking?'

'She's asking,' Anne yelled.

As he was drawn further into the throng, David drooped his mouth comically and shrugged. 'I'm dancing.' An instant later he vanished among the other heaving bodies.

Still laughing, Anne turned away from the dance floor and

walked slowly towards one of the doors. It was becoming rather too warm for her. She needed fresh air, and now seemed like a perfect time to get it, while David was otherwise occupied.

By stages, she found her way out on to the north-facing battlements. The night air was cool and scented; Anne stood for a minute by the door, sipping her champagne, then she walked slowly to the wall and leaned there, watching the sea.

After a minute she became aware that someone was watching her. She turned her head slowly to the left then froze, astonished. A man was standing at the far side of the battlements. He was in a white dinner jacket and he wore a gold sculpted mask. It was a replica of the face of Don Tierney. As Anne watched the man slowly removed the mask. Beneath it was Don's real face. He smiled.

Delighted, Anne put down her glass on the battlements and began moving quickly along the walkway towards him. He remained where he was, still smiling at her.

A masked man suddenly appeared in front of Anne, startling her.

'Have you been enjoying the view, Mrs Tierney?' He removed his mask.

'Oh, good evening, Herr von Reitz,' Anne gasped, flustered and annoyed at being intercepted. She glanced anxiously at the other end of the battlements. Don was no longer there. She felt her heart sink.

Von Reitz frowned at her. 'Is something the matter?'

Bewildered, Anne glanced at him. 'What?'

'You seem upset.'

'No, not a bit,' she said, recovering herself. 'I'm fine, thanks.'

'You are not leaving, are you?'

Anne looked back again at the empty walkway. 'No,' she said. 'Not yet.'

Inside the castle, David Bascombe had finally managed to

wrest himself away from the aggressive brunette. Not being able to find Anne, and having no wish to hang around the dance floor and be dragged into the maelstrom again, he armed himself with a fresh drink and made his way out into the corridor. Guiding himself by memory, he found his way to the reception hall where he had been with Anne, the first time they came to the castle together.

The door was ajar. David peered inside. There was no one about. He pushed the door wider and stepped into the hall. The portrait of Tibald de Montrefort was on the far wall; David crossed and stood in front of it. As he gazed up at the stern, bearded face, he began to notice that the eyes were as piercing and unnerving as Lavallière's.

'You are interested in my kinsman, Mr Bascombe?'

David jumped. The voice was right behind him. He turned and saw Raoul Lavallière standing a yard away, smiling politely. 'Ah, yes, I am,' David stammered, sipping his drink to calm himself. He looked up at the picture again. 'He was quite something.'

'A truly remarkable man,' Lavallière agreed.

'Looking at him, though, you wouldn't believe he was a murderer, would you? Or that he'd done business with the Devil.' David turned to Lavallière and grinned. 'According to popular belief, anyway.'

'I beg your pardon?' Lavallière said coolly.

'You *don't* know the full story, then. I mean why de Montrefort was here on Rhodes. Or what happened to him.'

'As to why he was here,' Lavallière said cautiously, 'my understanding has always been that he held this castle for the Order of the Knights of the Temple.'

David nodded. 'He did. Briefly. And on sufferance. But you won't find any mention of that in the history books.'

'Really.' Lavallière's eyes narrowed a fraction.

'No. And when I first saw that portrait it bothered me.' David gestured at the painting with his glass. 'I just couldn't work out how de Montrefort, as a Templar, fitted in on an island that was run by the Hospitallers.'

Lavallière sniffed. 'I believe that has always been something of a mystery,' he said distantly. 'To everyone.'

'There are no family records?'

'None have survived from that period.'

'And haven't you ever wondered?'

'I cannot say that I have ever given much thought to it, Mr Bascombe.' Lavallière tilted his head slightly. 'The past is full of unanswerable questions, is it not?'

David nodded. 'I'm happy to say I found the answer to this one.'

'So it would appear,' Lavallière said, a trifle acidly. 'With embellishments. May I ask where?'

David explained about the old records he had been sifting through when he found the Belabre manuscript.

'And you are saying, are you, that according to what you have discovered, the Compte de Montrefort was a murderer?'

'Among other things. He garotted his girlfriend, or so the story goes. A lady named Agnes Beauvoir'.

Lavallière glared at him stonily.

'Sex, violence, a touch of the diabolicals. Your family history's got everything going for it, Monsieur Lavallière.'

'How very interesting.' Lavallière glanced at the portrait, then at David. 'So please. From the beginning, if you would.'

Since she had been out on the battlements, Anne had been covertly searching for the man with the white dinner jacket – the man she *knew* was her husband. Pursuing him was necessary – Anne was sure she mustn't question that. It was an instinctive act, and she knew that instinct was everything in this new dimension their relationship had entered. Besides, she wanted to find him.

She edged her way through the guests standing on the perimeter of the crowded dance floor. The music was slower now, almost romantic, and each pulse of the strobe had been lengthened, so that the hall was bathed in its blue light for several seconds at a time.

During one bright pulse Anne saw him. He was standing among the crowd on the far side of the dance floor, still wearing the gold mask.

He appeared to see Anne in the same instant she saw him. He began moving towards her. Steadily, never taking her eyes from him, Anne eased her way through the guests; in the strobe's dark phases she maintained her steady gaze and each time the light flashed on again he was still there, getting nearer and nearer.

They met in the centre of the dance floor. The masked head, the gilded effigy of all Anne loved, inclined towards her for a moment, then he took her in his arms and drew her close. They began to dance.

David Bascombe was looking for a lavatory. So far, he had been along three different passages that appeared to offer every amenity but the one he was urgently seeking. As he climbed the great staircase a laughing woman guest came running down towards him. She was being chased by an eager suitor whose drunken state, in spite of the mask, was totally evident.

'Excuse me,' David said as the couple went racing past. 'I'm looking for a . . .'

They ignored him and went on their giggling way.

'Thanks a lot,' David called after them. 'Have fun. Break your necks.'

He got to the top of the stairs, paused, then went along the nearest corridor. There were two long rows of stout, iron-hinged doors on either side, none of them showing any particular promise. As David strode towards the intersecting passage at the end, he passed one door that was partly open. He paused, peering inside. It was Lavallière's study. The desk lamp was on, and so was the shaded strip-light over the large tapestry.

The urgency of his mission diminished suddenly. Intrigued by the tapestry, he stepped tentatively into the room and stood for a moment, making sure he was alone.

He stared at the tapestry. The stylized, two-dimensional technique of the period had done nothing to dilute the violence of the picture. David crossed the room slowly, his eye scanning the battle scene, the agonized faces of the knights' victims, the sombre, triumphant eyes of the sword-wielding victors.

He went behind the desk to take a closer look. The fabric of the tapestry, though it was obviously very old, showed no signs of decay. The bright threads used to weave the picture didn't appear to have faded much, either. It was a magnificent piece of work, he mused, and undoubtedly priceless.

As he stepped back a pace, gazing at the full width of the tapestry, he brushed against the desk and displaced three leather folders. The top one fell on the floor.

'Damn!'

He bent to pick it up, then paused. It had fallen open. He was looking at a photostated picture of Anne and Don Tierney. Bewildered, David flipped over the sheet and saw a copy of a medical report with Anne's name at the top. He picked up the folder and straightened with it, turning the pages, finding more detailed medical records and even a copy of the Tierneys' marriage certificate. Frowning, David began reading one of the clinical reports then stopped, realizing he was intruding on something deeply private. He looked up, his mind a jumble of half-formed questions. And then he saw the triptych on the desk.

He couldn't believe his eyes. He dropped the folder back on the desk and picked up the triptych, staring at the portrait in the centre. *Anne*, he thought, *it's a painting of Anne . . . Even the pendant . . .*

'God almighty!' His voice was a harsh, unbidden whisper as he read the scroll beneath the picture. 'Agnes Beauvoir!'

A sudden uneasiness closed on David. He wasn't alone.

Still clutching the triptych he swung round. A man in a white dinner jacket was standing in the doorway. His face was concealed behind a gold mask. It was sculpted into the living likeness of Don Tierney.

As David watched, the man closed the door and came across to the desk. His eyes flicked from the triptych to the open folder. Slowly, he took off the mask, revealing that he was Raoul Lavallière.

His eyes were holding David's. It was a grip as firm as any physical contact, a strong, unwavering lock that immobilized David. He was suddenly very frightened.

There was a sound beyond the windows, faint at first, a disturbing rustle that grew rapidly, mounting to a tremulous, angry chattering. David couldn't move, he lacked the power to trigger even one muscle as the hellish noise swelled. He blinked once, a massive effort at breaking Lavallière's hold. When he opened his eyes again terror constricted his throat.

'Oh my God . . .'

It wasn't Lavallière standing there. He had changed, hideously. The face was now the one David had seen carved at the main gate, the contorted, malevolent features of the devil Asmodeus. The eye socket blazed with fire.

The sound grew louder. David's head jerked aside, his face rigid with fear as he stared at the source of the noise. A thin trickle of fire oozed in under the window. A second and third rivulet sputtered in alongside the first and spilled on to the floor. They merged in a widening stream that slowy advanced on him.

Convulsed with terror, David found himself looking down at the triptych in his hands. The wooden panels were smoking. The paint began to blister and scorch, then the whole triptych burst into flames. The wood blackened swiftly as the fire licked around David's knuckles.

He screamed and dropped the blazing triptych. As it hit the floor he realized was standing in a pool of fire that lapped

170

over his shoes. Terrified, he ran screaming to the door, free now of the paralysing stare but surrounded by fire.

He ran into the corridor, the terrible noise pursuing him. Blind instinct led him down a steep flight of stairs and out through an archway. He found himself in the courtyard. The sound was close behind him, a grating whine that hounded him as he darted to where the Volkswagen was parked. He could see no fire now, but the smell of burning was rank in his nostrils. He jerked open the car door and hurled himself inside. At a high window, Raoul Lavallière gazed down impassively at the courtyard.

David's only impulse was to get away. He started the engine and threw it into gear, accelerating in a dangerous swerve as he aimed the vehicle down towards the valley road. The sound was still there, he could hear it raging close to the car. He slammed the pedal hard, shot past the gate house and out on to the road.

He was driving as fast as he could, but the raging sound was engulfing the car. Sweating with fear, David glanced through the left window. A large bush burst into flame as he sped past it. A sob erupted from him as he tried to gun the car faster, leaning forward over the wheel, desperately willing himself away from the ghastly noise and the fire it carried.

He braked suddenly, howling, as the road ahead burst into flames. The car spun once, slid across the road and thudded into a ditch, its engine stalled.

For ten breathless seconds David lay in the toppled vehicle, listening, anxiously watching the road. There was no sound, no trace of fire.

Shaking violently, he climbed out through the passenger door and staggered into the middle of the road. He dropped to his knees and covered his face with his hands. The sound of his own shuddering breath was all he heard as gradually, scene by hideous scene, the respite brought back all that had happened. It was crazy, no reasoning person could support an ounce of belief for any part of it. Yet it had happened, he could even smell the traces of smoke on his hands.

David's head jerked up, The sound was coming again, distant but growing rapidly.

'Oh sweet Jesus . . .'

Three hundred yards along the road there was a bright, fast moving river of fire, igniting trees and bushes on either side as it rushed towards him. Whimpering, David rose to his feet and looked around desperately. In the distance he saw lights. *Houses.* The discovery put urgent strength in his legs. He turned and began running as the fire roared towards him.

Time evaporated. There was only the imperative to outrun the flames. David hurtled along the road, seeing his own hands fly up and down before him, hearing his whimpering breath, dulled by the pursuing noise.

Recognition gleamed through his terror. He knew where he was. This road, the drives . . .

'Ismini!' he gasped.

Her house was here, it was close, he was sure of that. He glanced over his shoulder and saw the flames surge around the corner behind him.

He pumped his legs harder, seeing Ismini's driveway ahead. As he stumbled on to the path the fire suddenly rushed forward, roaring, surrounding his feet. He looked at the sleeves of his jacket. They were smouldering.

David threw himself up the drive, screaming wildly, slapping at his sleeves as they started to burn. He collided with the front door, punched the bell then began hammering the panels with his fists.

'Ismini! Help me! For God's sake! Please help me!'

He could feel the flames licking along the back of his jacket, touching his hair, his face.

'My God! *Ismini!* Help me!'

A light came on in the house. As David went on screaming, flailing at his clothes and head, the door was opened. Ismini stood there, her face alarmed, watching David writhing and slapping at himself.

'Put them out! The flames! Hurry! *Hurry!* Please! Don't let me burn!' He ran past Ismini into the house. She went after him, slamming the door shut behind her.

David was in the middle of the sitting room, hopping wildly, whining as he beat at his chest and arms.

Ismini stepped close to him, desperately concerned. 'What is the matter, David? What is wrong?'

'On fire!' he squealed breathlessly. 'Burning! Burning! Ismini help me! Help me!'

Ismini saw no flames. All she saw was David, bathed in sweat and writhing as if he were demented.

David, listen to me . . .'

He blundered across the room, knocking over a glass and smashing it as he pitched forward on to the settee. Ismini ran to him, sitting on the edge of the settee and grabbing his wrists trying to restrain him.

'Listen to me! You are all right. There is no fire. Nothing is wrong. You are not burning.'

'Flames!' David screeched. 'Flames everywhere! That terrible sound . . .' He struggled to free his wrists but Ismini held on.

'It is in your mind,' she told him firmly. 'Only in your mind. Believe me.'

David's chest was heaving now, he was gasping for air. 'Fire . . . Fire . . . The floor, walls . . . Everything . . . I . . . I . . . Run! Run! I can't . . . I can't . . .'

'You are imagining it,' Ismini said urgently. 'It is not real. You must believe me. It is not real. *This* is reality.' She drew back her hand and slapped his face twice, hard. 'That pain, that is reality.' She slapped him again. 'That, and the fact that you are in the house and that I am with you. Those things and this pain.' Her hand cracked against his cheek again. 'Everything else is in your mind.'

David had winced under the blows but Ismini could see she was achieving nothing. He tore his hands free suddenly and covered his face with them, his breathing harsh, laboured. His body was being racked by convulsions. He turned on his side and began clawing at the back of the settee, gibbering, trying to pull himself up over the edge.

Ismini reached down and snatched up a jagged piece of glass from the floor. She grasped David's right arm and hauled it across her knees. Flattening his hand, she put the shard of glass on his palm. With her fingers wrapped tightly around his, she snapped his hand shut on the razor-sharp edges.

David screamed and arched his back with pain. He tried to wrench his hand free but Ismini clung to it.

Abruptly, the convulsions stopped.

'David?'

His body sank back limply against the cushions. He was grimacing with the pain in his hand. His eyes flickered open, focusing slowly on the ceiling, then he turned his head and stared at his hand. Blood was dripping on to the floor. Mystified, he looked up at Ismini.

'It is all right, David.' She heaved a deep grateful sigh and smiled at him. 'You are safe now.'

Chapter Nineteen

It took twenty minutes to clean the wound, stitch it and put on a dressing. As Ismini worked steadily her medical bag open on the floor beside her, David told her what had happened.

'I'd just one thought,' he said. 'To run, to get away from the fire. I wasn't thinking about Anne or anyone or anything else.' He paused, watching Ismini winding the bandage around his hand. He was pale, still slightly in shock. 'I was terrified out of my skull. I was convinced the flames were after me and at any minute . . .' He stopped and put his left hand over his eyes, caught by the ferocious clarity of the memory.

'Gently,' Ismini said, putting her hand on his shoulder. 'Lie back.'

'Fire.' David stared at her, shaking his head. 'It's the one thing that's guaranteed to scare the hell out of me. Ever since I was a kid and saw one of my school friends burned to death.'

'That is why Lavallière used it against you,' Ismini said. She put a strip of adhesive tape across the bandage, securing it.

'But how did he know that?'

'By searching your mind for those areas of experience in which you are most vulnerable.'

David blinked. 'Is that possible?'

'Certainly. With hypnosis. I do it often with my patients.' She pressed the tape firmly into position. 'There. Do not even try to use that hand for a while. In a few days I will remove the stitches.' She closed her medical bag and began tidying away the kidney bowl, syringe and suture pack she had been using.

David was still considering what she had told him. 'Could you persuade someone under hypnosis that they were on fire?'

'Yes.'

'And if they went on believing it?'

Ismini put the bag and the other equipment on a side table. 'With a psychological reaction to fire such as yours – if the hypnotic suggestion was implanted deeply enough – then the subject would very quickly become deranged.' She thought for a moment. 'If he was convinced that he was burning to death, he would die of his burns – though there wouldn't be so much as a scorch mark . . .'

'Oh, come on,' David said impatiently. 'That's voodoo stuff. Black magic.'

Ismini sighed. 'There are Aborigines in Australia who die because a witch doctor has pointed a bone at them.' She came forward, her face very serious. 'Believe me, David, even you, a sophisticated European in the twentieth century, could have died tonight. Merely because you believed you were burning.'

'My God.' He stared at his bandaged hand, then looked up at Ismini again. 'Could anyone who can hypnotize pull a stroke like that?'

'No,' Ismini said, shaking her head. 'Fortunately. Although it is not difficult for someone with only a rudimentary grasp of the technique to bring about a hypnotic state in a willing subject – irresponsible amateurs do it for entertainment. But suggestion in depth, the kind to which you were subjected – that is altogether different.'

She went to the drinks trolley and began pouring a whisky. 'In the first place,' she said, 'it would normally require the subject to be totally relaxed, and to have absolute faith in the therapist. That is something which can only be built up over a long period of time. Even then, it would take a very knowledgeable and practised hypnotist to induce such an advanced hallucinatory state.'

'Then Lavallière's got to be a bloody past master at it.'

'Or something even more than that,' Ismini said softly, putting the cap back on the whisky bottle.

'But why?' David demanded. 'Why, all of a sudden, was I such a threat to him?'

Ismini brought the drink across and handed it to him. 'You had seen the file he has on Anne,' she said.

'All right, so he's got a bloody great dossier on her and I'd like to know why. I'd also like to know where he got the information from. But is that such a deep, dark secret that it made him desperate enough to kill me?'

Ismini frowned. 'This dossier. It is very detailed, you say?'

'It looks like a full biography, just about. Going way back, as far as I could tell. There's even photostats of Anne's medical records.'

'And Anne is unaware of this?'

'Totally.'

Ismini was still frowning. 'You are sure of that?'

'Positive. My God, if she *had* known she'd have raised hell about it.' David tilted his head at Ismini. 'Wouldn't you? If you suddenly found out that someone you've only met a couple of times had a file on you with your life history in it?'

'Yes,' Ismini nodded, 'I would.'

'And with good reason,' David snapped. 'So if she did know, she would've said something to one or other of us about it by now. Right?'

'I would have thought so.'

'She can't know about the picture on his desk, either,' David shook his head, remembering the shock he'd received when he saw it. 'She's as much a dead ringer for Agnes Beauvoir as he is for de Montrefort. Even more so, particularly tonight. If the Beauvoir woman was still around and she and Anne were dressed alike, I honestly don't think anyone could tell them apart.'

To Ismini, for whom logical deduction was an everyday tool, the underlying reason for the night's events seemed obvious. 'Lavallière's prime motive,' she told David, 'was to prevent you telling Anne these things.'

'Yes,' David grunted, 'that has to be it.' Sudden anger crossed his face. 'What the hell am I doing lying here?' He struggled up off the settee, spilling his drink as he reached out to support himself. His bandaged hand closed on the back of a chair. The sudden pain made him wince. He swayed, almost falling.

'What are you doing?' Ismini rushed to his side, steadying him and taking his glass. 'You must rest.'

'Don't you see?' David was staring at her, his face agitated. 'If Anne's the key to what happened tonight then she has to be at risk, too – you sensed you she was, practically from the first moment you met her. Only I didn't take it seriously. And I've left her up at the castle.' He began easing himself from Ismini's grip.

'You're going to charge back there and rescue her, is that?' Ismini demanded.

'Well, I'll get her out of there, anyway . . .'

Ismini stopped him. 'You are in no position to go anywhere. I doubt if you would get more than fifty metres before you collapsed.' As David made another attempt to cross the floor he began to sway. 'You see?' Ismini hissed. She put an arm tightly around his waist and guided him back to the settee.

'We must ring the police, then . . .'

'And what would you say to them, David?' Ismini eased him down on the cushions. 'The much-respected, rich and powerful Raoul Lavallière tried to kill you – is that what you'd say?'

'Exactly. Just that. He did.'

Ismini sighed at him. 'When we tell them how, they would believe us, do you think? We have absolutely no proof, have we?'

'Even so,' David groaned. He had turned very pale again. 'We can't just sit around doing nothing about Lavallière, and Anne's alone up there with him, among all those weirdos.'

'I do not think she is in any immediate danger,' Ismini said.

'How do you know?'

'It would be too much of an embarrassment, even for Lavallière, to have two of his guests die in the same night.'

David frowned at her.

'Look,' she said, 'I am quite sure that Lavallière doesn't imagine that you survived – if you had not had the strength to get as far as this house, you *would* be dead.' She smiled at him. 'Now you see what a sound investment those hours on the running track were. I will telephone the house and see if Anne is back yet. She may well be.'

Ismini put David's glass on the table and crossed to the telephone. She picked it up, dialled and waited. After a minute she put the receiver down again. 'There is no reply. I will try again later.'

'Yes,' David said wearily. 'And keep trying until she answers. If she's still not there in half an hour I'll . . .'

'You will do nothing. In half an hour you will be in bed. I will have given you something to help you sleep.' Ismini went to the bookshelves and started searching along the second row.

'Oh, for God's sake!' David glared at her. 'I couldn't sleep – not after what's happened. Not without knowing that Anne's OK . . .'

'As I said,' Ismini announced calmly, 'I doubt that Anne is in any physical danger, so long as Lavallière continues to think he has successfully disposed of you.'

'But there are so many questions that haven't been answered . . .'

'And I don't think that we will find satisfactory answers to any of them tonight. Ah!' Ismini pulled a book from the shelf. 'Except one of them, maybe.' She took the book to the settee and sat down beside David. 'The face that you believed had replaced Lavallière's – did you recognize it?'

'Yes,' David said. 'It was the face carved on the main gate of the castle. Some devil or other.'

Ismini nodded. 'So now, look through this book. It is Professor Matthofer's psychological study of demonology.'

'What?'

Ismini opened the book and laid it on David's lap. He riffled the pages. Apart from the text, there were dozens of drawings and photographs, many of them depicting devils and deities of various religions.

'See if the face you saw appears in any of the illustrations.'

David looked at her impatiently.

'Please,' Ismini said quietly. She stood up as David began turning the pages. 'Would you like another drink?'

'No thanks.'

Ismini went to the trolley to pour herself a vodka and tonic.

'What I can't get over,' David murmured, 'is that damned pendant thing Anne was wearing round her neck tonight.'

Ismini stopped what she was doing for a moment, staring gravely into her glass. 'Yes,' she said, 'that is strange.'

'And one hell of a coincidence.'

Ismini poured in the tonic carefully. 'You are sure it was identical to the one in the portrait of Agnes Beauvoir?'

'It looked that way to me,' David replied, still turning the pages. 'Damned near to it, anyway. For a moment I actually thought . . .' He shrugged. 'If Anne hadn't already told me where she got it from . . .'

'You have no reason to doubt that her husband gave it to her?'

David looked up. Ismini still had her back to him. 'Of course not,' he said sharply. 'Why would she lie about a thing like that?'

'Why indeed? And I am sure she did not.'

'That's all it can have been, a coincidence.' David returned his attention to the book. 'But it was weird. Her wearing it, then me seeing one exactly like it in the painting.' He turned another page and stiffened. 'Here. This is it. The figure in the carving.'

Ismini came across to the settee, leaving her glass on the trolley. 'What does it say under the picture?'

'I don't read German.'

Ismini took the book from him and read the caption. '"Asmodeus, the inciter of lechery and king of demons in Hebrew tradition",' she translated. '"The custodian of secrets and, according to Judaic legend, the builder of Solomon's temple".'

'Of course,' David said excitedly. 'I should have realized. Asmodeus!'

'The name means something to you?'

David nodded. 'And it fits perfectly with the Kastello Aghios Theodoros. The Knights Templar took their name from the temple of Solomon. The Inquisition accused the Templars of worshipping Asmodeus and some demon called Baphomet. More and more it looks as though they were right.' David looked at the picture again. 'My guess is that Tibald de Montrefort had that carving put up there as a final act of defiance.'

'And it would seem,' Ismini said thoughtfully, 'that Monsieur Lavallière has something of an affinity with it, too.' She looked at David. 'That is one question answered, at least.'

David shook his head. 'I don't see that identifying

Asmodeus answers anything.'

'No, I wouldn't expect you to understand. But it could be the answer to everything.' Ismini looked at him intently. 'One last thing before you sleep,' she said. 'I want you to tell me everything you know about Donald Tierney's accident and the hours that led up to it.'

Chapter Twenty

Anne awoke just after nine o'clock. For a moment she lay still, trying to remember what had happened. Peering over the sheets, she discovered she was in a curtained four-poster bed. Apart from the pendant around her neck and her wristwatch, she was naked under the covers. She blinked up at the canopy, waiting for clarification of those facts. After a minute memory flooded back, making her smile.

She had found Don again last night, after losing him twice during the course of the evening. First, he had vanished from the battlements, then, just as mysteriously, he had disappeared during a break in the dancing. But he had returned to her as she searched for him on the terrace outside the great hall. Their meeting had been mesmeric, wordless. He had led her to a bedroom in the castle and there they had made love. It had been splendid and gratifying, as always, and Anne had fallen asleep immediately afterwards.

Her smile faded as it dawned on her that she was alone again. She sat up, realizing that her presence there would require explanation. Or would it? Don had seemed so positive – it was as if the room had been laid on, yet no one knew about him except Anne herself . . .

In the midst of her confusion there was a tap on the door. A second later a uniformed maid came in. She closed the door behind her and smiled at Anne.

'Good morning, Madame. If it is too early for you I will come back later . . .'

A little surprised, Anne glanced at her watch then shook her head.

Reassured, the maid crossed to the window. She drew

back the curtains, letting in the morning sunlight. She then went to the wardrobe and slid back one of the doors. Removing an exquisite negligée, she brought it to the bottom of the bed and laid it there.

'Monsieur Lavallière has asked me to say that he will be delighted if you would join him for breakfast, Madame. I will run your bath for you.'

As the maid went through to the bathroom Anne sat further up in the bed, looking around for her clothes. They were nowhere to be seen.

As the sound of running water began in the bathroom she got out of bed and quickly put on the negligée. It fitted perfectly, as if it had been made specifically for her. She was looking at herself admiringly in the mirror when the maid came back into the room.

'Where are my clothes?' Anne asked her.

'Your dress is being pressed,' the maid replied. 'I have sent your underthings to the laundry.'

'I see.'

'They will be returned shortly, in no more than an hour from now.'

Anne frowned at her. 'What do I wear meantime?' She touched the flimsy negligée. 'I don't think this is really suitable to go down to breakfast in.'

The maid went to the wardrobe again and slid open the doors fully. The interior, from one end to the other, was hung with an expensive array of dresses and trouser suits; the shoe racks were full, and when the maid pulled out a drawer Anne could see that it contained lingerie.

'If Madame would care to choose.'

Bemused, Anne went over to the wardrobe. She trailed her hand along the row of expensive fabrics, then took out a dress. She held it against herself and looked in the mirror. Like the negligée, it was precisely her size.

'These things,' she said, 'they're all new! None of them has ever been worn.'

The maid smiled noncommittally and removed one of the trouser suits from the rail. 'May I suggest, Madame, that this would be very suitable this morning.'

Anne looked at it for a moment, then she made a small, bewildered smile. 'Yes,' she said, 'that would be perfect, I suppose.'

Out on the battlements, a table had been set up in the shade of a small watch tower. As before, a servant was in attendance by the serving trolley, while one of the young aides stood by the wall.

Raoul Lavallière and Dietrich von Reitz were standing a little way off from the table. For ten minutes they had been discussing business and now von Reitz, having received his orders for the day, was about to move off.

'I will take care of it personally, *Maître*,' he was saying, nodding his head sharply to underscore his efficiency.

'Good,' Lavallière murmured. 'Report back to me personally as soon as you have confirmation. Later I will want to go over the programme for the next three days with you – in detail. Is everything ready for this evening's arrivals?'

'Yes, all the necessary arrangements have been made.' Von Reitz glanced casually along the wall, then reacted with obvious shock as he saw Anne approaching. He shot a querulous look at Lavallière, who smiled faintly.

'Mrs Tierney will be leaving shortly after breakfast. But I warn you, Colonel, you may have to get used to her presence. Permanently.'

Von Reitz was clearly about to protest, but he checked himself.

Lavallière turned and smiled at Anne as she joined them. 'Good morning, Mrs Tierney.'

'Good morning.' Anne was wearing the trouser suit and carrying her evening bag. She was measurably embarrassed.

'After breakfast,' Lavallière told her, 'Herr von Reitz will have a car waiting to take you home, the moment you need it. Is that not so, von Reitz?'

'Indeed, *Maître*,' he said coldly. 'I will have one of the drivers put on standby immediately. Excuse me.' Von Reitz made the customary stiff bow and walked away.

Lavallière looked at Anne. 'You slept well, I hope?'

'Yes, thank you,' Anne faltered. 'But I think I rather outstayed my welcome.'

'Nonsense.' Lavallière indicated the table and escorted her to it.

'I feel terrible about this,' she said as he held her chair for her. 'I really don't have any explanation.' She stared at the table cloth. 'Please forgive me.'

Lavallière smiled expansively. 'My dear Mrs Tierney, there is nothing to forgive. Believe me, you are welcome here at any time, and for as long as you wish to remain.' He sat down and placed a hand on the table. 'The explanation for your being here is simple. It was getting late and you were tired. Please think no more about it.'

Feeling rather more at ease now, Anne asked the servant if she could have orange juice and coffee. 'I don't feel at all hungry,' she explained to Lavallière who was gazing steadily at her.

'You are looking particularly beautiful this morning, if I may say so. And I see you found something that pleased you.'

'It would have been difficult not to,' Anne said. 'There was such an incredible choice.' She touched the sleeve of the jacket. 'I'll have this cleaned, of course, and see that you get it back.'

'It is of no importance,' Lavallière assured her. 'If you like it enough, it would give me great pleasure if you would keep it.'

'That's very generous of you.' Anne felt herself blushing. 'But I couldn't do that.'

'It suits you so well,' Lavallière said persuasively. 'Really.'

'Just the same . . .'

He shrugged. 'As you wish.'

186

The servant brought the orange juice and poured the coffee. Anne sipped at the chilled juice for a few moments, then she sighed. 'I feel very guilty about David. I'm afraid I neglected him last night. He was probably looking for me everywhere.'

Lavallière waited until the servant had poured his coffee and moved off. 'No,' he said, 'I do not think that Mr Bascombe was too concerned. Perhaps he had other things on his mind. The last time I saw him he was enjoying the company of an attractive girl – he had been dancing with her for some time.'

'Oh, really.' Anne felt a little deflated. 'What time did he leave?'

'I have no idea.'

'He didn't say goodbye?'

Lavallière shook his head. 'I understand that he was in something of a hurry.'

Anne nodded absently. 'I hope he got home safely.'

After breakfast, Lavallière suggested they take a short stroll along the wall. The idea appealed strongly to Anne. As they moved off, she noticed that Lavallière dismissed the ever-present aide with a small wave of his hand.

At a point where the wall curved out to the north, Anne paused and looked out over the dazzling blue sea. 'Well,' she said, turning to Lavallière, 'have you decided?'

Puzzled, he smiled at her. 'I am sorry . . .'

Anne smiled back. 'The very first time I came here, you said that you were seriously considering giving me this view. I was just wondering if you'd made up your mind yet.'

'Ah.' Lavallière shook his head slowly. 'I cannot imagine why I hesitated.' He moved closer to Anne, his face growing a shade more serious. 'Tell me something. If a man could offer you everything you ever desired – more than that even, much more, more than you could imagine – and if all he wished in return was the pleasure of that giving and to have you as his wife, would you consider such a proposition?'

'No,' Anne said simply. 'I couldn't. I think you know why.'

'But if he told you he understood the way you still feel about your husband.' Lavallière moved closer still, his eyes wide, intense. 'If he said he was prepared to accept that fact, however long it might last. And if he told you the acceptance was another of his gifts to you.' He paused, looking almost vulnerable, searching Anne's face. 'If he promised that he would make no demands of you that you were unwilling to meet – beyond time, if need be – and that your only obligation would be companionship and to be close to him . . . What then?'

Anne saw nothing false or conniving in his expression. Indeed she had never seen such open sincerity. But she shook her head. 'It would be unfair, in so many ways,' she said. 'Children, for instance. A man with so much to offer would undoubtedly have a great deal of money and a lot of power. Someone like that would feel cheated if he didn't have a son or a daughter to inherit those things from him.' She looked out at the sea again. 'Circumstances would probably demand that he had an heir. With me, even if he was very patient and if, in time, I came to love him enough . . . Well, that wouldn't be possible.' She looked at Lavallière again. 'I can't have children, you see.'

'That is sad,' he said softly. 'For you. But what if he convinced you it was of no importance to him? That he even welcomed the fact?'

'I doubt if he could convince me of that.'

'But if he did,' Lavallière insisted. 'If the offer appealed to you in every other respect, and you didn't find him entirely unattractive – would you not at least think deeply about it before giving him your final answer?'

Anne stared at him, finding nothing in his eyes but the same naked sincerity. She nodded. 'If I was sure that he gave a similar depth of thought to what he proposed, and that this was what he really wanted, then I'd be obliged to consider my answer very carefully. I would owe him that.'

A smiled spread slowly on Lavallière's face. 'Good,' he murmured, then stood back, his manner becoming more brisk. 'Forgive me, I am keeping you.'

They began strolling back in the direction of the main courtyard. Anne felt confused, but rather exhilarated at the same time. She was flattered and – she realized it with a little shock – not particularly surprised at what had happened.

'Regrettably,' Lavallière was saying, 'I have business commitments which will take up my time for three or four days. However, if you are free next Wednesday, perhaps I could persuade you to have dinner with me.'

Anne looked at him, accepting the invitation with a slow, gracious smile.

A Mercedes limousine was waiting outside the main gates. As Lavallière and Anne approached it, an aide came forward and put a plastic protector bag, containing Anne's freshly cleaned clothes, into the boot.

Anne held out her hand to Lavallière. 'Goodbye.'

'*Au revoir*.' Lavallière took her hand and kissed it.

The sensation jolted through her again, spreading warm from her loins, slackening her thighs and tingling wildly across her abdomen and breasts. Anne stood transfixed, sure now that Lavallière knew the effect he was having on her. He prolonged the kiss, and when he withdrew his lips he still held her hand, looking up slowly into her eyes. Even if she had wanted to, Anne couldn't have turned her eyes away from this.

At last, he released her hand. 'Until Wednesday,' he said.

'Wednesday,' Anne echoed huskily.

She got into the back of the car. The aide closed the door then climbed into the driving seat. The engine purred into life and the car moved off smoothly. Lavallière stood watching until it was out of sight.

As soon as Anne got home, she went to the telephone and dialled David Bascombe's number. While it rang out, she gazed at the picture of herself and Don, sitting in its frame on the table. She smiled, not testing her feelings, simply responding to an accumulation of pleasant sensations.

David's landlord answered.

'Oh, hello,' Anne said. 'Is Mr Bascombe there, please?' She frowned. 'No, I'm sorry I don't . . . English. Do you speak English? No, Bascombe, I want to talk to David Bascombe. Mm? Sorry? Oh, this is ridiculous!' She spread her fingers in her hair, summoning her meagre vocabulary of Greek words. '*Boro na miliso o Kyrie Bascombe* . . . Yes, David Bascombe. What?' She shook her head, exasperated at the old man. 'I'm sorry, I don't understand. Then *ksero elenika* . . .'

Finally she put the phone down, promising herself she'd invest in a Greek crash course one day. She had no idea what the man had been saying to her, although she did get the impression that David wasn't there.

An hour after Anne had left the Kastello, Dietrich von Reitz reported to Lavallière in his study. Von Reitz had been out on the country road to determine what had happened to David Bascombe. He had not come back with the positive findings he had hoped for.

'I searched the area around the car thoroughly, but there is no trace of him.'

Lavallière considered that for a moment. 'Was the car badly damaged?'

'No,' von Reitz said. 'It had merely skidded off the road.'

Lavallière raised an eyebrow in surprise, but he didn't look too concerned by the negative information.

'So I went into Rhodes and asked for him at the house where he has a room,' von Reitz continued. He caught Lavallière's frown and hastened to reassure him. 'I merely said that, in conversation last night, Bascombe had agreed to lend me an old book on Rhodes which he has, and that I had arranged to pick it up this morning.'

Lavallière seemed to accept that as a valid subterfuge. 'He was not at home, of course.'

Von Reitz nodded. 'The people there said that they had not seen him since yesterday.'

'He will turn up soon,' Lavallière murmured.

'I will detail one of our people to watch his lodging and inform us the moment there is any news.'

'No,' Lavallière said flatly, 'that will not be necessary. We already have a reliable source of information. Mrs Tierney will be among the first to hear what has happened to him.'

Chapter Twenty-One

Ismini was showing Anne into the sitting room.

'They don't speak any English,' Anne was saying as they came through from the hall. 'And I don't understand Greek, so that didn't get me anywhere. When I called round, though, I rather got the impression that David hadn't been home all night. And then it occurred to me that you might know where he is. I did telephone but the line was engaged.'

Ismini looked tired. Her expression was grave, almost mournful. 'I was probably trying to reach you,' she said.

'It's not that I'm worried,' Anne said, unbelting her jacket, 'but he shot off last night without a word to anyone. I just wanted to make sure he's OK. Have you seen anything of him today?'

'Sit down, Anne,' Ismini said.

Anne remained standing, noticing Ismini's expression for the first time. 'What is it? Has there been an accident? Is he hurt?'

Gently, Ismini said, 'David is dead, Anne.'

The words were like a slap, in spite of the gentleness.

'Dead?' Anne blinked, not wanting to accommodate anything so monstrous. '*Dead?*' Oh, no, he can't be! She sank down on the arm of the settee, feeling the clammy cold spread in her stomach, as it had when she knew about Don. 'He *can't* be!'

'I am sorry,' Ismini said. 'There is no easy way to tell anyone such a thing.'

'I don't believe it. David. Dead.'

Ismini poured a large brandy and brought it to Anne. 'It will come as a great shock to many people, I think.'

'But what happened? Was it his car? Was he in a crash?'

'No,' Ismini said, 'it was not an accident.'

'What, then?' Anne took the glass, but she didn't drink from it. She stared up at Ismini, who averted her eyes.

'We will not know until after . . . It was a heart attack, perhaps. Or a stroke.'

'A heart attack?' Anne still wanted to reject what she was being told. She wanted to reverse it. 'That's not possible! David's a fit, healthy – I mean he was a young man.'

Ismini was pacing slowly by the fireplace. 'Regrettably it is not only the middle-aged and the old who are struck down by heart diseases. Or by cerebral haemorrhages. David may even have had a coronary condition without being aware of it himself.' She sighed. 'As I said, we cannot be sure yet what the cause was. But in my opinion, it was one of those things.' She glanced at Anne. 'Are you all right?'

Anne nodded, staring down into the brandy glass, making an effort to control herself. 'Where did it happen? When?'

'Here. Last night. It was quite late. I was in bed but I was not asleep. I heard David banging on the front door. When I opened it he collapsed into the hall. I tried to revive him but it was no use. There was nothing anyone could have done for him.'

'I just don't understand,' Anne said wanly. 'He seemed perfectly all right when we were at the Kastello. He was dancing, making jokes, enjoying himself.'

'You say he left in a hurry?'

'So I was told.'

'You were not with him, then?'

Anne was momentarily thrown by the question. She couldn't tell Ismini what really happened. She hesitated, then to cover her confusion she took a sip from the brandy glass. 'We got separated,' she murmured. 'You know how it is at parties. I was . . .' she shrugged. 'I don't know where I was.'

'Then I would say that David must have suddenly been taken ill.' Ismini took a swift look at Anne, gauging her reaction. 'I expect he looked for you but then, feeling much worse, he decided he needed medical attention. Quickly.'

'Why didn't he say anything to anyone?'

'The people there would all have been strangers to him, would they not?'

Anne sighed. 'He could have told Raoul . . .' She stopped herself, but her use of Lavallière's first name had already drawn a quick look of concern from Ismini. '. . . Monsieur Lavallière,' Anne continued. 'I'd be very surprised if he doesn't have a doctor on his staff.'

'Perhaps he could not find him either. But, in any case, I imagine he probably thought it best to try to reach his friend, Doctor Mavros. The effort of driving, though, could have become too much for him and he lost control of the car . . .'

Anne raised a surprised, querying look towards Ismini.

'He was on foot when he arrived here,' Ismini said. 'Earlier today I went looking for his car. It is lying in a ditch on the roadside about three kilometres away.'

'So it could have been an accident!'

'No.' Ismini was careful again to look at Anne for only a moment, evading the probing of her eyes, the perception that could go beyond the surface. 'The car is only a little damaged. And there are no marks on David, apart from one or two bruises. What happened would not have helped him, of course. Walking would have placed a terrible strain on a man who, by then, was almost certanly desperately ill. Because my house is so much nearer than the town, he clearly changed his mind and came to me instead of Mavros. But too late . . .'

'Where is he now?' Anne asked.

'They have taken him to the mortuary.'

'Can I see him?'

'Now now. A post-mortem examination is necessary. Tomorrow, perhaps . . .'

Anne nodded. Her misery had stooped her, clutching the

brandy glass with both hands like a crystal ball that foretold nothing but gloom. After a minute she stood up, went to the trolley and set the glass down on it.

'This is a sad day for both of us,' Ismini said. 'But I have had time to accept. For you, though hearing about David in this way . . .' She slapped a hand helplessly against her skirt. 'I telephoned you at your house, of course, soon after it happened. But you were not there. I called again this morning but there was still no reply.'

'I wasn't . . .' Anne began, then stopped herself for the second time. 'I didn't get back until the early hours. And this morning I was probably out shopping when you rang.' She moved restlessly across the room, then turned to Ismini. 'I came by taxi. Will you drive me home?'

'Of course. But why not stay here?'

Anne shook her head. I'll go home, if you don't mind. I'd like to be on my own for a while.'

'I understand.'

Suddenly, impulsively, Anne threw herself into Ismini's arms, giving in at last to the sharp pain of grief. Ismini held her, her face remaining grave as she stroked Anne's shoulder and told her, over and over, that soon she would feel better.

It was half an hour later when Ismini's car entered the square in the old city and stopped. Opposite, a champagne-coloured Mercedes was parked near the mouth of the street where Anne lived. Both women were rather surprised to see the limousine.

They got out of Ismini's car and stood on either side, looking. Lavallière was in the forecourt outside a taverna, a lone figure in an island of empty tables. His aide was the only other person nearby, standing by the taverna wall, discreetly on guard.

'Monsieur Lavallière,' Ismini murmured.

Anne glanced across the car at her. 'I'll introduce you.'

195

'I would rather you did not.'

Anne nodded at once. 'You're right, of course. It's hardly the moment, is it?'

Ismini opened the car door again. 'I will telephone you this evening.'

'Yes, please do.' Anne's eyes were unsteady as she smiled across the car. 'Thank you, Ismini. And forgive me, please. I've been very selfish up to now – thinking of it as my loss and forgetting he was your friend, too. And for longer.'

Ismini nodded, showing her understanding. 'We will talk more later.' She got into the car and started it up, then she moved off slowly, drving around the square, aiming for a narrow exit street beside the taverna.

As she drew level with Lavallière she glanced at him. His eyes were on her, sharp, probing. Ismini looked away smartly and accelerated down the street.

Anne walked slowly across to where Lavallière was sitting. As she reached the table he stood up. He looked troubled.

'One of my staff reported that he had seen Mr Bascombe's car overturned on the side of the road,' he said. 'I was very concerned and I could not reach you on the telephone.' He gestured to the little street. 'When I found that you were not at home, I thought I would wait a little for your return.' He studied Anne's face carefully. 'What is it, my dear? What has happened.'

Anne decided to invite Lavallière back to the house before she explained. Once they were inside she told him about David. Lavallière stood by the sideboard holding the picture of Anne and Don, examining it as he listened.

When Anne had finished he went on gazing at the photograph. 'I cannot tell you how sorry I am,' he said. He put down the photograph again. 'If only he had come to me and told me that he was feeling unwell. There is a doctor in residence at the castle.'

'I thought there probably was,' Anne said. 'That possibility can't have entered his head.' She put a trembling hand to her eyes. 'If I'd stuck close to him he'd probably still be alive . . .'

'Oh no, Anne!' Lavallière crossed quickly to her. 'You must not blame yourself in that way.' He turned her to face him, placing his hands on her shoulders. His touch, this time, was simply comforting and friendly. 'A man of his age, full of life and apparently so fit – there was no way you or anyone could have foreseen such a tragedy.' He put his face close to hers, his voice dropping almost to a whisper. 'Promise me you will dismiss that thought from your mind. Forever.'

'I'll try to . . .'

'You must.' His eyes held Anne's again, probing deep, searching. He relaxed after a moment, shaking his head sadly and taking his hands from her shoulders. 'If only he had been nearer to Doctor Christoyannis' house when his car left the road. Then, perhaps, she might have saved him.'

'There are so many "if only's",' Anne sighed. 'As it was, he was beyond help by the time he got to her. He must have died seconds before she got to him.'

'And without a word,' Lavallière murmured sombrely. 'If there is anything I can do, anything at all, please do not hesitate to ask. I expect that his family would like him buried in England, in which case my private jet is at their disposal Please see that they are told this.'

Anne looked at him, her face brimming with gratitude. 'Thank you. You're very kind.'

'I hope you will allow me to help you, too, in this moment of sorrow – as I wish I could have done when you lost your husband.'

'It's such a pity that you never met Don,' she said, smiling wistfully. 'You would have liked him, I think. And he would have liked you.' She took Lavallière's hand in hers. 'As much as I do,' she said softly.

Von Reitz emerged from the main entrance to the keep at

almost the same instant the Mercedes drew up at the bottom of the steps. He descended the steps quickly and stood by the car, waiting as Lavallière got out.

'Has Mrs Tierney heard anything?' Von Reitz sounded particularly anxious.

Lavallière nodded. 'Bascombe is dead.' He moved on, heading for the steps.

'And the cause?'

Lavallière paused and gazed at the fretful, restless-eyed face. 'A heart attack, it would seem. Much as I expected.' He turned again and started striding up the stairs.

Von Reitz stood watching him, his lips working soundlessly, as if he were chewing something tiny and stubbornly tough. Time and again he was left with answers which only filled his head with more questions. There was so much about the *Maître* that he still didn't understand.

Chapter Twenty-Two

Late that evening Ismini telephoned Anne. It was clear, from the sound of Anne's voice, that she had been crying.

'How are you?' Ismini asked.

'I'm fine,' Anne said listlessly. 'And you?'

'I would like to see you. I thought perhaps we could spend the evening together. Unless you would prefer to be alone.'

'No, that would be good for both of us, I think.'

Ismini asked if she should drive over to Anne's house. Anne said no, she needn't take the trouble. 'I'll get a taxi out to your place.'

'Fine,' Ismini said. There was a pause. 'How did Monsieur Lavallière take the news?' she asked tentatively.

'He was appalled.'

'Yes.' Another pause, then, 'He would have been, of course.'

'And very sympathetic,' Anne added. 'He's offered the use of his private jet to fly David back to England.'

'How thoughtful.' Ismini's voice sounded almost cold. 'I will see you soon, then. *Andio.*'

The sun was setting as the taxi arrived at Anne's house. A short distance away, at the harbour, Dietrich von Reitz and two of Raoul Lavallière's aides were waiting by the side of a Mercedes, parked at the head of the steps leading down to a small stone jetty. For several minutes they had been watching a motor tender, approaching from a yacht lying at anchor outside the entrance to the harbour.

As the motorboat drew alongside the jetty von Reitz went forward to the top of the steps. A well-dressed man in his late fifties emerged from the boat's day cabin. With the assistance

199

of a sailor he climbed ashore and slowly ascended the steps. At the top von Reitz stepped forward to greet him, his left hand extended.

It took the taxi fifteen minutes to reach Ismini's house. She opened the door as the car pulled into the drive and stood waiting as Anne paid the driver.

The two women embraced briefly in the doorway, then went inside. Ismini led the way to the sitting-room, leaving the door open behind them. She stood for a moment, noticing how dejected Anne looked.

'What would you like to drink? Whisky and water?'

'Yes. Thank you.' Anne wandered aimlessly across the room as Ismini went to the drinks trolley. 'Something suddenly occurred to me on the way over here,' Anne said. 'I should have thought of it before. Do you know if anyone's been in touch with David's family? Or the university, come to that? I mean, is it something we ought to do?'

Ismini brought the drink and handed it to Anne.

'Thanks.' Anne took a sip, frowning over the rim of the glass. 'I don't know what relatives he had. Or where to reach them. Do you?'

'There is no need to contact his family,' Ismini said, facing Anne squarely. 'David is not dead.'

The words took a second to penetrate, stunning Anne as they did. 'What are you saying? Not dead?' She couldn't accept the cancellation of her sorrow; it was too abrupt, too unbelievable. 'Of course he's dead! You told me he was. You described . . .'

'I lied to you. He is alive. He is here.'

'I don't understand.' All day the grief had churned in her. Now she was being told it had no focus. 'He can't be alive.' Anne stared at Ismini, struggling suddenly for a foothold on reality. 'You lied? About something like that? It's not possible. You wouldn't do that . . .'

Ismini was looking across at the doorway. Anne turned

her head, following her gaze. Shock hit her, almost making her drop the glass. David Bascombe was standing there.

'I'm sorry we had to do this awful thing to you, Anne,' he said. He closed the door and came into the room. 'Honestly, there was no other way.'

Every tumbling emotion in Anne was swept away sharply by sudden, swamping anger. 'Why?' she screeched at Ismini. 'How could you? How could you be so cruel to let me think, to let me believe that . . .' Tears stung her eyes as she turned on David. 'And you! For God's sake! You must have known what it would do to me! And so soon after . . .'

'David cannot be blamed for this,' Ismini said firmly. 'It was only after much persuasion that he agreed to do it.'

Anne rounded on her again. 'Why? For what possible reason?'

'It was essential you convinced Lavallière that I was dead,' David said.

Ismini nodded. 'To do that, Anne, you had to believe it yourself. There could be no doubt whatever in your mind, so that when he looked into it he would find nothing but comfort there.'

A fresh wave of bewildered anger washed over Anne. 'What the hell are you talking about?' she demanded. 'What's he got to do with this?'

'Tell her what you found at the Kastello last night,' Ismini said to David. 'And tell her what happened to you.'

For ten minutes, David sat and explained everything that had happened, starting with his discovery of the dossier, right up to the moment when Ismini dragged him free of the lethal nightmare Lavallière had raised up around him.

Anne was deeply sceptical, although she couldn't doubt David's sincerity. He was telling her the truth, *his* truth, a version of events that was coloured by his own reaction to them. The deception no longer seemed so cruel, either, since it was well-intended. But strong doubt persisted; Anne knew, more than most people, how reality and imagination could overlap.

'That's not something that could have really happened,' she said, looking at David as he sat back nursing his bandaged hand. 'Not the way you've told it. It can't be real, any of it.'

'It was all too real,' David assured her. 'It's only because of Ismini that I survived it.'

'But no one has that kind of power. It's not possible to make a person believe that . . .'

'It is possible,' Ismini said flatly. 'Accept that. It's incredible, perhaps, and how it was done is even more incredible – but it *is* possible. Hold on to that, Anne, because the other explanation is almost unthinkable.'

Anne stared at her. 'What do you mean?'

Ismini's eyes became evasive. 'There is no reason why either of you should have to face the possibility, until it is all that is left to us. For now, I would rather we clung to everything within our grasp. Extraordinary it may be, but it is feasible.'

'If it's feasibility we're looking for,' Anne said, 'let's start with that picture of Lavallière's. She turned to David. 'OK, so you saw some resemblance to me in it. The shape of her face, the eyes, the colour of her hair. No problem, I'll go along with that. But there couldn't be more in it than those similarities – however striking. To see her as my twin, well, that could have been your imagination working overtime. That's feasible, right?'

David shook his head firmly. 'No way, Anne. I saw what I saw. You're her double. It could be a picture of you, only it's not. It's a painting of Agnes Beauvoir. The woman Lavallière's look-alike strangled.'

'Are you suggesting I'm in some kind of danger from him because of that?'

'I think the three of us are in danger because of it,' Ismini said. 'But you most of all.'

'I don't believe it,' Anne snapped.

Ismini sighed. 'After what he did to David?'

'I'm not convinced of that. Oh, I don't think David made it up, not just for the hell of it. Why should he? But you, Ismini – you know better than any of us the kind of tricks the mind can play.'

'Yes,' Ismini said, 'I do. But as you've learned from your own experience, that is often no more than an easy explanation. In this instance, I have no doubt at all that from the moment Lavallière discovered him in the study, until shortly after he arrived here, David could not be described as sane. His mind was being manipulated – and in such a way as to destroy him. Accepting it on that level, we are still left with the question why.'

'Exactly!' Anne said, a small light of triumph in her eyes. 'Why should Lavallière give a damn about what David saw?'

David leaned forward. 'Are you forgetting that file he's got on you?'

Anne immediately looked evasive. 'I can think of a possible explanation for that,' she murmured.'

'Oh?' Ismini stared at her. 'And what's that?'

'It doesn't matter. It's just not that odd, that's all.' Anne made to avert her eyes, but Ismini's stare was fixed, penetrating. Their minds collided, Anne felt the balance of her memory shift as it was probed.

After a few moments Ismini looked down, frowning. 'A man does not normally compile a dossier on a woman before he asks her to marry him, does he?'

Embarrassed, feeling terribly vulnerable, Anne stood up and moved away from them, avoiding David's startled look. 'A man in Lavallière's position might well do,' she said lamely.

'And what exactly is his position?' Ismini demanded.

'An extremely wealthy man.' Anne said defensively. 'He would have to be careful.'

David's face was stark with disbelief. 'Lavallière asked you to marry him?'

'Yes, indirectly. Which hardly points to the fact that he means me any harm, does it? In any case, what could he stand to gain from any of this?'

'It could be more a question of what he might lose,' Ismini observed. Tell me, Anne, that pendant you wore last night . . .'

Anne's hand flew to the bodice of her dress, as if she were reassuring herself the pendant was still underneath. 'What about it?'

David says your husband gave it to you.'

'He did.'

'May I ask when?'

Anne moved a little further away, flustered, taking care to avoid Ismini's eyes. 'It was some time ago.'

Ismini crossed the room and took Anne firmly by the shoulders, swinging her around to face her. 'When exactly?' she demanded urgently.

'I don't remember.' Anne's eyes were fixed on the floor, trying to avoid Ismini's searching stare.

'When, Anne? I want the truth. Tell me.' Anne tried to break free but Ismini's fingers tightened on her. 'You must. Look at me.'

'A few days ago,' Anne said, almost whispering.

'He can't have!' David's voice was a harsh admonishment. 'That's not . . .'

Ismini silenced him with one swift, angry glare, then turned her eyes to Anne. 'Look at me . . .'

Anne raised her head slowly and met Ismini's gaze. She was hesitant at first, blinking, then gradually defiance hardened her mouth as she opened her eyes wide and fixed them on Ismini's.

Ismini drew in her breath sharply, as if she were in pain. She closed her eyes momentarily. As she opened them again she released her hold on Anne but continued to study her, a look of tenderness spreading across her face. 'How often did he come to you like that?'

'Several times,' Anne said.

'Since when?'

'The day of the festival at Arhangelos. It happened the first time that night.'

David was leaning forward in his chair, his face shocked.

'And when was the last time?' Ismini asked.

'Last night.'

'At the Kastello?'

Anne nodded.

David was on his feet. 'You saw your husband there?'

'And each time,' Ismini intoned softly, 'you have made love, yes?'

Again Anne nodded.

'Oh, my God!' David looked sickened.

'But you said nothing.' Ismini kept her voice level, gently eliciting the truth. 'Not even that you had seen him again.'

'I couldn't!' Anne's face twisted with anguish. 'At first I thought it was a dream, even though it was all so real. But then . . .'

'He gave you the pendant and in the morning you still had it, so you knew it was not a dream.'

'He had come back to me,' Anne said in a wavering voice. 'But I still couldn't be sure it would last. I was afraid that if I said anything . . .'

'On these visits, has Don ever spoken to you?'

'He doesn't need to. It's enough that he's there.'

'I understand.' Ismini took Anne's hand. 'Help me, will you? We must try to reach your husband again. Tonight. Now. It is desperately important for you that we do.'

Throughout the evening, by boat, plane and helicopter, imposing-looking men of several nationalities were arriving

205

on Rhodes and being warmly greeted by Dietrich von Reitz. A tightly observed schedule ensured that every visitor received the same courtesy and attention, the identical swift transfer by limousine from his landing point to the Kastello Aghios Theodoros.

In his study, Raoul Lavallière sat in full evening dress, the insignia of his office around his neck on a black and white ribbon. He signed documents as he waited for von Reitz to come and announce that the others were ready for him. Occasionally, Lavallière looked up from his papers and smiled at the portrait of Agnes Beauvoir on his desk.

Anne and Ismini were sitting on the couch. Opposite them, at a slight angle, David sat in an armchair, watching, his head in partial shadow.

'Take my hands,' Ismini said.

'Why is this necessary?' The closer this moment had come, the more Anne's resistance to it had grown. 'Donald and I . . . We're no longer apart. I'm content.'

'Don't fight me, Anne, whatever you do,' Ismini pleaded softly. 'I beg you.'

Reluctantly, Anne reached out and joined hands with her. 'It didn't work the other day,' she murmured. 'What makes you think we'll be successful tonight?'

There had been time for Ismini to consider their previous failure. Tonight, she was confident she knew the reason. 'When we tried before, Anne, what image of your husband were you holding in your head?'

'I pictured him just as I'd seen him that afternoon, in the village.'

Ismini nodded, surer still. 'Now I want you to remember him at some happy time you spent together in England. A time long ago, if you wish. Dismiss all memories of him on Rhodes.' She tightened her grip on Anne's hands. 'Try to do that.'

Open-eyed, Anne began to concentrate, bringing the picture together in layers, like before. As it strengthened she felt the immediate intrusion of Ismini's mind, probing, sensitive to the image. Colour and firmness built up rapidly until Anne held the scene clear and bright in her head – Don, with her beside him, posing for the photograph that Anne now treasured.

'Good!' Ismini breathed, staring into Anne's eyes. 'Good! Now keep that image firmly fixed.' She closed her eyes and tightened her fingers. The transference began as a dimming of her consciousness, a shift to a state of trance where her power thrummed like a spiritual dynamo. 'Yes, Anne . . .' Her voice was a telepathic extension now, unheard in the room. 'Yes. I see him clearly. This time. This time . . .' The finger grip intensified as Ismini's breathing grew fast, shallower.

Anne was holding the picture with almost perfect clarity. Around it, the pull of Ismini's psyche throbbed implacably, taking the details across, the million fragments in the unique permutation that was Don Tierney's face.

The picture faded, making Ismini pant softly, holding on. 'Nearly,' her telepathed voice encouraged. 'Nearly. Almost there.' The picture became firm again, bright, the smiling face of a happy man. 'Stay with me, Anne. Stay with me . . .'

Synchronous impulses from the women's minds touched momentarily and meshed. The picture was suddenly shared between them, a doubling of its strength that cleared all obstructions to contact.

'Now!' Ismini's voice sang triumphantly in Anne's head. 'He is here! He is in the room with us! Do you feel his presence?'

'Yes . . .' Anne knew he was there, close enough for her to reach out and touch. 'I feel it. He's near. Oh, my darling, Don. You're here . . .'

Smiling radiantly, Anne opened her eyes, knowing

precisely where to look. Her head swung round in a gentle, confident arc, her eyes widening expectantly. The smile receded and died. Anne's face creased in a frown.

David Bascombe, sitting back with his head in shadow, leaned slowly forward into the light. His face was expressionless, his eyes fixed and staring. He moved his lips, stiffly at first, then more naturally. There was no sound for a moment until a long sigh escaped. 'Thank God, Anne love!' The voice was perfectly clear; it was Don Tierney's, panting softly, relieved. 'At last! At last!'

Chapter Twenty-Three

There could be no mistake. Anne wanted to reject this counterfeit, this near-obscenity. Her husband was her husband, indivisible, *whole*. To look at another man and hear Don's voice issuing from his mouth was repugnant to her; but there was no mistake, no trick. Anne glanced at Ismini, who still had her eyes tightly closed.

'He has chosen this way to reach us,' Ismini's transmitted voice said. 'He is using David as a channel. We can ask no more than that. It is enough.' Ismini turned a fraction, speaking aloud. 'Anne needs your help. Take us back. Back to the time when you were on Rhodes, to that last night. Will you do that?'

'Afterwards . . .' Don's voice was laboured, struggling. 'I tried. In London . . . I tried to reach. Many times. I wanted to tell her what . . . It was important. . . .'

'Yes, I know,' Ismini said. 'I know. So now, tell her.'

Anne was watching Bascombe, seeing the tension in his throat as the invading voice shaped it to its own needs.

'It wasn't an accident, Anne. He made it happen.' Now Don's voice was becoming stronger. 'Lavallière. He's . . . He's . . .'

'Go on,' Ismini urged.

'The day I arrived. Spotting Joseph Marcus . . .'

Now it was more than a voice. Ismini could see what Don was telling Anne. His speech was becoming the commentary to a series of vivid images.

'That was the first surprise. According to the television news, just before I flew to Greece, Marcus was supposed to be with the Prime Minister that weekend.' The voice had

209

grown confident, controlled. 'So what was he doing on Rhodes? Being met off a private jet and whipped away smartish from the airport?'

'Yes, yes,' Ismini coaxed softly, 'go on.'

'I didn't think much more about it, though. The meeting at Chequers could have been called off, for all I knew. And a man like Sir Joseph needs to keep a low profile.'

Ismini watched the scene shift to the harbour. She saw von Reitz greeting a man from a motor launch.

'That night when I spotted Emric Niedermann with the same fellow, well that got me really curious. The top man from the world's largest multinational and the biggest private banker in Switzerland – both slipping into Rhodes on the same day! And the same reception committee for each of them! So where was the party? Who was throwing it?'

Anne stared at Bascombe as her husband's voice took on the familiar, beloved tone of the seasoned raconteur.

'I found out,' he went on. 'The following day.'

The road above the Kastello, the helicopter, a man being welcomed; Ismini saw it clearly. She saw Don taking photographs from behind the rocks.

'Remo Manzini, tipped to be Italy's next Prime Minister. This was getting to be quite a gathering. I had to get closer to that castle, although I couldn't see that I'd be welcome. I was right.'

There was no need for Ismini to concentrate. The graphic images flowed with perfect clarity. She saw Don being refused entry to the castle, then Lavallière staring from the limousine, the way he had stared the first time she encountered him. She saw the jeep swerve as the headache struck Don, just as it had attacked her.

'I wasn't going to leave it at that. I couldn't get into the castle by the front door. In that case I'd come back when it was dark and try some other way.'

In flashing summary Ismini witnessed Don drive up the

valley road, climb the castle wall, then ease himself over the top.

'It was easy. Too easy. I should have realized that. But how was I to know that I was expected?'

The image was flawless. Ismini saw Don push open a small door, checking to make sure there was no one about before he went through. He moved silently along a corridor, pausing occasionally to listen at the doors. Hearing footsteps approaching, he stepped into a recess; two of Lavallière's aides went past without seeing him.

Anne could still hear Don's voice clearly, but it dimmed in Ismini's ears as the sounds of the re-enactment became married to the images. She saw Don in another corridor, moving stealthily, and she heard a raised voice from beyond the door to the gallery over the main hall. The sound was muffled; Don pushed open the door a fraction. It was von Reitz speaking: '. . . therefore in accordance with the Rules as prescribed on the foundation of our noble parent order . . .'

Don eased his way around the door and on to the gallery. He crouched and moved quickly to the balustrade, keeping low. He looked down into the hall.

At the far end, facing a large audience of men, Raoul Lavallière sat in a high-backed wooden chair. He was in full evening dress. Draped over his shoulders was a long white hooded cloak with a red cross emblazoned on the left breast. On top of the cloak he had a short cape of white sheepskin, and over that a token cape of silver chain mail. The cloak was fastened by a clasp bearing an elaborate insignia.

Slightly behind Lavallière and to either side sat six other men, among them Sir Joseph Marcus, Emric Niedermann and Remo Manzini. Their dress was similar to Lavallière's, except for the sheepskin cape. On Lavallière's left, Dietrich von Reitz was standing before his own chair, holding a sheet of parchment. Further behind were more men, dressed in dinner jackets and black ties and wearing brown hooded cloaks. The atmosphere of solemn ceremony was rich, awesome.

'Let the examination begin . . .' von Reitz intoned. He sat down. A man in a white cloak with a simple silver clasp stepped forward and stood before Lavallière.

Ismini was holding Don's point of view on the gallery; she was aware of everything he did. As he checked the light in the hall and raised his camera to his eye, she saw the image in the viewfinder, the moments of darkness each time the mirror flipped up to permit an exposure. Simultaneously, she could hear the ceremony proceeding.

'Are you, Wilhelm Ruiter, any man's serf?' Emric Niedermann asked the man standing before Lavallière.

'I am not.'

'Are you aware of the great hardness of this House?' Joseph Marcus asked him.

'I am.'

Remo Manzini spoke: 'Will you willingly undergo everything you may be called upon to undergo, and be a servant and slave to this House, for all the days of your life?'

'I will,' Ruiter said.

'Do you now forswear and renounce any vow of fealty,' Lavallière asked, 'any allegiance or subscription hitherto made by you?'

'I do.'

'In what do you believe?' Niedermann demanded.

'In the supremacy of the Order, above all else,' Ruiter replied, 'and in the justness of our cause.'

'Which is?' Joseph Marcus asked in his turn.

Ruiter stood straighter as he replied, framed neatly in Don's viewfinder. 'Right to those born to it. Might to those who use it to that end. The humiliation and destruction of those who oppose it, for the common good and by any means.'

'Brother Knights,' Lavallière said, 'this man, having been examined and having answered well, stands on the threshold of this Brotherhood. If there is anyone among you who knows of any reason why, according to our Rule, he should not be fully admitted, say so now, for it is better that such a thing should be said before, rather than after he has come among us.' He paused. No one spoke. 'Is it your wish that he joins us?'

In unison, the Brother Knights cried, 'In the name of us all let it be so!'

Ruiter knelt. Lavallière rose and advanced towards him, followed by von Reitz, carrying a cape of silver chain mail and a clasp fashioned in the seal of the Order.

'Sire,' Ruiter said, 'I have come before the Brothers of this Order to beg and require you to accord me your company and the benefits of this House as one who will henceforth always be its servant and slave.'

'Good Brother,' Lavallière said solemnly, 'you ask a great thing. To achieve it will you swear, on pain of death in default, that henceforth, all the days of your life, you will obey the Master of this Brotherhood and any Commander placed above you? That you will uphold the custom of our House and that you will never desert this Order – neither through strength nor weakness, neither in worse times nor better?'

'I do so swear.'

Lavallière nodded slowly. 'Then so be it.' He took the chain mail cape from von Reitz and draped it over Ruiter's shoulders. 'Arise, Chevalier Wilhelm Ruiter, Knight of the Brotherhood of the Survivors of the Thirteenth.'

Ruiter stood up and Lavallière handed him the clasp.

'*Baucent!*' the assembly cried. '*Baucent! Baucent!*'

Ruiter bowed to Lavallière, turned and took his place in the front row of Brother Knights. As he did, Don snatched another photograph.

213

'I'd heard it and seen it all,' Don's voice said to Anne, 'but I could hardly believe it. Some of the most powerful men in Europe, banded together in a fascist brotherhood based on an old order of knights. Incredible. But it was real. It was happening in front of me. And I'd caught it, the story of the century. With pictures.' He paused. 'But then it happened.'

Behind tightly-shut eyelids Ismini saw it; Lavallière down in the hall, raising his head slowly and gazing up at the gallery.

'Good evening, Mr Tierney,' he said.

There was immediate consternation in the hall. Everyone was looking at Don now, demanding to know who he was Von Reitz, furious, made an urgent signal to the confreres at the back of the hall. Several of them moved to obey, heading for the door to the gallery.

Lavallière put up his hand. 'No,' he said firmly. 'That is unnecessary. Remain where you are.' His eyes widened a fraction as they locked on Don's.

The images tumbled rapidly now. Ismini saw Don, transfixed, held rigid by Lavallière's stare. For an instant she saw the carved face of Asmodeus, then Lavallière again, his eyes narrowing in concentration, probing Don's mind.

Suddenly there was a noise, disturbing, dangerous. Don looked down at his feet and gasped. He saw rats. There were dozens of them, brown and grey and black, teeth glinting dully as they crawled over his shoes and clawed at the legs of his trousers. He looked up and saw more, on the balustrade and the stairs. Hundreds of them. He stumbled through the door and began running, terrified, his feet scything through the horde of squeaking, angry rodents.

The images were kaleidoscopic now. Ismini saw the wall again, the shadow pouring over it. She heard the terrible chattering noise as Don ran from the castle and threw himself into the jeep.

'I couldn't shake them off,' Don was telling Anne

breathlessly. 'There were rats everywhere. They were after me. Hundreds of them. You know how it is with me and rats. I can stand most things, but not rats. Not rats!'

Ismini saw the darkness, the sudden stillness as Don braked the jeep. No noise, no rats, just silence and gratitude.

Then the noise slammed back and they were there, on the road and leaping into the jeep in a hairy, menacing stream, rats in their dozens and hundreds, crawling over Don and clawing on to his back and shoulders.

'I could feel them, smell them. Horrible. Horrible! They were everywhere . . .'

It was like a torrent of clawing feet and rank, hot bodies. Whimpering, flailing at the rats crawling in his hair, Don started the jeep and drove blindly, feeling the hideous writhing on his legs and arms. The road suddenly went crazy. Don swerved, one hand coming off the wheel to brush a rat from his neck. Then there was no road, the jeep was bouncing over grass and boulders.

It came up suddenly, a wall, dead ahead. There was no time to brake, no time to realize what was happening before the jeep smashed into the building and Don hurtled through the windscreen.

The fuel tank exploded. There was fire everywhere, showering down across Don's body, enveloping the jeep. Ismini moaned, experiencing Don's shift from life to the dimension beyond, hearing the dying echo in his brain – 'Anne! Anne! Anne!'

Anne was crying, appalled by what Don had told her. As she watched, David Bascombe's body shuddered and Don's voice made a low, sorrowful moan. Tears were streaming down David's cheeks.

'That's it, Anne . . . That's how it was. I wanted to tell you before, my love . . .' The voice was becoming stilted again, losing its power. 'I tried . . . but I couldn't make it.'

'I saw you, Don,' Anne whimpered. I saw you. But no one

215

would believe me. They said I was mad.'

'I wanted you to know . . . Everything . . . But I drifted, further and further away . . . Until now, thank God! Until now.'

Anne was shaking her head. 'No, Don! You only left me for a little while. I found you again. You were waiting for me. Here. I saw you. You were in the pictures I took. And you've come to me, taken me in your arms, more than once. You gave me a pendant, remember?'

'Couldn't get through to you,' his voice said feebly. 'Not before. I wanted to . . . Did try. Not until now. At last.' With an obvious effort the voice regained its fluency for a moment. 'I loved you, Anne. Always will. Don't screw up your life because of this. Find someone else. Someone who'll make you happy. Find someone.' The voice faded again. 'Promise me. Promise me . . .'

In a torment, Anne wrenched her hands free of Ismini's and ran to David's chair. Ismini cried out sharply, as if she'd been hurt. A swift, violent tremor passed through her body and her eyes opened suddenly.

'It's you I want,' Anne moaned, kneeling by David and grasping his arm. 'No one else, Don. Just you. As it is with us now. That's enough . . .'

David's eyes fluttered and closed. His head sank forward as he slumped back in the chair.

'No!' Anne howled. 'Don't leave me, Don! Please! Don't leave me! Not yet!' Sobbing, she tugged desperately at David's sleeve. 'Don! Don!'

Ismini was exhausted. She looked across at Anne, shaking her head. 'The contact is broken,' she said. 'I could not have held it for much longer, anyway.' She stood up, crossed to Anne and helped her to her feet, putting her arms around her and comforting her.

David stirred and opened his eyes. After a moment's confusion he sat up in the chair, staring dumbly as Ismini

216

and Anne returned to the settee and sat down again.

He moistened his lips. 'What the hell . . . ?'

Anne stared at Ismini. 'He was murdered,' she said, her voice trembling. 'By Lavallière. He killed him the same way he tried to kill David.'

Ismini nodded, letting Anne set the terrible facts before herself and confront them.

'He murdered him, cruelly, coldly. And then yesterday he asked me to . . .' She shuddered, clamping her lips tightly together.

'I need a drink,' David mumbled. He got up and went to the trolley.

A thought struck Anne. 'I don't understand. Don could have told me that before. He should have.'

'You heard him,' Ismini said. 'He tried. He couldn't.'

'Not in London, perhaps. But since. Here. On Rhodes. That first night he came to me, surely he could have . . .' She saw Ismini's frown and misread it. 'You don't believe me, do you? You think he's never been with me like that. I imagined it all. Or dreamt it. That's what you think, isn't it?'

'Anne . . .'

'He must have!' Anne cut in. 'I told you, each time . . . I felt – I – it was so real, it couldn't have been a dream. And earlier this evening, you as good as said so yourself.'

David feeling disorientated and irritable, had moved to the far side of the room with his drink. He stood with his back to the settee, finding the conversation unbearable.

'No,' Ismini told Anne, 'It was not a dream. The pendant is proof of that. But Donald is dead. There can be no physical contact between you. You know that. So this apparition that has visited you . . .'

'Oh, you don't understand!' Anne said angrily. 'It wasn't a phantom, a *wraith* that made love to me. It was a warm, vital, exciting being with my husband's face, my husband's body. So it had to be Donald.' She let out a humourless, exasperated little laugh. 'Who else could it have been?'

David spun round, staring worriedly at Anne. Ismini was holding her gaze, allowing her to look into her mind and discover the answer to the question.

'No . . .' Anne breathed, shaking her head. 'No . . .' a look of desperate, agonized horror spread on her face. '*No!*' Her strangled, whimpering moan rose suddenly to a scream, long and hysterical, tearing at her throat as the full, unbearable weight of the truth descended on her.

Chapter Twenty-Four

Towards midnight David helped himself to his third large whisky. Ismini had been upstairs with Anne for ten minutes, calming her. During that time David's agitation had grown. He was being hounded by a notion – more than that, a belief – that he could scarcely confront. It troubled him more than Don's revelations and his own part in them. And no amount of scotch, it seemed, could dull the edge of his unrest.

Ismini came back into the room.

'How is she?' David asked.

'Distraught, naturally. But calmer. I have given her a sedative. How are you?'

'Nothing like that's happened to me before. And I hope to God it never does again.'

Ismini came and stood by him, touching his hand. 'I was also surprised,' she said. 'You have a psychic receptivity which neither of us suspected.' She stood back, tilting her head thoughtfully. Tell me, during the time you were taken over by Tierney, were you aware of everything?'

'It was like I was there with him. But as an observer – separate, detached if you know what I mean.'

Ismini nodded. 'That is interesting. Did you feel this great empathy that day when you met him?'

'Not especially.'

'Clearly he did, though.'

David took a long swallow from his glass 'You saw everything too, did you?'

'Yes, I did. What did you make of that ceremony?'

'Well, it's like Tierney said. The Kastello's obviously the headquarters of some kind of cabal – a bloody powerful one, it would seem. Modelled on the Knights Templar. A sort of neo-Nazi freemasonry.' He shook his head. 'It's frightening.'

'You are certain?' Ismini asked. 'The Templars are the root of this organization?'

'Positive. The costumes, the regalia, the induction ritual – that's almost exactly the way a postulant was admitted to the Order in the old days. The name, the Brotherhood of the Survivors of the Thirteenth, that's practically proof on its own.'

'Oh? Why?'

'Because it was on the thirteenth of April, 1307, that the Master of the Templars and most of the Knights in France were arrested.'

'But not Tibald de Montrefort,' Ismini said.

'No. He was one of the original survivors. And he went on surviving for a good few years.'

'What do you suppose is their purpose?'

David looked at her as if the answer should have been obvious. 'They're setting themselves up as a power block. A political and economic mafia. They've probably gone a long way in achieving it, with their kind of money and influence. Plus the backing of the businesses and organizations they control. He swallowed some more whisky. 'Like I said, it's frightening. Since they're a bit more corrupt than the Templars, they might even be going in for a few orgies, as an extra-curricular activity.' He glanced at Ismini, who had sat down on the settee. 'I suppose they could even have gone the whole hog and got into Devil worship.'

Ismini considered it, then shook her head. 'No. In these permissive times sexual indulgence is freely available, in all its forms. It is a growth industry. And the worshipping of false gods of one kind or another is an everyday activity, encouraged on all sides. You no longer have to meet in secret to indulge in sin.'

David nodded. 'They probably just have an insatiable

hunger for more and more power – the greatest, most dangerous vice of all. The one Lavallière will go to any lengths to hide. Even murder.'

'Probably not for the first time. There's no question that he meant to kill you.'

David sighed. 'So, knowing what we now do, where do we go from here? You've already done a good job persuading me we can't contact the police.'

'They wouldn't believe us.' Ismini sighed. 'Even if they did, they would not risk offending Lavallière by attempting to secure the necessary evidence to support our story.'

David was on the move again, pacing, preoccupied. Ismini watched him thoughtfully for a moment, then appeared to come to a decision.

'Let's face it, David,' she said pointedly, 'there is much more to this than Tierney's murder and the existence of the organization, isn't that so?'

David stopped and frowned at her. 'Such as?'

'Speak your thoughts,' Ismini said. 'Trust me with your suspicions.'

'I don't know what you're on about,' he said, colouring. 'Suspicions! We've been over those already. And they're a hell of a sight more than suspicions, aren't they? I mean, we *know* that Lavallière killed Tierney. We *know* that he's the leading light in a revival of an old military order.' He made a strained laugh. 'It was probably his idea in the first place – a memorial to his illustrious ancestor.'

'Tibald de Montrefort,' Ismini said. 'Of whom, as you have already told me, Lavallière is the twin.' She stared at David. 'De Montrefort. In your words, the original survivor.'

David stared back. 'What are you suggesting?'

'I am telling you that the thing you suspect – but dare not say – is true, in my opinion. I believe that Lavallière does not only resemble de Montrefort – he *is* de Montrefort.'

'Oh, thank God!' The change in David was instantaneous.

221

The brooding frown left his face. He closed his eyes and let out a long sigh of relief. 'I thought maybe I was going mad, just considering the possibility.'

'When did you begin to suspect it?'

'The very first time I saw the portrait. It was a flight of fancy at that point, of course. Tonight, though, seeing Lavallière through Tierney's eyes – seeing him wearing that cloak, sensing his power – it suddenly seemed conceivable. More than that, even.' He paused, trying to frame his feeling accurately. 'It seemed *likely*, Ismini.' He frowned again. 'It can't be possible, can it?'

'It is no less possible than it is for someone to assume the shape and substance of a dead man in order to seduce his widow.'

'Even allowing that that ever happened . . .'

'It happened, David,' Ismini said firmly.

'But how could she?' He winced visibly, finding the idea painful to contemplate. 'She's not stupid. Deep down she must have known . . .'

'She was not thinking. He was there, the man she loved, still loves. It was a miracle, something she did not want to question. And do not forget Lavallière's skill – you believed in the fire, didn't you? There was no doubt in your mind. Tierney didn't doubt the presence of those rats, either.'

After a moment David nodded, half way to accepting the unthinkable. 'You're positive it was Lavallière who came to her?'

'You are not?'

'I don't know! The whole business is so incredible. I suppose I don't want to believe any of it.'

Confident in her reasoning, Ismini stood up again before she stated the case for her own certainty. 'Anne has the pendant her lover gave her,' she said. 'The same pendant Agnes Beauvoir wore in the painting you saw. That jewel was never in Donald Tierney's possession.'

'I see that,' David murmured. 'But the other thing – Lavallière being de Montrefort. I have this damned near-certain feeling about it, but logic keeps getting in the way. The pendant doesn't prove anything in that direction, does it? It could have been handed down to Lavallière through the family.'

'Yes, it could have,' Ismini agreed. 'But we know how Anne received it. Even if we are wrong about Lavallière's true identity, we are left with the certainty that it was he who appeared to Anne as her husband. Knowing that, we know that we are confronted with a force which can only be supernatural. We also have plenty of evidence that it is malignant force.'

David raised an eyebrow. 'Satanic?' he ventured.

'Yes.' Ismini paced for a moment, thinking. 'I do not subscribe to the concept of Satan as a being. But the existence of Evil as a potent force is indisputable. I believe Lavallière is just one facet of Evil – a part of the whole negative force aligned against Good. A vital part, perhaps even the core.'

David was nodding, catching her line of thought. 'And Evil,' he said, 'is a continuing thing.'

'Precisely. Originating who knows where. In this case, after many metamorphoses, taking the form of Tibald de Montrefort. Then, through succeeding transformations, becoming Lavallière.'

'That's only a hypothesis,' David pointed out. 'A pretty tenuous one, at that.'

'Is it?'

Ismini took his glass and went to the trolley. She poured another scotch and made a vodka and tonic for herself. She came back and handed David his drink.

'Think, David. When Anne returned here unexpectedly after her husband was killed, Lavallière must have seen her as a threat. Had she come back because she suspected

Tierney's death was no accident? Did she perhaps know something? Had Tierney told her about the mysterious Kastello before he was disposed of?' She sipped her drink. 'Lavallière's first inclination would have been to get rid of Anne, too. As a precaution, if nothing else.'

Ismini moved squarely in front of David, warming to her point, holding his attention by the sheer certainty in her voice. 'Something, I doubt if Lavallière was sure what it was, prompted him to invite Anne to the Kastello first. Seeing her, he would have had an enormous shock. He found himself face to face with what must have seemed the reincarnation of a woman who died almost six hundred years ago.'

'If he was shocked,' David said, 'he hid it bloody well. Although I must admit, he hardly took his eyes off her. But carry on.'

'Well, now that he'd seen her, he no longer wanted her harmed, even if she *was* a threat. He certainly didn't want her dead. So, having gathered the dossier on Anne, he learned from her medical records that she had recently had a breakdown. He decided it would be simple insurance to cast further doubts on her mental stability. Her credibility would be undermined. Anything she might say or reveal, even unknowingly, would not be taken very seriously.'

'The images of Tierney Anne saw on the photographs,' David murmured; 'are you saying it was Lavallière who conjured them up?'

'Exactly that. As he was also responsible for the apparition Anne saw that day the three of us went to Arhangelos.' Ismini wagged a finger for emphasis. 'And that is why I could not contact Tierney the first time we tried, because Anne's mental picture was not of him at all. I was reaching out to Lavallière, not Tierney.'

The deductions were tight and carefully considered. From the moment Lavallière knew that Anne was trying to contact her husband, Ismini continued, he would have known his plans were being meddled with, and in an area where he was vulnerable. Anne had to be dissuaded from trying it again. That was why Tierney began appearing in Anne's bedroom, Ismini reasoned. That way, Lavallière achieved two objectives. First, he diverted Anne from trying to contact her husband any more; she had no need to, the thing had happened apparently by itself, and further seances might destroy the 'contact'. Second, Lavallière achieved possession of Anne's body. It would have been the perfection of his own dream, to have someone who so closely resembled the only woman he had ever loved.

'So,' Ismini concluded, 'we have convincing evidence of Lavallière's true identity.' She saw David frown. 'Think. It was not Raoul Lavallière who loved Agnes Beauvoir and who shared her bed, was it? Just as it was not Lavallière who strangled her, to protect himself against the prophecy. It was Tibald de Montrefort.'

Chapter Twenty-Five

The grey pall of certainty had settled on Anne. Time, rest and the sedative had combined to make her accept.

'Accept,' she whispered, rising in the darkness of the bedroom. She had trained herself to acceptance, it was a state of mind that had seemed, at one time, to offer comfort and a balanced outlook on her situation. Now, she had achieved a balance that was arid, desolate.

She put on the dressing gown that had been draped on the end of the bed. Silently, she crept out of the bedroom. The house was quiet, Ismini and David had probably gone to bed. Anne went downstairs, hesitated, then made for the kitchen.

Three minutes later she was back in the bedroom. She closed the door carefully and went to the window, drawing aside the net curtain. Motionless, she gazed out into the night. Acceptance of the truth didn't oblige her to acknowledge defeat. Anne knew that perfectly well. And the balance could still be adjusted, it could be tilted to put at least a trace of comfort in her heart.

She raised her left hand slowly and grasped the tear-shaped diamond at her throat. She held it tightly, concentrating.

At the Kastello Aghios Theodoros dinner had been over for almost an hour, but Lavallière, von Reitz, the Marshal and the Commanders of the Order were still sitting at the high table. The port and brandy were circulating and all of the men, with the exception of Lavallière, were smoking cigars.

'In the interim,' Lavallière was saying to Remo Manzini,

'we will see to it that there is continued civil unrest.'

Manzini nodded. 'That is essential, *Maître*. And on an increasing scale. Otherwise, when I take office I will not be in a position to suspend the Constitution.'

'Don't worry,' von Reitz said. 'That has already been attended to. Three weeks from now will see the start of a major terrorist offensive.'

Lavallière looked at Emric Niedermann. 'The necessary funds for that will be made available to them soon, I trust.'

'Yes, *Maître*. In several donations. All of which will be easily traced back to left-wing revolutionary sources.'

Lavallière smiled. 'But not too easily. We must let the security services earn their salaries.'

As the discussion moved to other areas of the Brother Knights' activities, Lavallière began to shift restlessly in his chair. Von Reitz had noticed, but thought it better to say nothing. When Sir Joseph Marcus raised the matter of his company's enclosure of other major organizations, Lavallière began to look even more restless.

'It must be realized,' Marcus said, 'that it will not be possible for ACI to secure a monopoly overnight. We will need to proceed very carefully.'

'No one is suggesting any other course,' Lavallière said. 'We all appreciate, fully, that this is something which . . .' He broke off suddenly, looking puzzled. To von Reitz, it appeared as if he were listening to something far off.

After several seconds, as Lavallière continued to sit there, frowning at the table, von Reitz cleared his throat nervously and leaned forward.

'*Maître*?'

Lavallière looked up at him coldly, then glanced at the others around the table. 'That is enough for tonight,' he said. 'There are a number of despatches which require my urgent attention.' He stood up. The others did the same. 'We will continue this discussion tomorrow. Goodnight.'

'Goodnight, *Maître*,' they said in unison.

Lavallière pushed back his chair and walked brisly to the door. One of the aides opened it hastily, letting him through.

He went quickly to his study, closed the door and leaned back against it. He was excited, smiling, gazing across at the picture of Agnes Beauvoir on the desk.

Anne had moved away from the window. She was sitting on the edge of the bed, staring down at the floor, her hands folded in her lap.

Gradually, she became aware of another presence in the room. She turned her head slowly, but did not raise it. On the edge of her vision she saw Donald Tierney step out of the shadows by the window. He looked at Anne and smiled.

She stood up. With her arms by her sides and her eyes still demurely lowered, she walked to the end of the bed. Don came to her and closed her in an embrace.

Slowly, Anne brought up her arms and curved them around his shoulders. The fingers of her right hand closed around the handle of the knife that had been concealed in her dressing gown sleeve. She turned the blade, pointing it at his back. As his embrace tightened Anne lifted her face to him, the expression blank, the eyes filled with loathing and hurt.

He went on smiling at her. The knife moved back a fraction, ready to strike. Her forearm tensed.

Anne froze. His dear face, so close, the beloved features . . . She couldn't do it. She knew it was an illusion but it was so perfect, it was Don . . .

She set her teeth, forcing herself to ignore the likeness, poising the knife again.

His face changed suddenly as he looked deep into her eyes. Anne saw surprise, alarm. Then she saw anger.

A cold voice invaded her mind. 'Drop it.'

Transfixed by his gaze, Anne opened her fingers and let the knife fall to the floor.

The eyes probed deeper. The face of Don Tierney became twisted with rage. 'Bascombe is still alive!' the voice shouted in Anne's head. 'You know it all. That is a pity.'

With a swift movement he grasped the chain at her throat and twisted it. The fine links bit into her flesh. He twisted it again, tighter, making the blood pound in Anne's ears as she

228

coughed, choking, desperate for air. Trying to pull free from him, she swung herself along the side of the bed. Her leg struck the night table and it crashed over on its side.

The chain snapped. Anne sucked in air through her open mouth an instant before he grabbed her again, his fingers encircling her neck as he bent her back over a table. His thumbs pressed savagely on her throat, throttling her. Anne fought, she punched and kicked at him, but the grip got tighter. Her vision began to darken as the pounding in her ears mounted. Her arms and legs felt heavy, too heavy to move. The thumbs pressed harder, the enraged face panting in the effort to shut off her life.

The door flew open. Ismini stood there in her nightdress, paralysed, unbelieving. Even in the darkness she could see who the man was. Lavallière. He was in a rage, merciless, completely unaware of her. *He was trying to kill Anne!*

Ismini saw the knife glinting on the carpet, three feet away. In one bowing sweep she had it, was closing both hands around the handle as he straightened and raised her arms above her head.

Anne's eyes rolled back, submitting to darkness. The hands on her neck tightened murderously, clamping out air and life.

Ismini brought down the knife with all her strength. The blade struck Lavallière's back with a thud and sliced through flesh and cartilage. Blood spurted over Ismini's hands as he arched, roaring with pain.

David Bascombe came rushing to the room, tightening the belt of his bathrobe. Horrified, he watched as Lavallière levered himself away from Anne, wrenching the knife hilt from Ismini's fingers as he lurched across the room. In bizarre slow motion he tried to pluck the weapon from his back. He staggered against the wall and pivoted on his shoulder, facing the door.

David ran across and pulled Anne up off the table. She was conscious, coughing, hanging on to his shoulder as he led her hurriedly to the door.

Leaning by the wall, Lavallière was gripped by a spasm of

pain. He groaned, his face an amalgam of agony and rage. He raised one trembling finger and pointed it at the three of them around the door. Immediately there was a noise, shrill and unsettling, mounting within the room, growing to a scream.

David looked terrified. The two women, bewildered, put their hands over their ears as the screech became unbearable. Lavallière mustered his feeble strength and staggered towards the French window, grunting, dragging his feet. He put out his hand, seeking support as his legs buckled. He swayed, then he let out a long cry of anguish and pitched forward through the panes of glass.

The sound stopped instantly. Recovering themselves, David and Ismini eased Anne gently on to the side of the bed. When they were sure she was all right, Ismini ran to the balcony as David went downstairs and opened the front door.

David searched around the house and Ismini scanned the steet, but there was no sign of Lavallière's body. David looked up from the path to Ismini on the balcony, shaking his head. He moved along the path, across the lawn and into the bushes. Nothing. Lavallière had disappeared.

Up in the bedroom, Ismini was staring at her arm, covered in dark blood. On the bed, Anne sat gazing at the floor, her expression blank as she absently massaged her bruised throat.

Early next morning, Dietrich von Reitz tapped the door of Lavallière's study and entered, his document folder tucked under his arm. As he turned from the door he paused, surprised not to see the *Maître* at his desk.

He moved further into the room, opening the file, removing some papers. He placed them on the centre of the desk, then realized suddenly that something was wrong. The desk lamp was gone, files had been knocked out of place. He stepped around the desk and gasped.

'*Maître.*'

Raoul Lavallière, still in evening dress, was lying on the floor. His fingers were twined around the cord of the lamp, which was lying broken beside him. In his other hand he clutched the triptych. The hilt of a kitchen knife protruded from his back. Trembling, von Reitz knelt by his master. He was dead, no doubt of that. Murdered.

Von Reitz straightened, staring at the body, his mind racing. The Kastello was inviolable, secure. No one could have entered from outside. Yet Raoul Lavallière had been killed. Murdered.

Slowly, von Reitz turned and gazed at the door, his face turning grim as the clear implication dawned on him. The master was dead. And someone in the Kastello had killed him. The Brotherhood, von Reitz realized bleakly, could never be the same.

Four days later, powerful men from every corner of the world gathered in the main hall at the Kastello. A funeral bier stood in the middle of the hall, draped with the Templars' standard. On it lay the body of Raoul Lavallière, wrapped in his white cloak and the other vestments of the Grand Master of the Order. On the floor at each corner of the bier stood a large candlestick with an equally large candle burning in it.

Facing the bier was Dietrich von Reitz, dressed in the full regalia of Seneschal, his head bowed in reverence. Massed behind him were the Brother Knights, the Brother Sergeants and the Confreres, each dressed according to his rank.

It was an occasion for solemn ritual, an event of the greatest moment. It was also, von Reitz thought, the prelude to discord, accusation and counter-accusation, dissent, power-struggles, chaos. The rumblings had started already, dark allegations had been laid and suspicion was rife. The unity of the Order had been attacked at its foundation, and without unity they were nothing.

Von Reitz sighed, raising his head for a moment and looking at the coffin. It could have all been so different. With the leadership of the *Maître*, his iron will and his unique understanding of power, they would have eradicated every barrier to the realization of their goals. In a few short years they could have taken the world in their grasp. As it was, von Reitz saw no hope of continuity, no passing-on of power. He doubted there would even be a Brotherhood by the time this year was ended.

Chapter Twenty-Six

The loudspeakers crackled and the airport announcer made the final call for the flight to Athens. While a porter carried the metal camera case and the holdall to the hand-luggage security point, Anne stood by the door to the departure lounge, saying her farewells to Ismini and David. As the two women embraced David stood apart from them, trying to hide his dejection.

'Goodbye, Ismini. I wish that . . .'

'So do I,' Ismini said, smiling ruefully.

'I'll write,' Anne promised. 'And the next time you're in London you'll give me a call, won't you?'

'Of course.'

Anne went across to David and kissed him on the cheek. ''Bye, David.'

'Take care.' His voice was dry, husky. As Anne told him quietly that she'd miss him, he forced a smile. 'I'm glad to hear it.'

'See you when you get back to England?'

'If you'd like that,' David said.

'Yes I would.' It was more than an empty pleasantry. 'I'd like that very much.'

'Rely on it, then.'

Impulsively Anne reached her arms out to him and kissed his cheek again. She stepped back, looking for a moment from one friend to the other, then she turned and walked quickly away.

David stepped close to Ismini. They watched Anne climb the stairs, where the porter waited with the camera cases. At the top of the stairs Anne turned and waved briefly, then walked into the checkpoint.

David sighed. 'She is going to be all right, isn't she?'

'Yes.' Ismini nodded. 'I think so.' She glanced at David, appraising his concern. 'On the way back we will stop and light a candle for her, shall we?' She squeezed his arm. 'Two candles, perhaps. One for Anne, and one for all of us.'

On a narrow road on the north-western coast of Scotland, sixty miles south of the Sutherland boundary, a dark limousine was travelling at speed. In the front passenger seat, beside the chauffeur, Robert McLelland made a proprietary smile at the sunlit countryside. He was in his fifties, a man with bright, intelligent eyes and a well-fed sheen on his skin. He wore an immaculately-tailored business suit and an expression that suggested he was permanently eager to please.

As the car passed a village signpost McLelland pointed to an imposing structure half a mile ahead, a thirteenth-century castle standing in extensive, carefully-tended grounds.

Half turning in his seat, he said, 'You've made a really excellent choice.' He beamed at his passenger, transmitting his own enthusiasm. 'A choice I am sure you'll never regret. It's a truly magnificent property, eh? And very private.'

In the rear of the car, Raoul Lavallière touched the button to lower the window. He leaned forward, staring impassively, taking in the view of the castle and its tree-lined gardens. After a moment he nodded, a barely perceptible movement of his head, then sat back again. The window glided shut as the car took the curving path up to the castle and swept in through the tall gateway.

Dr Phillimore opened his office door and made a brief smile of welcome. His visitor, he noticed at once, looked troubled. He ushered her into the room and closed the door.

'I can't tell you how grateful I am to you for having come all this way, Dr Christoyannis. And so promptly, too.'

234

'Naturally I was concerned by your telephone call,' Ismini said, taking the chair Phillimore had indicated by the desk. 'And knowing what I know about Mrs Tierney's recent mental state . . .'

'Exactly.' Phillimore sat down behind the desk. 'It was because of what you know that I got in touch with you.' He folded his hands on the blotter. 'Frankly, I need your help.'

Ismini shook back her hair, watching the doctor's eyes as he framed what he had to say. Like her, he was trained to find a proper beginning before he launched into any explanation.

'I can get very little out my patient as to what exactly happened to her on Rhodes,' Phillimore said at last. 'Almost nothing, in fact. Now clearly, it is there that the root of her problem lies. During one of our sessions, though, she did mention your name – I got the impression she looks on you as a close friend, not just another psychiatrist.' He paused and smiled. 'Having once heard you deliver an impressive paper on anticipatory trauma to the International Association, I thought perhaps that as Mrs Tierney's friend, and as an admired colleague, you might . . .'

'Of course,' Ismini said, anxious to get to the point. 'She tried to kill herself, you said.'

Phillimore nodded. 'With an overdose of sleeping tablets.'

'When?'

'A week ago today. Fortunately, she was discovered by her cleaning woman before it was too late to save her.'

'And you re-admitted her to this nursing home.' Ismini noticed Phillimore's questioning look. 'I am aware that Anne was in your care for a time after her husband was killed,' she explained. 'She told me everything.'

'Ah.' Phillimore nodded. 'Well, I'm glad she did. That helps a lot.'

'What I do not understand, though,' Ismini said, 'is that since she returned to England, none of her letters to me

235

carried even a hint that she was under any great stress. In fact I was greatly encouraged by them.'

'When did you last hear from her?'

Ismini thought for a moment. 'Two weeks ago,' she said. 'Perhaps three.'

She would not have been finally convinced then.'

'Convinced of what?'

'That she's pregnant,' Phillimore said.

Ismini stared at Phillimore, shocked. 'Pregnant? But I understood that . . .'

'That she can't have any more children? That's just it. She can't.' Phillimore picked up a folder and stared at it. 'In her case it's not merely a psychological or emotional problem. It never was. With Mrs Tierney it's a physiological impossibility.' He handed the folder across to Ismini. 'Here's the report of a specialist she and her husband finally consulted. As you'll see, it would require a miracle to correct the deficiency.'

Ismini opened the folder and began scanning the closely-typed pages.

'There has been *no* divine intervention, I can assure you of that,' Phillimore went on. 'Nevertheless, Mrs Tierney not only believes firmly that she's going to have a baby, she's showing just about every physical sign that she is.'

Ismini looked up, frowning at him.

'It's nothing more than a fantasy on her part. The fact is, she's pregnant only in her mind.'

Upstairs in the nursing home, in her cheerful, sunlit room, Anne sat fully dressed on the side of the bed. Her expression was dull, listless.

She had capitulated slowly, after long days of suffering the shock and the burning shame of what had happened. *Of what was happening*. Now that death had eluded her, Anne had become a passive receptor. What was taking place inside

236

her body was inescapable, she believed, something she must withstand. It was an enactment of some bleak justice.

She sat motionless for a long time before she looked down at her right hand, open in her lap. Without feeling, she stared at the tear-shaped diamond pendant lying on her palm, still attached to its broken chain.

Coffee had been brought to Dr Phillimore's office. He sat on the arm of a chair, sipping from his cup, while Ismini stood opposite him. They were still discussing the nature and history of Anne's delusion.

'When she first began to believe she was pregnant,' Ismini asked, 'did she not consult her doctor?'

'She consulted *a* doctor,' Phillimore said. 'But not her regular GP. And that's most significant, I believe. The man didn't know anything about her medical history. On the evidence she gave him, he naturally told her it was almost certain she'd conceived.'

'But he would have carried out all the normal tests, surely?'

'That's right.' Phillimore nodded. 'Only Mrs Tierney never went back for the results. I don't think she ever intended to. My guess is that the doctor's initial diagnosis was enough for her. Her fantasy had been given all the medical confirmation she needed.'

'So,' Ismini said, 'she took an overdose.'

'That same day.'

'And since then?'

'There have been no further attempts.' Phillimore drained his cup and put it down. 'It's as though, having failed to kill herself, she's become reconciled to what she considers to be inevitable. The birth of her child. The most disturbing aspect of this case, I think, is that she looks on this imagined child as some terrible form of punishment that she has to endure.' He stared at Ismini. 'What in the name of God did happen to her on Rhodes?'

237

Ismini laid her cup down on the tray. Her affection and concern for Anne were interfering with her objectivity as a doctor. She felt it would be a violation of her friend's privacy to give any account, however carefully edited, of what had taken place on the island.

'May I see her?' she asked Phillimore.

'Of course.' He stood up and went to the door.

Ismini picked up her handbag. As she turned to the door she saw a small Indian figurine on a side table. She paused, gazing at it. Something had been triggered; the fragments of a notion began gathering in her head. She moved closer to the figure, staring intently.

'Are you interested in Indian art?' Phillimore asked her.

'Yes,' Ismini said absently. 'As part of a general interest in the deities of all the ancient religions.' She nodded to the figure. 'It reminded me for a moment of Kali-Ma.'

'Sorry?'

'The black mother. Conqueror of demons.' She looked up. 'The most ruthless of all avengers.'

Vengeance, she thought. *Retributive punishment*. It ran like a mainstay though every culture. No human being was complete without the impulse. Something she'd picked up as a student – a fragment of ancient, tribal philosophy – came to her as she looked across at Dr Phillimore. *Righteous vengeance that lifts all shadows from the soul . . .*

'Tell me, Doctor,' she said, 'during all the time Anne has been here, have you been able to shake her conviction that she is pregnant? Have you made her question it at all?'

He shook his head. 'Up to now I haven't even tried. I don't consider it would be a wise course of action at this stage.'

Ismini nodded. 'I agree entirely. Her delusion must be allowed to run its course, I think. For the time being, at least. But her spiritual wellbeing . . .' She stopped, fearful of saying too much. She smiled at Phillimore, who was still holding the door partly open. 'I'm sorry. Shall we go?'

Phillimore pulled the door wide. As Ismini passed through she paused, looking at him.

'What do you know about the Australian Aborigne practice of pointing the bone?' she asked.

Phillimore made a puzzled face. 'Not a great deal. It's a form of witchcraft, isn't it?'

'That's right,' Ismini said. 'A prophecy, always a harmful one, is fulfilled when the victim learns that the bone has been pointed at him, from however far away. He believes his fate to be inescapable, you see. His own fear is used to destroy him.'

Phillimore smiled lamely. 'And does it work?'

'Hopefully,' Ismini said, going out through the door. Dr Phillimore followed her, looking mystified.

Lavallière had just climbed the steps from the garden. He stood on the front terrace of the castle, gently breathing the clean air, his eyes roaming over the fine geometry of lawns, flower beds and topiary. The peaceful isolation of the place wrapped itself around a person. He began walking again, heading towards the main door.

He stopped suddenly, aware of a disturbance. It was something distant, disquieting. Lavallière frowned. Slowly, he turned and gazed down into the avenue of trees lining the central path through the grounds. As he stared, the impassive set of his features surrendered to a twitch. His eyes widened and sweat broke on his forehead.

At the far end of the avenue tree branches were moving, an agitated, angry rustle in the windless air. As Lavallière watched, the movement advanced along the avenue, a formless shadow, fast, swirling the leaves and fanning turbulent whorls through the grass.

His mouth twisted in sudden alarm. A sound, alien and chilling, had swelled among the trees, hammering the air as it raced nearer. It grew as it moved, swelling to match the wild churning of trees and earth, building to a merciless, guttural roar.

Lavallière stood open mouthed, paralysed. Earth and torn leaves swirled madly and branches cracked. A scream rose in his throat as the noise closed on his head. The malignant shadow seethed up towards him, relentless, engulfing.